Break Me First

A BWWM Dark Billionaire Power Exchange Romance

Fortuna Lux

Break Me First written by Fortuna Lux

Edited by: Jordyn Young
Cover Design: Fortuna Lux

Contents

Also by

Say You'll Stay

Say You're Mine

Canvas of Our Souls

Laid Bare in D Minor

Ruthless Desire

Santa's Sinful Secret

Ava After Midnight

Break Me First

Ruin Me Twice

Rapture in Ruin

Second Skin

Celine: A Book Slut's Revenge

Tenderness & Torment: Part One – Red String of Fate

Content Warning

This book is intended for mature audiences (18+). All sexual encounters are consensual between adults, even when exploring consensual non-consent and power exchange dynamics. Please read with care.

This book contains mature and potentially triggering content, including but not limited to:

- BDSM dynamics (Dominance & Submission)
- Explicit sexual content
- Breath play / choking (consensual)
- Light impact play (spanking, flogging, slapping)
- Restraint (ropes, cuffs, blindfolds)
- Power imbalance (boss/employee)
- Age gap (slight; power dynamic based)
- Mafia/criminal family ties
- Blackmail, coercion (non-sexual, family/political)

- Dubious consent themes (consensual non-consent play)
- Voyeurism & public sex acts (semi-public play)
- Workplace sexual conduct (consensual)
- Possessive / obsessive behaviors
- Intense psychological intimacy
- Toxic family dynamics
- Family legacy pressure (arranged marriage threat)
- Emotional manipulation (non-abusive)
- Threats of violence (non-sexual)
- Crime family politics / organized crime backdrop
- Stalking (protective surveillance)
- Gaslighting (from side characters)
- Mild pregnancy fantasy / breeding kink mentions
- Rough sex
- Aftercare & emotional vulnerability

Dedication

For the ones who understand that surrender isn't weakness, it's trust.

And for the ones who were brave enough to kneel — and be worshipped.

Chapter 1

Body Like a Threat

Naomi

By the time I realize I'm tasting blood and unclench my jaw, the damage is already done. My grip on control has slipped, and the spiral is already pulling me under.

The moment is small. Barely a ripple. My thoughts scatter like marbles on tile. My focus fractures, slipping through my fingers like steam. Then... the truth hits like a slap: I'm unraveling.

The fluorescent lighting in the Leviathan Tech women's restroom is aggressively honest. It catches the sheen of sweat slicking my edges and my tired eyes staring back at me from the mirror—tight smile, blouse clinging like a threat, and a reflection I barely recognize anymore.

"Breathe," I whisper, gripping the cold porcelain sink like a lifeline. "Just make it through the meeting."

The door swings open behind me. I brace.

"Naomi, there you are." Kelly from marketing. Size zero, lip-filler smile, and a voice that always lands a half-octave too high when she's trying to sound casual. "You might want to, uh, freshen up. You've got lipstick on your teeth."

I bare them in a feral grin. "Thanks, Kelly. I'll fix it right after you pull the stick out of your ass."

Her eyes go wide. She blinks, gives a nervous laugh, and disappears. I take a breath that tastes like cheap soap and shame.

This place is killing me slowly. Polished glass towers and open-concept oppression. The kind of startup culture that sells itself as disruptive while bleeding women dry from the inside.

I push away from the mirror, heels clicking sharp against the tile. Today is my third month at Leviathan. Three months of subtle digs, impossible deadlines, and being talked over by men who repeat my ideas like they invented them. I've perfected the tight smile. The blazer-as-armor. The careful silence after meetings.

As I gather my things, Ethan strides past, murmuring into his phone in clipped Italian I can't begin to parse. His jaw ticks.

"No, we'll handle it. But they need to be patient."

He catches me watching, and his expression smooths into that CEO-neutral calm.

"Long day?" I ask, like I haven't just eavesdropped.

"Always," he says lightly, but his smile doesn't quite reach his eyes.

Another problem I'll never be paid enough to know about.

And then there's him.

Gideon Hawke. CEO. Phantom. The legend who built an empire before thirty-five and makes boardrooms quake with a glance. I've seen him in person yet—but the things I've heard...

The elevator dings. I step in, fix my expression, square my shoulders. It's fine. I can survive this. A few more months, a promotion, a better offer. Then I disappear, and maybe—finally—breathe.

My phone buzzes.

Zoe: *Tonight. Asylum. Non-negotiable.*

I smirk despite myself.

Me: *That place gives me hives.*

Zoe: *Hives you can cum through. Pack a dress.*

A laugh slips out—sudden, real. God, I need that. Need her. Need to remember I exist outside of fluorescent lights and status reports.

Back at my desk, someone's left a protein bar with a sticky note: *Hangry?* with a smiley face. I don't know who it's from, but I can guess. Someone who thinks it's helpful. Or worse, funny.

My stomach turns.

I close my laptop, ignoring the Slack notifications piling up. Let them pile. Let the world tilt.

Tonight, I'm not Naomi the Reliable. Not Naomi the quietly competent doormat.

Tonight, I'm slipping the leash.

Zoe meets me at my apartment just as the sky starts to bruise with twilight, fire in her eyes and a garment bag that looks like it could double as a murder weapon. She's wearing black leather and zero shame, her lipstick fierce enough to count as a threat. She looks like sex and vengeance, and I feel better just breathing the same air.

"You look like a librarian in crisis," she says by way of greeting. "Time to unleash the slut within."

She tosses me the bag and I unzip it to find crimson satin and strategic cutouts. I raise a brow.

"This screams midlife crisis."

"And yet, it's perfect for your quarter-life spiral. Put it on."

Minutes later, I stand in front of the mirror in a dress that hugs every inch of me like a scandal. My breasts are basically a declaration of war, my ass looks like it could cause accidents, and the shade of red makes me feel dangerous.

Zoe beams. "That's my girl. Now let's go remind the city that soft doesn't mean weak."

The heavy thump of bass thrums through my bones as we slip through Asylum's dark entryway, anonymous bodies grinding in a fever dream of shadow and strobe. My heart pounds in my throat with each sway of my hips, deliciously aware of every devouring stare snagged on my rolling curves. Let them look. Let them crave the raw, unapologetic woman I'm unleashing tonight.

Zoe leans in close, cinnamon eyes glinting as she scopes out the room like a lioness clocking a herd of sacrificial lambs. "Damn girl, we've hit the jackpot," she purrs in my ear. "Pick a snack, any snack. Mama Z's treat."

Laughter bubbles out of me, edged in simmering mischief. But then I see him.

Or maybe, he sees me first. It's hard to tell with men like that—the ones who look like they've been waiting all night for a reason to devour someone alive.

Lounging against the onyx bar like a jungle cat cloaked in Armani, one elegantly brutal hand draped over the back of his barstool. Predator personified. He's stupidly gorgeous in that austere way that makes a woman's head feel stuffed with cotton candy. But it's the power rolling off him in near-tangible waves that kicks me in the solar plexus and steals my breath. Every precise shift of sinewy muscle seems to declare: This is my domain. My playground. Avert your gaze, little mouse, lest I strike.

There's a darker edge to him, though. Not just wealth. Not just arrogance. Something colder simmering beneath, like violence carefully leashed.

Eerie glacial eyes pin me in place, twin lasers stripping me down to the pulsing heat of my core. I shiver as his gaze drags over me, a physical caress igniting my blood.

God, the sheer size of him. The width of those shoulders testing the confines of his impeccable suit. The powerful thighs sprawled indolently, one Italian leather shoe crossed over the ankle in a move of pure, arrogant insouciance. And that mouth—a study in cruelty and promise, lips lush enough to be obscene yet bracketed by grooves of unforgiving command.

He doesn't look away. Doesn't blink.

I take a step forward. Then another.

But I don't go to him. Not yet. That would be too easy—and I've spent too long letting men set the pace.

Instead, I let the heat of his gaze linger on my skin like sunlight through glass and pivot away, hips swaying with purpose. Zoe notices instantly, her eyes gleaming with approval.

"That's right," she whispers. "Make him work for it."

Asylum is alive around us—neon lights flickering across exposed skin and shadows, the air thick with heat, sweat, perfume, and possibility. Bodies press close on the dance floor, pulsing to the beat like a shared heartbeat. It smells like lust and rebellion.

We slide into the rhythm. I dance. Really dance. Hair sticking to my neck, thighs clapping with every move, the kind of full-bodied joy that dares anyone to look away. And they don't.

Sweat slicks the nape of my neck, curls sticking to my skin, and still I don't stop moving. Every beat sinks into my hips, low, slow, and heavy. Each roll of my body feels like an act of reclamation.

People notice. Men. Women. Some with parted lips, some with the slack-jawed awe of people watching a solar eclipse—equal parts awe and disbelief. A pair of femmes near the bar give me a toast with their drinks. Someone shouts, "Yes, queen!" as I spin, grinning.

I don't shrink. I shimmer.

A woman with locs and a silver septum ring slides beside me, matching my rhythm with ease. Her smile is all heat and approval. "You look like power," she says. "Like velvet wrapped around a blade."

"Damn right," Zoe calls over the bass. "She's the whole damn storm."

A man in leather and too much cologne leans close, hand hovering near my waist. "Can I buy you a drink?"

I brush past him with a polite smile and a shake of my head, the scent of bourbon and entitlement clinging to my skin like static. Another guy tries to catch my hand as I twirl past—he misses.

None of them are him.

My gaze flicks back to the bar. He's still there.

One hand loosely holding a tumbler of something dark, the other perched with calculated ease on the edge of his stool. He waits like the room bends around his stillness.

He thinks I'll come to him.

Cute.

I dance closer to someone new, letting him spin me by the wrist. Our bodies never quite touch. When I lean in, I let him catch the scent of my perfume, let him imagine a fantasy I have no intention of fulfilling. He laughs, dazed, as I drift away.

And I know that he's still watching.

When I glance back, that man at the bar hasn't moved—but his mouth has. A flicker of something. A smirk, maybe. Or a warning.

Good. Tonight, I'm not prey.

I'm the one circling the cage, testing the bars, deciding who's worth breaking a few rules for.

And he just made the shortlist.

Chapter 2
Touch, Taste, Take
Gideon

The first time I see her tonight, she's spinning on the dance floor, laughing like sin in silk. Crimson clings to her like a secret, hips rolling to the beat with deliberate abandon. Her hair sticks to her shoulders, thighs flashing beneath slits meant for the kill shot. And when she turns, laughing at something her friend shouts—she looks straight at me.

My heart punches once, hard and low.

Naomi Walker.

My new cybersecurity hire. And the woman currently dancing like no one's watching. Except I am.

I should walk away. Go back to the penthouse. Drown myself in the file I've been building on her for months. But she doesn't look at me like I'm a man. She looks at me like I'm her way out. Her bad decision. Her invitation to ruin.

For one perfect moment, it's easy to forget the calls I dodged all day, the texts from uncles who think blood buys obedience, the noose of family expectations tightening by the hour. But then she turns, and none of it matters. Only her.

So I don't walk away.

I watch.

Her gaze lingers, bold and curious. And then—she turns away. Not disinterested. Testing me.

A grin tugs at my mouth, slow and predatory. She plays. I'll play back.

I order a drink just to give my hands something to do. I don't taste it. Can't. My attention's a tether locked to every shift of her hips, every brush of her hand down her own body like she's daring someone—anyone—to take her up on the offer.

When she glances back and finds me still watching, something like satisfaction flickers across her face. She's not prey. Not tonight. And that makes her all the more dangerous.

By the time she's danced through two more bodies and ghosted half a dozen hands reaching for her, she's flushed and glowing and walking straight toward me. She doesn't slow until she's close enough that I can see the pulse in her throat flutter.

"Buy me a drink?" she asks, voice smoky.

"Only if you let me decide what it is."

Her brow arches. That same, defiant tilt from the elevator last week. The one I pretended not to see.

"I'm not in the mood for sweet."

"Good," I say, downing what's left of mine. "Neither am I."

She lets the moment stretch before finally nodding toward the side hallway leading out of the main floor. No words. Just a look.

I let her lead.

The sound fades with each step we take, the throb of bass softening to a distant pulse. Asylum's main floor gives way to a curated underground—an architectural warren carved for secrets and indulgence. Low archways curve into velvet-draped corridors. Wall sconces flicker with real flame, casting gold over black steel and crimson wallpaper patterned with blooming orchids and wolves' teeth. Here, the air changes. Thicker. Hungrier. Mirrors and velvet ropes line the corridor, the air growing cooler, quieter. Her heels click in rhythm with the beat, but it's her breath I'm attuned to—shallow, quick, threaded with want.

I key open the final door—one of a dozen private suites designed for anonymity and excess—and step aside.

Naomi walks past me into the room like she owns it.

Low crimson light and shadow spread across the space—plush velvet chaise, steel anchors embedded in the walls, rope neatly coiled, candlelight glinting off dark-polished wood and chrome. She pauses in the center and turns, chin tipped up like a queen awaiting tribute.

"This where you bring all the girls you eye-fuck from the bar?"

I close the door behind us with a soft click, letting the lock slide into place.

"Only the ones who look like they might eat me alive."

She smirks. "Smart man."

"Debatable."

I step closer, the air heating with each inch I close. Close enough to catch the scent of her—cinnamon, sweat, something wild and hot. Not perfume. Her.

My hand hovers near her waist. Not touching. Not yet.

"You know who I am?"

She tilts her head. "A man who watched me dance like he wanted to ruin me."

I could. God, I could. Map every inch of her with my mouth. Make her forget her name. Rebuild her around the weight of my hands and the sound of her own pleasure.

But not without permission.

I lift a hand, stopping just short of her skin. "Do you want me to stop."

She doesn't. Instead, she steps into the space between us. Her breath brushes my jaw as she whispers, "Make me forget everything but your name."

That's all I need.

I close the final distance in a single breath, one hand curling gently at her nape as the other settles on her hip. Our mouths meet, slow and electric, heat blooming between us like a spark catching dry tinder. Her lips part with a gasp that melts into a moan, her fingers fisting in my shirt like she's already afraid I'll pull away.

I don't.

I guide her gently backwards, each step choreographed by instinct until the backs of her knees meet the velvet chaise. She lowers herself slowly, never breaking eye contact.

I follow her down, knees on the rug, hands on either side of her thighs.

She watches me with wide, molten eyes, breath coming in soft pulls as I slide my hands slowly up her legs. The heat radiating from her center is a magnetic force. My palms skim the slick insides of her thighs until she shudders.

"Still want this?" I ask.

Naomi nods, then, clearer. "Yes, Sir."

That word. From her mouth.

I close my eyes for half a second and let it brand me.

Then I dip my head and begin to worship.

I taste her—not just the sweetness between her thighs but her pussy, hot and slick and already dripping for me. Her clit swells beneath my tongue, and the way she gasps, trembling, tells me she's sensitive—already wound tight. I flatten my tongue, press into her with slow, deliberate pressure, and she whimpers. Fuck, the sound shoots straight to my cock, thick and hard against the zipper of my pants. It's a dull, punishing throb. I want to feel her clench around me, feel how tight her pussy grips when she comes apart—but I pull back just a fraction, breath ragged.

I should stop.

I won't.

She gasps when I circle her clit again, slower this time, then faster—testing. She's so wet I could drown, her cunt practically begging to be filled. I groan against her, letting that flicker of guilt feed something deeper—something twisted. If I can give her this much pleasure, maybe it makes up for the deception.

Maybe.

Ethan's warnings echo in the back of my mind. The family won't wait forever. But tonight, I'm not theirs. Tonight, I'm hers.

Her thighs quake around me, flexing and twitching as I drag two fingers through her soaked folds and slip one inside her pussy. She moans—sharp and broken—and when I curl it just right, her whole body jumps. She's close. So close.

And all I can think is: What happens when she finds out who had her pussy on his tongue before she ever learned his name?

Not tonight, I tell myself. Let me have tonight.

Because tonight, I'm not just worshiping her.

I'm burning myself to the ground in the shape of her name.

She whimpers when I curl my finger again, so I give her more—slip a second inside, twisting deep, my mouth sealed around her clit as I suck just hard enough to feel her body lock up. Her pussy tightens, her thighs tremble, and she gasps, "Sir—oh fuck, I'm—"

"Let go," I growl at her. "Come on my fingers. I want to feel you come, Naomi."

She breaks like a wave, shuddering apart under my tongue with a cry that echoes in the candlelight. Her cunt clamps around my fingers, slick and pulsing, wetness gushing across my hand. Fuck. It's messy and undeniable and raw.

I slow my rhythm, letting her ride it out, then kiss her thigh, her belly, the inside of her knee, all reverent while she pants above me, glowing and limp.

When I rise, her eyes are dazed, lashes stuck to her cheeks, lips parted. She looks wrecked. Beautiful.

I wipe my mouth with the back of my hand, then brace over her, caging her in without touching.

"I haven't even started yet," I murmur. "Do you want more?"

She nods, breath hitching. "Please, Sir."

I reach for her hands and guide them up the chaise. "Then stay open for me. I'm going to teach you how to beg like a good girl."

My cock strains, thick and aching with every beat of blood behind it, but I don't give in. I hold steady. That's who I am. That's who I've always been.

But with her, it's unraveling. I feel it in every slow breath, every pulse of heat where our skin meets. My restraint isn't a weapon tonight. It's a fucking lifeline.

She doesn't know who I am. Doesn't know that she's already mine, not just here in this room—but on paper, in payroll, in the corner of every hallway she's walked since her first day. And I can't decide what's worse: that I haven't told her... or that part of me doesn't want to.

Because if she knew, she might stop looking at me like this.

Like I'm the only thing she'll ever trust to break her right.

I trail my fingers back down her stomach, slow and possessive, until I reach the soaked heat between her thighs. She's still twitching, her cunt fluttering from aftershocks. I dip two fingers in again.

Not to push, just to feel. She moans, soft and open, like the sound's pulled straight from her core.

But I don't give her more. Not yet.

I pull back, fingers slipping free, and tap them gently against her inner thigh. "You want more, sweetheart?"

"Yes," she breathes, voice gone wrecked and warm.

"Then beg better."

She shifts, hips tilting, hands still pinned where I placed them. "Please, Sir. I want your fingers. Your cock. I want to feel full."

"That's more like it."

I press my mouth to the inside of her knee, then the dip of her hip. Let my breath ghost over every inch I don't touch. When I drag her dress up, it pools around her waist in a rippling mess of silk. I let my knuckles trail over the exposed curve of her stomach, then skim higher. Her breath catches as I finally cup one of her breasts, thumb brushing the peaked nipple.

"Christ," I mutter. "Look at you. Your tits are fucking perfect. Soft and full and made to be in my hands."

She arches under the praise, chest rising like she's offering herself up for more.

I take it. I devour her.

Mouth at her throat, my hand at her breast, my knee nudging her thighs wider again just to hear that stuttered gasp.

Only then do I move back, standing slowly, keeping my eyes on her as I undo my shirt one button at a time. Her gaze drops as I bare my chest, my abdomen, then the trail of hair leading down into my waistband.

When I strip the slacks off, my cock is thick and heavy, flushed dark and leaking at the tip.

Her eyes go wide.

"Still with me?" I ask, voice low.

She nods, breathless. "Yes, Sir."

I wrap a hand around the base, stroking once, slow. "Then I'm going to give you everything. And you're going to take it all."

Chapter 3

Ruined and Revered

Naomi

His hand curls around my throat as he guides me toward the floor-length mirror. My breath hitches, not from fear—never from fear—but from anticipation so sharp it borders on pain. The lights are low, casting soft amber over our reflections, but I see everything.

"Look," Gideon growls against my ear, voice thick with command. "Watch how you come apart for me."

His other hand slides beneath the hem of my dress, fingers dragging upward, knuckles grazing my trembling thighs until he finds my soaked center. He doesn't ease in—he presses, deliberate, two thick fingers sliding deep inside me, making my knees buckle instantly.

"Sir—" I gasp, but the sound is already broken.

"You can take it." His teeth scrape my earlobe as his fingers fuck into me, wet sounds echoing in the quiet, obscene and perfect. "I want you to see yourself like I see you. Wrecked. Desperate. So fucking beautiful."

The mirror doesn't lie. My mascara is already smudging beneath wet lashes, black streaks cutting down flushed cheeks. My mouth falls open, breathless, a whimper on repeat every time he curls his fingers just right inside me.

"Please," I sob, hips grinding down on his hand without shame.

"Please what? Use your words, pretty girl."

"I need your cock. I want to be ruined again."

His growl vibrates through my spine. In one fluid motion, he withdraws his fingers, slick and shining, and brings them to my lips. I suck them in greedily, tasting myself, eyes locked on his through the mirror.

"That's my good girl," he praises. "Open for me. Always open."

His belt drops with a metallic clink, pants shoved down just enough for his cock to spring free—thick, hard, and flushed dark with need.

"Hands on the mirror," he orders. "I want to watch you fall apart."

I obey, palms flat against the cool glass, arching my back as he positions himself behind me. The head of his cock teases my entrance once—twice—before he buries himself in one deep, punishing thrust.

"Fuck!" I cry out, tears spilling freely now, blurring my vision but not enough to hide my reflection. "So full."

He doesn't give me time to adjust. His hands grip my hips, pulling me back onto him, setting a brutal rhythm that sends my breasts bouncing with every thrust. The slap of skin fills the room, obscene and addictive.

"Look at you," Gideon pants, thrusts growing harder, deeper. "Mascara running, mouth open, desperate for me. You're perfect like this."

"Yes, Sir," I sob. "Yours. Always yours."

His hand returns to my throat, applying just enough pressure to make my head swim, vision narrowing on the sight of myself completely wrecked in his arms. Mascara streaks, glassy eyes, mouth trembling.

"You're going to come for me again," he growls. "Right here, watching yourself break."

The coil snaps violently, pleasure detonating through my entire body. My legs give, but his grip keeps me upright, fucking me through the aftershocks as I scream his name.

"Good girl," he groans, hips stuttering as he spills inside the condom, head dropping to my shoulder.

We stay like that, heaving, connected, our reflections in the mirror painting the aftermath of our shared destruction.

I'm still flying.

Not the high, glittery kind. The kind where your body feels used—in the best way—like every muscle's been wrung out and repurposed for pleasure. My legs won't hold steady, and my brain's somewhere back in that room, still leaking moans into candlelight.

Sir's hand is on my lower back. Not pushing. Just there. Warm. Steady. Solid.

The contrast fucks with me. How he went from having his mouth on my clit like it was oxygen—to tucking my dress up over my shoulders and whispering praises into my hair. That whiplash should scare me. But it doesn't.

It feels earned. Honest.

I lean into him as we walk, heels wobbly, thighs shaking. He doesn't gloat. Doesn't smirk. Just keeps pace with me, like it's the most natural thing in the world to escort a woman out of a sex club looking like she's been loved within an inch of her life.

When we reach the exit, the air hits my skin like a slap—humid, thick with the buzz of a New York summer night. And with it, the noise starts up in my head.

What the hell did I just do?

I let a man I don't know put his fingers in me, make me scream, make me cry. I let him see me unraveled. And I didn't just like it—I *begged* for it.

Shit.

Shame bubbles up fast, hot and stupid. My chest tightens. My heels click unevenly on the sidewalk.

"I can practically hear you spiraling."

His voice cuts through it—cool, but not cold. I stop walking. He turns me to face him with hands that know how to hold, not force.

"You think you fucked up?" he asks, brows raised, like the answer should be obvious.

"I think I let a stranger wreck me in a dungeon and liked it a little too much."

His mouth twitches. Not quite a smile. Not judgment. Just something softer.

"You let yourself *want* something. That's not reckless. That's honest."

I look down. He lifts my chin back up.

"You didn't lose control in there. You *chose* it. Big difference, Naomi."

My throat works around a lump. There's no script for this. No tidy box to shove it into and call it experience. I run threat models for a living. I monitor breaches and patch holes before anyone knows they're exposed.

But this? This was a deliberate breach.

And God, did I want it.

I laugh, sharp and a little unhinged. "Guess I need to update my firewall."

That earns me a real grin.

"There she is," he murmurs. "My brave, brilliant girl. Overthinker. Smartass. Sensual as hell."

I feel heat crawl up my throat for an entirely different reason now.

"Just wait," he adds, leaning in. "By the time I'm done with you, you won't know where the pleasure ends and the pain begins. And you'll beg me to take you there again."

And the worst part? I believe him.

Because he didn't just take my body.

He got under my skin—and I'm already aching for another fix.

"Please," I whisper, the word already breaking apart on my tongue. My thighs clench, slick with the want he stoked hours ago and never truly let settle.

"Tell me what you need, pretty girl."

"I need your cock. I need to be ruined. Please, Sir."

His mouth curls, wicked and reverent all at once. "You want to be my good girl or my filthy little slut tonight?"

I flush. Burn. Ache. "Both."

"Smart answer."

He peels my dress down my body like unwrapping something sacred and obscene. His hands are everywhere—gripping my tits, dragging nails lightly down my belly, slapping the inside of my thigh when I try to close them.

"Keep these open. Show me that perfect pussy like you're proud of it."

I whimper, legs trembling, but I obey. I always do.

He slides two fingers through my folds, then spits directly on my clit and rubs it in with a slow, filthy swirl.

"Look at you. Dripping already. You want my cock that badly?"

"Yes, Sir."

"Then beg."

"Please," I gasp. "Please fuck me. I need it—I need to be stretched and filled and used. I want to be wrecked by you."

"That's more like it."

He strokes himself slowly, deliberately, watching my eyes track the motion.

"You're going to take every inch like a good little whore, aren't you?"

"Yes. Please, Sir. I want it so bad."

The first thrust knocks the breath from my lungs. He's huge and merciless, filling me in one deep, punishing slide.

"Fuck, you're tight. Like you were made to take me."

I cry out, nails digging into the sheets. My body stretches, gives, clenches around him. I'm soaked and trembling and already teetering.

He sets a rhythm—slow at first, then brutal. His hand grips my throat lightly, not enough to choke, just enough to anchor me in the now.

"You love this, don't you? Getting fucked like the filthy little girl you are."

I nod, moaning. "Yes, Sir. I love it. Love how you use me."

His praise is savage and sweet. "Good girl. My good girl. Taking it so well. Crying on my cock and still begging for more."

I feel the tears spill over. Not from pain. From everything. From how full I feel. From how seen I feel.

He notices.

"Look at that. My pretty girl is crying because her pussy's so desperate for it."

I come hard—body convulsing, cunt clenching around him like a vice. But he doesn't stop.

"Don't you dare tap out yet," he growls. "You've got more in you. And I'm going to drag every last scream out of that sweet little throat."

He flips me over, yanks my hips up.

"Ass up. Face down. Keep that mouth open."

I do.

He slaps my ass, hard enough to sting, then shoves back in. Faster. Rougher. His balls slap against me with every thrust, his hand wrapped tight in my hair.

"Say it," he pants.

"I'm yours," I cry out. "Your slut. Your good girl. Your fucking toy. Anything you want, Sir. Just don't stop."

He grabs my jaw, leans in close to my ear.

"You're everything. Every fucking thing. Mine."

One more thrust, deep and brutal, and I come again—loud, broken, raw.

He follows with a growl, spilling into the condom, collapsing half on top of me, his weight grounding me like gravity.

Silence. Only breath. Only heat.

Then his hands turn soft again. Stroking my back. Kissing my shoulder.

"Good girl," he murmurs, like a benediction. "So fucking good."

And all I can do is melt into the sheets and hold that praise in my chest like it's holy.

He doesn't move for a long time, just lets me catch my breath while his fingers stroke slow patterns into my spine. Each pass of his hand coaxes me back into my body, soft where he'd just been brutal. Worshipful where he'd demanded. I've never felt so completely wrecked—and so completely safe.

Tears cling to my lashes, not from shame, but from the quiet hum of being seen, handled, cherished. I feel cracked wide open and somehow stronger for it.

"I've never let anyone see me like this," I whisper.

His response is a kiss to the curve of my shoulder. "And no one else will ever be allowed to."

I should feel owned. I don't. I feel chosen.

And I want more.

But he doesn't press. Doesn't push for another round or reach for his cock like he owns the rest of the night. Instead, he pulls me close, one palm at the nape of my neck, the other stroking gently down the curve of my back as I come down.

He murmurs praises between soft kisses to my temple, my shoulder, the shell of my ear. Wipes the dampness from my thighs with a warm towel he must've stashed nearby. Cleans me like it's sacred, like I'm something holy he's just offered up to the gods.

Then, with hands reverent and slow, he redresses me. Slides the straps of my dress over my shoulders, smoothing the fabric where it clings. Fingers through my curls with care. Not erasing the wreckage—just helping me gather myself piece by trembling piece.

And through it all, he never stops watching me. Not like he owns me. Like he's witnessing something rare. Like he knows exactly how close I came to shattering—and how much more I have left to give.

When I finally steady on trembling legs, he offers me his arm like a gentleman and guides me to the door. The quiet click of the suite unlocking feels like a shift, a return to reality neither of us is quite ready for.

We walk down the hallway together, past velvet walls and flickering sconces, his touch still warm on my back, anchoring me as the bass from the club grows louder with every step toward the exit.

Outside, the air is still. He hails a car like he's done it a thousand times, then opens the door for me.

"Get some rest, little red." His thumb grazes my knuckles as he hands me inside. "You'll need it."

The door shuts before I can respond. He doesn't follow. Just watches the car pull away with that same devastating intensity, like he's memorizing the moment.

Gideon's phone buzzed once in his pocket, vibrating against his thigh. He didn't reach for it.

He already knew who it would be.

The family was getting impatient.

But for tonight, for this moment, Naomi Walker was the only dangerous thing he wanted to handle.

In my bed, hours later, I lie tangled in sheets that smell nothing like him. My body aches in the best way. My thighs, my throat, my heart.

I close my eyes and replay the moment he leaned into the open car door, heat still radiating off his skin. His voice was low, just for me.

"I want to see you again. Tomorrow."

The words didn't settle—they itched under my skin all night like static. Like something unfinished that keeps you too wired to sleep.

I grope under the sheets until I find my phone, face-down and still warm from the charger. My fingers fumble with the screen as I unlock it.

Then text my bestie...

ME: Zo... he asked to see me again. What the fuck do I do?

ZOE: Girl. You *know* I'm gonna say yes, so do me a favor—let's skip the pros and cons list—wear clean underwear and walk with electrolytes. You're gonna need both.

BREAK ME FIRST

Chapter 4

Black Lace and Green Lights

Naomi

When did I even decide the answer was yes?

Was it last night when I said goodbye and still hoped for more—or the second I slid into that black dress and ordered the Uber like it was already decided? I told myself I wouldn't come back.

That one night was enough.

But here I am, slipping into Asylum like an addict chasing a high—about to give myself to a man I still only call Sir, and barely know at all.

Twenty-four hours. That's all it took for him to worm his way into my blood like a virus. My skin still remembers the shape of his hands. My cunt clenches at the memory of his mouth. And my pride? That bitch didn't even put up a fight.

Zoe didn't say it out loud, but I saw it in her face when I got dressed tonight. That look of giddy, concerned support only your best friend can pull off. She handed me my black lace and didn't even try to lecture me. Just arched a brow and said, "Hydrate. Stretch. And don't let him fuck you on carpet. Your knees will never recover."

The club's the same, but I'm not.

Last night I walked in pretending to be HER, when I really wanted to hide. Tonight, I glide in draped in skin-tight black, eyes unbothered beneath a mask, skin flushed with confidence and sin. Every step is a silent fuck-you to every voice that's ever told me to shrink. I don't. Not tonight.

Tonight, I'm that Bitch.

And then—

He's there.

I don't see him so much as *feel* him. That pull in my chest like my body already knows its place. My gaze drags across the crowd until it finds him—sprawled in shadow like he owns the night. And maybe he does.

The second our eyes lock, I know I'm not getting out of this untouched.

And I don't want to.

He doesn't move toward me. He waits. Like he's daring me to come to him. And God help me—I do.

Each step feels like peeling off another layer of hesitation. When I reach him, I don't speak.

Neither does he.

He just stands and offers his hand.

I take it.

The music swells and the world narrows until it's just me and him, and the gravity between us. He leads me down a hallway I didn't notice before. Past other rooms, closed doors, whispered sounds.

When he finally pushes one open, I barely register the space before his hand is on the back of my neck, guiding me inside.

"You came back," he murmurs.

"I told myself I wouldn't."

"But here you are."

"Here I am."

His smile is slow and dark and devastating.

"Color?"

"Green."

He locks the door.

And ruins me again.

Not fast. Not like last night.

Tonight, he takes his time.

His fingers brush the edge of my mask, tracing the shape without lifting it. "You wore this for me?"

"Yes, Sir."

"Good girl."

He tilts my chin and studies me like he's checking for cracks. I feel his gaze travel my body, warm and invasive. "You remember your safe word?"

"Yes, Sir."

"You'll use it if you need to?"

"Yes, Sir."

His palm cups my throat—not choking, just enough pressure to remind me who's in charge. "Take off your clothes. Slowly. I want to watch you unwrap all this power you pretend you don't have."

I move like he owns the air around me. Pull the straps down my shoulders, inch the fabric over my hips. When my dress puddles at my feet, I don't try to cover myself. I let him look. Let him want.

"*Cazzo,*" he breathes. "Look at you. Look at what you bring me. Lush. Unapologetic. Mine."

The possessiveness in his voice sends a flood of wetness between my thighs.

He strips too, methodical and unhurried, eyes never leaving me. When he's bare, he doesn't press me down or drag me close. He just waits.

I step to him.

And he meets me halfway.

He brushes his mouth along my jaw—not a kiss, not yet. Just a warning.

"You ready for me, *bella*?" he murmurs against my skin, the last word curling, foreign and fond on his tongue.

I don't need a translation. The question trembles through me, curling low and tight in my belly.

"Yes, Sir."

"Good."

He walks me backward until my knees hit something padded and plush. I sit without being told, thighs already parting for him like my body knows its role. He kneels between them like a man in prayer.

"Look at this body," he whispers, hands coasting up the outside of my thighs. "*Così perfetta...*" the foreign words slip out low and reverent, like a secret meant only for him. "You were made to be worshipped."

His palms bracket my knees, spreading me wide, and I let him. I spread for him like an offering, brazen in a way that would've made me blush yesterday. But not tonight. Tonight, I want him to see it all.

"You don't hide from me. Never hide, okay?"

"I won't."

He hums, low and pleased. "Good girl," he says, then adds something soft in Italian I don't catch—but it sounds like worship.

His mouth is on me a breath later—hot, unhurried, deliberate. He doesn't dive in. He tastes. He *explores* me. Long, slow licks that map every inch of my cunt, like he's trying to commit it to memory.

It's not enough. Not even close. I arch into him, chasing friction, need, *everything*—but he just laughs, breath warm against my folds.

"So greedy already," he murmurs, dragging his tongue flat over my clit, then retreating. "You want to come, *bella*?"

"Yes, Sir." I gasp, already panting.

"Then earn it."

His tongue flicks fast, then slow, then stops completely. My thighs shake from holding still. I try to grind against his face and he grabs my hips, holding me in place with bruising control.

"No, no," he purrs. "You'll take what I give you. Nothing more."

Tears sting. I'm desperate, soaking, on the edge. But then—

His mouth seals over me, sucking hard, tongue circling my clit in tight, perfect spirals. My vision goes white.

"Look," he growls. "Look what I do to you."

My eyes flick to the mirror across from us—and I see her.

Me.

Hair wild. Eyes glassy. Legs spread. Lips parted around a scream I haven't even let loose yet.

"Who is she?" I whisper.

He answers without stopping. "*You.*"

The orgasm rips through me. Violent. Loud. Shaking.

He doesn't stop. His tongue presses harder. His fingers join in—two, then three, thrusting deep and curling.

I break again. And again.

By the third time, I'm crying. Not from pain—from release. From being seen, fucked, wrecked, *worshipped*.

He finally pulls back, his mouth glistening, and presses a kiss to my trembling thigh.

"There she is," he murmurs. "My goddess. My ruin."

Then he's standing—slow and fluid—and pulling me up with him. My legs shake, my pulse a drumbeat in my ears. I lean into him, wrecked and wet and still greedy.

He turns me around to face the mirror, one large hand at the nape of my neck. The sight of myself—hair wild, mouth swollen, skin flushed—punches the air from my lungs.

"Open," he says, sliding two fingers between my lips.

I suck them in without hesitation, tasting myself on his skin.

"You see her?" he asks, his voice low and dark behind me.

I nod, unable to look away.

"That's my girl. Look at the mess you've made of yourself. So beautiful. So fucking desperate for it."

He pulls his fingers free with a soft pop, then brings one hand between my legs. Spreads me open. Lines his cock up against the slick heat of my entrance.

"Beg for it."

"Please, Sir," I whisper, meeting my own eyes in the mirror. "I want your cock. I want to come with you inside me. I need it—please, fuck me."

"That's it," he growls. "Good fucking girl."

He sinks into me with a groan, stretching me inch by inch until I'm full to the point of madness. My hands brace against the wall as his hips press flush to my ass.

"You were made for this," he says, thrusting slow and deep. "Made to take me. To shatter on this cock until all you remember is how it feels to be mine."

The rhythm builds—harder, filthier, his voice a litany of praise and filth in my ear. I watch myself unravel in real time. Watched. Owned. Worshipped.

"I want you to come like this," he pants, voice shredding. "On my cock, looking yourself in the eye. Knowing exactly what you are—mine."

And I do.

I squirt around him with a cry, hips jerking, vision blurring. My cunt clenches, milking him as he holds me through it, whispering praise that sinks straight into my skin.

He follows seconds later with a guttural curse, thrusting deep and stilling as he spills inside me, arms tight around my waist.

We stay there, trembling and tangled, staring into the mirror like we've just survived something holy.

Eventually, he presses a kiss to the top of my shoulder and murmurs, "Come on. Let me clean you up."

I nod, too wrung out to speak, and he guides me toward the en suite. The bathroom is warm and dim, candles flickering beside soft towels and a rainfall shower already steaming. Of course he thought of this.

He steps in first, pulling me in after him until we're surrounded by heat and spray. I brace against his chest as he lathers a cloth and begins to wash me—slow, reverent. No hurry, no shame. Just touch. Just care.

Neither of us speaks. He runs soap over my back, between my thighs, down my legs. Washes away the sweat and slick but not the ache, not the claim. I lean into him with a shuddering sigh, let myself be held.

He kisses the crown of my head. "You okay?"

"Yeah," I whisper. "Just... floating."

A hum of approval in his chest. "You did so good for me, Naomi. Took everything I gave you."

"Thank you, Sir," I murmur. "For... all of it."

"Always."

We step out, wrapped in towels and silence. He helps me into one of his shirts, hands brushing my shoulders, smoothing the fabric like it's armor.

He doesn't ask me to stay.

He just reaches for my hand and laces our fingers together as he leads me to the bed.

We lie in the quiet.

As he pulls the shirt over my shoulders, his phone buzzes on the nightstand. He doesn't look at it.

"Later," he murmurs. "They can wait."

Whoever *they* are, I don't ask.

There's a tightness in his jaw he tries to hide, like he's holding back something heavier than the softness he shows me. Like letting me stay this close is a risk he's no longer willing to resist.

And for the first time in a long time, I sleep without bracing for impact.

Chapter 5

The Morning After

Gideon

Naomi's number glows on my screen like a landmine.

One text. That's all it would take. A single string of words to tether her to me again. Something light. Easy. Maybe:

Had fun last night. Can I see you again?

Delete.

Dinner tonight? My place?

Delete.

I scrub a hand down my face, the glow of the city bleeding through the floor-to-ceiling windows behind me. I haven't slept. Not really. Not since I walked her down to that car and watched her drive off like she hadn't just wrecked me from the inside out.

Her fingerprints are scorched into my skin. The stretch of her mouth around my fingers. The heat of her cunt clenching when she begged to be ruined. Her voice, hushed and reverent, whispering *thank you* like I hadn't just taken her apart piece by piece.

I should have told her.

Should have explained who I am—who I used to be. Who I'm still tied to.

But instead, I opened the door and let her walk away without a word. Now I'm staring at a glowing contact I should never have saved in the first place.

Naomi Walker. Sweet Red. Goddamn poison.

I push off the barstool and pace, barefoot and restless across polished concrete. My laptop sits open on the marble island, still displaying her employee profile. I've read it five times. Ten. Memorized the goddamn thing like it'll give me a reason to stay away.

Lead Cybersecurity Developer. Six years of experience. Flawless work record. Degree from Howard.

I click open the internal security audit from last month. Her annotations are sharp, surgical. No fluff, no wasted words. It makes sense. The woman I met didn't mince anything. Not her mouth, not her heat, not her hunger.

I should let her go.

I should wipe her file, delete the contact, and forget any of this ever happened. But I don't. I don't move at all. I just stare at the glowing screen like it might answer for me.

And then my phone rings.

I don't have to look at the name to know. Only one person still calls this early.

I answer with a clipped, "Vito."

"*Gideone,*" comes from my uncle's warm, snake-slick voice. "I trust you're behaving yourself."

"Define behaving."

He chuckles like I'm still twelve. "The engagement dinner. Three weeks. I've confirmed the venue with Claudia's father. You'll attend. No excuses."

My stomach turns. "I told you, I'm not marrying her."

"You think walking away from the business means you're free of the family?"

"I built Leviathan with clean money. You know that."

"You think image is what matters? You forget who gave you your first loan? You forget what you owe?"

The silence buzzes. A quiet threat wrapped in tradition.

"You play your games with tech, with your pretty little ghost company," he says, voice tightening. "But don't think we don't see you. The board watches. Your name is still Hawke. And you will do what's expected."

A beat. Then, casually:

"How's your new cybersecurity lead, by the way? Naomi, isn't it? Quite the hire."

Every muscle in my body locks.

"Is she any good? Or just good for blowing off steam?"

My jaw clenches. "If you touch her—"

"*Tsk, tsk.* Such language. I'm only asking. You're a smart boy. Don't give us reason to look closer."

The line clicks dead.

I stand there, pulse hammering in my neck, blood a slow boil beneath my skin.

They're watching. Of course they are. Probably have someone inside already. Maybe more than one. If they find out what Naomi means to me—what she could become...

They'll use her. Like they use everything else.

Her profile still glows on my screen. Not just a file. Not just a fantasy. A target. A liability.

I tell myself inviting her here is strategic. Control the risk. Control the narrative.

But even I don't believe that lie anymore.

I grab my phone.

Open the contact.

Me: Dinner. Tonight. My place.

I hesitate.

Me: *And leave your mask at home*

I attach the pin drop for the penthouse address and hit send. She'll know where to find me.

The rest of the day unspools in static—meetings I don't remember, hours I can't account for. By the time the sun sets, I've already lost the fight I swore I'd win.

I prep the penthouse like I'm staging a crime scene—every glass wiped twice, every light dimmed to the perfect softness. I swap shirts three times. I check the time four. I'm not this man—fidgety, unsure. But she makes me forget how to breathe evenly.

I want her undone. I want her whole. And I have no idea how to hold both wants in the same hands.

When the elevator dings, I catch a glimpse of her on the security monitor—black dress, hair loose, confidence sharpened into armor. No mask. God help me.

I buzz her in, heart hammering like I'm the one being hunted.

She steps inside, eyes roaming over the space like she already knows the blueprint of my control. "This place is exactly what I pictured."

I arch a brow. "Sterile and obsessive?"

Her mouth twitches. "Surgical. Seductive. Like you."

I lead her to the table. Small. Intimate. Two glasses of wine already poured.

"You cook too?" she asks, eyeing the plated meal.

"I order exceptionally well."

She laughs. I want to swallow the sound.

We eat. Talk. Dance around the real things. She asks about my work. I ask about her degree, her start in cybersecurity. Her mouth is quick and sharp, but I catch the flickers—the way she flinches at praise, the way she shifts when I say she's brilliant.

She doesn't know how luminous she is. Not yet.

Then she tilts her head. "Why me?"

I blink. "What do you mean?"

"You could have anyone. Any submissive, any pretty little thing in that club. Why me?"

The question guts me. Not because I don't have an answer.

Because I have too many.

"Because you see me," I say quietly. "Because you fight back. Because the second you walked in, I wanted to know what your voice sounded like moaning my name. And because I knew you'd never let me keep you in a cage."

Her breath stutters. She doesn't look away.

"You always talk like that?"

"Only when I mean it."

She drains the last of her wine and sets it down.

"Then maybe I want to see what else you mean."

I rise and offer my hand.

"If I take you upstairs, Naomi, it won't be for release. It'll be to learn every inch of you. So when I do ruin you again... it'll be permanent."

Her fingers slide into mine.

And she follows me into the dark.

But I don't take her straight to the bedroom.

Instead, I guide her through the penthouse, past the glass, the shadows, the curated perfection, and toward the kitchen.

She arches a brow, breath catching. "I thought you said upstairs."

"I did," I murmur. "But first... dessert."

Her laugh is soft, a little breathless. "You're feeding me again?"

"Oh no, sweetheart." I press her gently until she bumps into the marble counter. "Tonight, you're my dessert."

Her lips part. She starts to speak—but I silence her with a look. One hand finds her lower back, steadying her, while the other reaches for the small drawer beside the fridge.

From it, I pull out a sleek black bib. Not childish. Silk. Monogrammed.

She blinks. "You have a bib."

"I plan ahead."

Her breath hitches when I snap it around my neck and smooth it into place.

"You're insane," she whispers.

I step between her legs, my voice a low growl. "And you're sweet enough to ruin me."

Her eyes darken. She's already pulsing beneath the silk of her dress. I can feel the heat radiating from her. She's not just aroused—she's aching.

"Up." I tap her thigh.

She obeys instantly, allowing me to lift her onto the counter like she weighs nothing. Her legs spread around my waist as I step closer.

"You trust me?" I murmur against her ear, hands sliding up her calves.

"Yes, Sir."

"That's my good girl." I praise her. "I want you to spread for me. Right here. Sweet, wet, and begging."

Her breath shudders when I slowly peel the fabric of her panties aside, exposing her swollen pussy. She's already soaked, glistening under the dim lights.

"God, look at you," I whisper. "Desperate for my mouth."

I drop to my knees between her thighs, hands bracing beneath her ass to pull her closer to the ledge of the marble. Her heels dig into my back instinctively, seeking to anchor herself somewhere.

"Hands behind you. Brace yourself."

She obeys instantly, fingers gripping the edge of the counter.

I glance up once—locking eyes with her, letting her feel every second of this.

"You are," I murmur, "the sweetest fucking thing I've ever tasted."

And then I devour her.

My tongue presses flat against her swollen clit, slow at first, savoring the tremor that rips through her body. The taste of her coats my tongue—warm, honeyed, addictive.

I slide two fingers inside her, curling deep, hitting that spot that makes her thighs quiver and her breathing stall. A moan catches in her throat, chest rising with each flick of my tongue.

"Sir—" she gasps, her voice already fracturing.

"That's it, pretty girl." I growl, voice muffled against her cunt. "Let me drown in you."

Her thighs start to shake around my shoulders, muscles locking as the pressure inside her finally breaks. A fresh wave gushes against my tongue, cum soaking my beard and dripping down my chin. I groan into her, savoring the taste like a man starving.

"Fuck, just like that," I rasp against her, voice thick. "Let me drink you down, pretty girl. Don't hold anything back."

Her mascara starts to smudge as her head tips back, eyes fluttering shut, mouth parting on a ragged moan.

I tighten my grip under her ass, holding her steady as I increase the pressure, tongue circling, fingers thrusting deeper.

"So close already." I tease against pulsing heat between her thighs. "Such a perfect, desperate little thing."

Her knuckles go white where they grip the counter. Her thighs tremble violently.

"Sir—I—oh fuck—"

"Be a good girl and come for me."

The command detonates something inside her.

She breaks with a sob, back arching as her thighs clamp around my head. Cum gushes across my tongue, wetting my beard, dripping down my chin like she's pouring herself into me.

Her entire body trembles—violent, helpless, beautiful. I groan into her, licking her through every spasm, savoring every drop like she's feeding a hunger I never knew how to starve.

But I'm not done.

Her breathing slows, I ease my fingers free and drag my tongue one last time through her lips, determined to taste her until there's nothing left but the tremble in her breath.

"You're not tapping out yet, are you?" I smirk, voice thick.

Her breathless laugh is wrecked. "I—no, Sir."

I rise slowly, unfastening the bib and tossing it aside, my lips and chin coated with her cum.

"Good girl." I cradle her jaw gently, tilting her face up to mine. "You'll give me another one."

Her ruined mascara trails faint black lines down her flushed cheeks, and I've never seen anything so fucking beautiful.

Her voice cracks, needy and eager. "Please."

I ease her back flat onto the island, eyes locked on hers as I shift above her. Her breath catches when I hook my arms beneath her knees, spreading her open as I crawl forward.

Hands on my thighs," I command. "Keep your mouth open."

She obeys instantly, gripping my legs for balance as I straddle her chest, cock heavy against her lips. The moment she parts for me, I slide in slow, groaning as the heat of her mouth swallows me inch by inch. At the same time, I drop my head to her cunt again, tongue plunging into her as I feast like a man starved.

We move together—a filthy rhythm of moans, licks, and choked breaths—as her lips stretch around me and my tongue plunges into her, both of us lost in the perfect depravity of it.

Because dessert isn't finished until I've devoured every part of her.

Her throat tightens around me with each thrust. She gags slightly, breath catching, while her hips tremble beneath my mouth. My beard is already drenched from her release, tongue driving her higher as she struggles to take me deeper.

"Good fucking girl," I growl into her, voice dark and wrecked. "Taking my cock while you squirt in my mouth."

Her moans are muffled around me, helpless, needy.

She gags and swallows, her throat flexing as I control the rhythm, rolling my hips slowly while I flick her clit with my tongue in perfect sync. Every pulse floods my mouth, coating my chin as I fuck her throat.

Her legs start to shake beneath me, thighs quivering uncontrollably as the tension insider her snaps. She lets out one more desperate moan around my cock, her body jerking as another stream of cum squirts against my mouth.

I groan, pulling back just enough to watch the mess I've made, her chest heaving, mascara streaked, lips swollen.

"Look at you, my beautiful fucking mess."

Her voice is hoarse, barely a whisper. "Please... take me upstairs."

I grin, wiping my mouth with the back of my hand. Rising from the counter, I step between her trembling thighs and slide my arms beneath her.

"Good girl," I murmur. "Let's finish what we started."

And I carry her upstairs—her body still shaking, slick coating my beard, both of us wrecked and nowhere near done.

Later, after we've thoroughly drowned in each other—stripped bare in ways that had nothing to do with clothing—the world narrows to the hush of skin and breath.

Her fingers trace slow, thoughtful patterns over my chest.

"When I'm with you... I can breathe," she says, voice low and raw. "At work, I have to track every breach, monitor every flag, and be two steps ahead of everything. It's constant pressure."

She hesitates, then adds with a crooked smile, "But you? I like when you take the reins. When you tell me what to do. It's like—for once—I don't have to hold the world up on my own."

A dry laugh escapes before I can help it.

She tilts her head up. "What?"

I shake my head, lips twisting. "Just ironic."

She watches me for a beat, then lets it go. "Would it be insane to ask if we could keep this going? Maybe twice a month? Something I can look forward to. Where I don't have to be in charge. Where I can just be—"

"Yours," I echo, low and certain.

She nods. "Yeah. That."

And it guts me.

Because I don't deserve it. Not when I'm keeping the one thing that could break her trust completely. Not when she's handing me her softest truth, and I'm sitting on a secret that could raze it all to ash.

The worst part? I want to say yes. I want to give her what she's asking for—this space to surrender, to let go. But every word out of my mouth would be built on omission. On a lie.

I bring her hand to my lips, kiss each knuckle like a vow.

But my chest aches. Because I know what I should say.

Her phone buzzes non-stop on the nightstand.

A groan. A stretch. She grabs it, squinting.

"Work. I've gotta take this."

She slips out, trailing curls and warmth and everything I didn't know I needed.

And just like that, the weight slams down.

She gave me her trust. Her submission. Asked me to be the one place she could fall apart.

And for one selfish second, I'm grateful for the interruption. Because the weight of her trust is suffocating, and the coward in me is too relieved to face it head-on.

God help me.

Because when she finds out who I really am—who her boss is—

I won't just lose her.

I'll deserve it.

My phone buzzes this time. Another message from the private line.

Unknown: You're slipping, Gideone.

And maybe they're right.

Because one more night like this, and I won't have the strength to keep them away from her.

Chapter 6

A New Normal

Naomi

Rock bottom doesn't sneak up on you. It kicks the door in wearing yesterday's lipstick and zero shame.

One minute I'm riding Sir's cock like my orgasm depends on it—because it absolutely did—just one "please, Sir, make me your Twinkie," greedy, needy, and ready to be filled to the brim like a good little cumdumpster.

But no. I get yeeted into a work emergency instead of taking his cock like the depraved pillow princess I was born to be. Capitalism wins again.

I stumble into my apartment at 4:00 a.m. like a glitch in the matrix—blouse askew, boots dangling from one hand, mascara staging a comeback tour down my cheeks. I don't even make it to the bed. Just face-plant onto the couch and blackout before the spiral can catch up.

Then the alarm screams.

I groan, slap it, mutter "five more minutes," and bury my face in the pillow like I'm negotiating with death.

I blink.

It's 9:00 a.m.

My phone is having a panic attack. Notifications everywhere. I lurch upright, stub my toe, scream, and knock over yesterday's iced coffee. Chaos greets me like an old friend.

Three-minute war-crime shower. Emergency caffeine. I yank on the first clean-ish blouse I can find. My eyeliner crooked, my earrings don't match, and my hair's doing something that defies physics. But I'm vertical and moving.

I burst into Leviathan's marble lobby just shy of 9:50 a.m., iced coffee in one hand, phone in the other, moving fast enough to earn a Fitbit medal. There's foundation smudged under my jaw and my concealer is losing the will to live, but I made it.

"Naomi Walker," Marissa sing-songs from reception, one manicured brow arched. "Fashionably late or just regular-degular irresponsible today?"

"Girl, I saved a Fortune 500's ass while you were dreaming about your next Botox touch-up. You're welcome."

She fake-gasps. "Rude. Accurate. But rude. Also—have you not checked your calendar?"

I blink. "Should I have?"

She gestures toward the elevator. "CEO, CFO, and COO are all on-site today. Big strategy meeting. You're not in the loop?"

Stomach, meet floor.

I whip out my phone. Flagged memo. Sent at 7:12 a.m. Missed it entirely while elbows-deep in encrypted logs and caffeine fumes.

"Fuck me sideways," I mutter.

"Not without dinner first," Marissa chirps.

I stab the elevator button and mentally prepare to fake composure. Upstairs, the energy's shifted. Department heads are peacocking. Shiny hair. Sharper blazers. Everything extra.

"Where's the fire?" Nate from QA leans across the hallway divider.

"I am the fire," I shoot back without stopping.

My desk is a battlefield—half-empty energy drinks, fiber bar wrappers, and a Post-It with the word *Breathe* written in eyeliner. But I slot into my chair, plug in, and start triaging the security feed from last night.

I catch a potential breach—a subtle DNS reroute—before anyone else does. Flag it. Document it. Fix it.

By 10:17, I've already written a patch, isolated the intrusion source, and submitted a detailed post-mortem to the client. By 10:45, the COO's executive assistant pings me personally to say, "Well done."

I roll my eyes, but yeah—I feel that spark. That dopamine zing when someone finally notices you're good at the thing. The proof I didn't just hallucinate my competence through a cloud of sleep deprivation.

I slip away to the atrium—Leviathan's little oasis tucked behind the data ops floor. It's all real greenery, soft lighting, and ambient noise machines that sound like rainfall in a bamboo forest. Officially, it's the wellness lounge. Unofficially? We call it the Detangler—where fried nerves and frazzled brains go to untwist.

I curl up in a corner pod, letting the hush wash over me, and finally open my phone.

The text started at 6:17 a.m.

Sir: Everything okay?

Then again at 7:03

Sir: Problem solved?

7:46—*Make it home safe?*

8:30—*Thinking about you.*

9:12—*Are you going to work today?*

And then the last one, just after ten.

I don't normally worry, but should I be concerned?

I never answered. Not because I didn't want to—but because I didn't know how. I read every one in the blue glow of a screen and still couldn't find the words. Now, sitting here in the green hush of the atrium, I call the one person who might get it.

"Hey girl," Zoe answers, voice thick with last night's bourbon and this morning's sarcasm. "You alive?"

"Barely. I left him to put out a five-alarm cyberfire and then ghosted for a solid eight hours."

"Wait—you ghosted your sex god aftercare king?"

"I didn't *mean* to. I had to work. It was chaos. But now I feel like a flaming trash bag because he's probably wondering if I fell off the earth."

"Bitch, please. He's probably wondering how to lock that magical pussy down in three business days."

I snort. "Should I tell him I wasn't ghosting, just drowning in a sea of data? That the night didn't end the way I wanted it to, but the sleep sacrifice was worth it."

Zoe hums, then goes quiet. "Okay, but like...did it feel like more?"

I hesitate. "It felt...like something. But I don't want to name it yet. Just...ride the wave."

Before she can reply, a shadow falls across the frosted glass wall.

Vivienne appears—still all stilettos and perfectly arched disapproval, this time with an even sharper edge. "Ms. Walker," she says crisply. "The CEO would like to see you in his office."

My brain immediately fills in a disaster bingo card: Unprofessional. Irresponsible. Possibly fired. Definitely not promotion material. I haven't even made it to lunch and I'm already starring in my own anxiety spiral.

My stomach nosedives, but I manage a nod. "Okay..."

With a muttered curse I can't quite make out, Zoe hangs up and a second later, my phone pings.

Zoe: Heard everything. Good luck. Hopefully it's a promotion and not an HR violation.

I'm still snorting at that when another message rolls in.

Sir: Still thinking about you.

Guilt coils low in my belly. I thumb open the thread and type.

Me: Hey. I wasn't ignoring you. Just fried. Last night spiraled into a whole saga. Not how I wanted it to end, but worth the sleep deprivation.

I stare at it, thumb hovering. Then hit send before I can spiral.

I wait, watching the typing bubble flicker on and off, heart thudding like it might answer for me. Maybe he's not mad. Maybe he is. Maybe he thinks I'm a flake who can't manage her inbox, her sleep, or her post-coital etiquette.

And now I've got the CEO waiting to eviscerate me for skipping out on the one meeting that actually mattered.

A second later, another message follows:

Sir: I'll see you soon enough... you can make up for it then.

My chest does a weird achy thing I don't want to unpack.

Right then, I realize Vivienne is already halfway down the corridor, heels clacking like a countdown. I'm still frozen in place, phone in hand, when she glances back and pins me with that trademark glare.

"Ms. Walker," she calls, sharper this time. "I said now."

My stomach backflips into my throat, but I manage a nod. "Of course."

I smooth my blouse out of habit—like that's going to erase the fact that I rolled in late after skipping the most important meeting of the quarter.

The CEO came to HQ—*in person*—for the first time in years, and I wasn't in the room. The man who only ever existed as a disembodied voice actually left because I wasn't there.

And now he wants to see me. Alone. That can't be good.

I trail after Vivienne like a condemned woman, my pulse pounding in my ears. Every step feels louder than the last. Too loud. Too slow. Too late.

We stop outside a set of glass-paneled double doors—the ones no one ever uses. The ones that scream "you're either getting fired or knighted."

Vivienne opens one and gestures inside. "He's waiting."

I step through the threshold, heart in my throat, every nerve ending on high alert.

The office is sleek and imposing. All clean lines, concrete authority, and money. There's a view of the city so sharp it could cut glass. And at the center of it all, behind a massive obsidian desk...

...is *him*.

My brain shorts out. My body stutters to a stop.

Sir is the CEO.

My CEO.

My fucking boss.

Oh god.

Chapter 7

Damage Control

Gideon

This was never how I pictured our reveal. Me behind a desk. Her ten feet away, looking like the floor just vanished beneath her heels.

Her taste still lingers on my tongue. Her laugh echoes somewhere behind my ribs. And my brain hasn't stopped spitting out a dozen filthy daydreams since the moment she left. My bed, my desk, hell—even the kitchen counter. All starring her.

Now she's staring at me like I just set fire to everything good.

If I wasn't ready to see her again, why the hell did I summon her? Why haven't I figured out how to stop her from pulling away, especially when I can't get her out of my system?

Fate doesn't ask for permission. It throws the grenade and watches.

Her name leaving Vivienne's mouth this morning nearly knocked the wind out of me. I'd been hoping—maybe stupidly—that she'd show up to work, answer one of my messages, and give me something. Instead, silence.

No text. No emoji. Just a haunting, aching nothing until five minutes ago.

Now she's here. And I'm watching in real time as the gears behind those gorgeous brown eyes lock into place. The mask slides down. Her spine straightens, lips pressed together.

Naomi Walker, cybersecurity badass. Wounded. Walled.

She doesn't move. Doesn't blink. And I'm still behind my desk, pretending to be composed while my stomach free-falls.

"Naomi," I say. Her name cracks something loose in me. I stand slowly, like I'm trying not to startle her. Like she's something wild I've already hurt too much.

She flinches. Barely. Most people wouldn't catch it. But I do. Because I know her now. I know what it means when she goes still. That stillness is defense mode. Code red. Lockdown.

I want to go to her. Cross the room. Tell her everything.

But I don't.

Because for the first time in a long, long time, I don't know what the right move is.

Her voice, when it finally comes, is low. Flat. "You're the CEO."

"Yes."

Her arms cross. She hugs herself like she's holding in pieces. "And I'm the idiot who thought you were just some guy at a club."

"You weren't an idiot."

She laughs once, brittle. "No? Then what would you call it?"

I step around the desk. Slow. Measured. She retreats before I can get too close, like my presence physically offends her.

"You knew who I was." Her voice wobbles, then sharpens. "You knew, and you still—"

"I did." My voice is rough. "The second I saw you. I knew. And I still—God, Naomi, I couldn't walk away."

The slap comes fast, sharp, and loud. Her palm connects with my cheek, and the sound echoes in the quiet office.

The sting blooms slowly. I don't move. I don't even breathe. She stares up at me, trembling.

"Did you ever plan on telling me?" she demands, voice cracking like thunder.

"I was going to. I didn't want to lose what we had before I even got to have it."

She nods once, jaw clenched so tight I see the twitch. "You know what's funny? I've worked my ass off in this company. Clawed and coded and outpaced half the department. I finally get summoned to the executive floor because the CEO I've been fucking wants to do damage control."

"I didn't bring you here to manipulate you."

"Then what?" Her arms drop, fists clenched now. "What do you want from me, Mr. Hawke?"

The use of my name hits harder than any title. And maybe that's the moment I decide. Screw the optics, the timelines, the long, strategic reveal. Screw all of it.

"I want this. All of it. Out in the open. No more pretending it's less than it is."

"You mean something messy. Problematic. Career-ending."

"Possibly," I admit. "But also real. And worth it."

She exhales sharply, then walks toward the door.

I panic.

"Naomi—please."

She pauses, hand on the handle. Doesn't look at me.

"Don't call me into your office like I'm a problem to solve, then tell me I'm worth it." Her voice is quiet now, broken in ways I know because I've lived them. "You don't get to play both sides. Decide what you want—and if it's me, figure out how to make it safe. Because right now, all I feel is small."

The door clicks shut behind her.

And for the first time since I built this empire, I realize I might lose the one thing I didn't even know I was building it for. The room still smells like her—cinnamon, sweat, and a hint of shame.

Where she stood is warmer. Charged. I catch myself staring at the carpet, at the faint indentation from her heel. One perfect puncture wound. Her mark. Her warning.

Turns out, the most valuable thing I ever touched is the one I never earned.

I stand there, motionless, the sting of her slap still burning on my cheek like a brand. Not from pain. Not even humiliation. But from the truth.

Because I deserved it.

The door's barely stopped vibrating and already the silence feels punishing. The absence of her is louder than any scream.

I drag a hand through my hair. Exhale hard. What the fuck did I think would happen? That I'd summon her, confess half the truth, and she'd throw herself into my arms like some corporate rom-com?

No. Naomi Walker was never built for delusion.

Smart. Fierce. Sharp enough to gut a man with a glance. And I just handed her betrayal, gift-wrapped in opportunity.

My phone buzzes on the desk. I nearly don't check it, assuming it's Vivienne or security.

But it's Ethan.

ETHAN: Where are you?

I stare at the screen before typing.

ME: My office.

The reply comes fast.

ETHAN: Perfect. I'm two floors down. On my way up. You just saved me a drive.

Shit.

I don't have time for this. Not for Ethan's smirking commentary. Not for whatever deal he's about to throw at me. Not when Naomi's scent still hangs in the air and my center of gravity is tilted.

Before I can take a breath, the screen lights up again.

Unknown Number.

I answer on instinct, bracing.

A smooth, familiar voice slides through like oil on glass. "Gideon."

Every muscle in my body tightens.

"Uncle."

"I hear you've been making waves. Impressive ones. But waves, nonetheless."

My hand clenches.

"I'm not coming back."

A pause. A soft chuckle, devoid of humor. "I wasn't calling for a discussion. You know how the family feels about disobedience."

The tone shifts. Darkens.

"You should pay us a visit before we come knocking. It'd be a shame if your tech empire suffered... setbacks. Or if someone inside it slipped. Hard to trust so many moving pieces, isn't it?"

My jaw tightens. "Don't threaten me."

"No threat, Gideon. Just... a family courtesy."

The line clicks dead.

I stare at the screen, heart hammering, the cold press of old fear clawing up my spine.

Footsteps. Ethan.

I barely have time to shove the phone in a drawer before the door swings open.

"Evening," he says breezily, holding two coffees. "You look like shit. Want to tell me who put that look on your face—or do I get to guess?"

I don't move. Even when Ethan sets the coffee down and slumps into the chair like he owns the place.

"You look like hell," he repeats. "She hit you because you finally get laid and forget how to play it cool?"

I don't answer.

"Ah," he says, nodding. "So that's a yes."

He sips, eyes steady. Sharp. "So... Naomi Walker. That's the woman who's got you pacing like a junkyard dog?"

My head snaps up. "How do you—"

He smirks. "Please. You're as subtle as a jackhammer. Vivienne said you summoned her—and she left like she was ready to torch the building. Let me guess—you called her in just to see her face. And she made damn sure you paid for it. That bruise speaks volumes."

I say nothing.

He sighs. "You fall for her?"

I nod. Once.

"Well. Shit."

There's a reason I trust Ethan. He sees the cracks before they split wide. And he's never looked away from the mess I am beneath the crown.

Ethan sets down his cup. "Then I should tell you—your family called."

My stomach drops.

"When?" I ask, bracing.

"Ten minutes ago. Tried my direct line first. Said if you didn't return their messages, they'd handle it. Whatever that means."

I exhale slowly, hands curling into fists. "It means they're done being patient."

"You think they know about her?"

I shrug, but the cold in my chest answers for me. "They know. They've been circling since I resurfaced. Now they're just waiting for leverage."

Ethan's quiet for a beat. Then, "And if they go after her?"

"I'll burn every last one of them to the ground."

He nods. "Good. That's the only acceptable answer."

I sink into my chair. My palms still sting from the memory of her skin, her voice cracking, the sound of the slap ringing in my ears.

"I can't stay away from her," I say. "Even if I should."

"Then don't." He rises, straightens his jacket. "Just make sure you've got the armor ready before the next attack comes."

He pauses at the door.

"And maybe... apologize like a human next time. You're not bulletproof, G. She saw through the armor—and hit where it hurt. She knows now. Fix it before she walks away from you and the company for good."

Then he's gone.

And I'm left alone. With my ghosts. My legacy. I rerun a silent audit on the internal firewalls. Again. Third time this week. Ethan says I'm paranoid. I say he's not paranoid enough. There's a difference between watching your back and being watched.

I don't trust the quiet anymore.

And with that, one brutal truth hits.

If I want Naomi safe, I have to become someone dangerous again.

Not just a CEO. Not just a Dom.

But the man I tried to bury long ago.

Chapter 8

System Breach... Heart in Danger

Naomi

I should've aimed lower. Gut shot, maybe even a well-placed knee to his groin. Something to ruin his week without leaving my handprint on his face.

Instead, I slapped Gideon Hawke across the face like I was starring in some glossy C-Drama and walked out of the executive suite with my dignity dragging behind me like a ripped hem.

Now I'm back at my desk, trying to breathe around the earthquake still rattling my spine. Lines of code blur on my screen—something I'm supposed to be debugging. But every time I blink, I see him. The man whose mouth was on me two nights ago. The man whose tongue spelled out worship between my thighs. The man whose title is embossed in chrome on the glass office door I just stormed out of.

He owns the company, Naomi. You cannot Sir. Or your dom. That's your boss.

I grip the edge of my desk like it might keep me tethered to this timeline. My brain is screaming, looping, crashing. The slap. His face. That look—like I'd carved open his ribs and reached for the thing he keeps locked away.

Good. Let him feel it.

But underneath the fury, shame coils low and hot. Part of me isn't just angry. Part of me is still wet.

I hate that. Hate that my body hasn't caught up with the betrayal. That my thighs clench when I remember the way he growled my name. That somewhere under the outrage, I miss him. And fuck me, I miss how he made me feel—seen, claimed, wrecked in the best possible way.

I type three lines of code. Then delete five. My fingers are shaking. I'm supposed to be brilliant. Controlled. The fixer. But I can't fix this. Not when everything inside me feels scrambled, like someone yanked the power cord mid-process and now I'm glitching too deep to debug.

Toni passes behind me and taps a sticky note on my second monitor. "Lunch?"

I blink at her, like she's speaking another language.

She tilts her head. "You okay?"

"I'm good," I lie. "Just... a headache."

She gives me a look like she knows better, but nods and disappears.

I grab my phone and duck out of the open floor before I spiral in public. Head down. Eyes forward. I make it to the atrium without breaking into a full-blown panic jog. The rooftop garden is quiet—just the faint burble of the water feature and the hum of my inner collapse.

I sit on a bench and bury my face in my hands. The echo of his voice keeps repeating in my skull. I want this. All of it. Real. Messy. Worth it.

And because the universe is a petty bitch, my phone buzzes.

ZOE: You dead or what?

I type back with shaky fingers.

ME: I slapped him.

ZOE: Omfg.

ZOE: Was it hot or HR?

ME: Both??

ZOE: Explain.

So I do. The whole thing spills out in frantic, misspelled bursts. His face when I walked in. His voice saying my name. The slap. The silence that followed. The shame. The ache.

ZOE: Babe.

ZOE: That's cinema.

ME: That's a career-ending, libido-complicating nightmare.

ZOE: Or it's a power move.

ME: It felt like breaking something that can't be unbroken.

ZOE: Maybe it needed to break.

She calls. I answer with a sigh that feels like it's been aging in my chest for a decade.

"Please tell me you're about to talk me off this ledge."

"Oh no, I'm here to pour tequila on your open wounds and yell affirmations."

"Zoe."

"What? You slapped your dom-slash-boss. That deserves a toast. Or a lawyer. Or both."

I groan and lean back against the bench, staring up at the too-blue sky.

"He lied to me."

"He flinched. There's a difference. But yeah, it still cuts."

"Is there?"

She sighs. "Do you want to be done? Really done?"

I don't answer. Because I don't know.

The silence stretches. Then she softens. "You're allowed to be hurt. You're also allowed to want more. Just don't confuse your pride with your boundaries."

My throat tightens. "I think I wanted him to fight for it. For me."

"Then tell him that. But don't beg. Just let him know the door isn't locked. Yet."

"I don't even know what we are anymore."

"That makes two of you. But at least you've got a head start on honesty."

I hang up not long after, a little steadier but still pissed. Still turned on. Still tangled in the mess of what he is to me now.

Back at my desk, I sit down like I haven't been emotionally eviscerated and try to remember how to function. I code in fits and starts, but it's mechanical. Hollow. I can't stop replaying everything.

The slap. His stillness. The way his mouth parted like I'd knocked something loose inside him.

I should feel triumphant. But it's not triumph humming in my blood. It's something heavier, low and hungry. The kind of need that only goes quiet when he's touching me.

Fuck.

I stare at my phone for a full minute. Then decide to say one last thing.

ME: We're not done.

Minor panic attack.

ME: But if you want this to mean anything, you better show me it's worth the fallout.

Send. Okay. Now I'm done.

I don't wait for a reply. I put my phone face down, crack my knuckles, and finally start to code like I'm not unraveling. Even if I am.

Toni nudges the salad container closer like she's offering up a peace treaty. The lid clicks too loudly in the silence, and she flinches. I just blink at it.

"Okay," she says dryly, "you're officially scaring me. You haven't touched your food and you love crunchy salads. You haven't blinked, and your 'I'm fine' face looks like it's buffering."

I force a laugh that tastes like static. "I'm just tired after this morning's security breach. You're lucky you got to go home after we secured the server. I had to stay and do paperwork."

Toni tilts her head, mock offended. "You would lie to your wife?"

"I'm not lying. I am tired."

"Really, babe? You're vibrating at a frequency only dogs can hear. Spill. The. Tea."

But I don't. Not yet. I stab at my food without really seeing it, because every whisper behind us sounds like a coded message.

Toni narrows her eyes. "Did something happen? You get a weird performance review? Passive-aggressive email? Did Marissa from HR pull another drive-by smile?"

I shake my head. "Worse."

Toni raises one brow. "Worse than a Marissa drive-by? Damn."

She leans in. "Spill or I'm texting Zoe. And you know I've got her number saved as 'Ride or Die.'"

I open my mouth. Close it. Stab a cucumber like it insulted my lineage.

And just like that, food's off the table. This isn't just paranoia anymore. Every glance feels a few seconds too long. I'm building conspiracy theories from casual silence.

Which wouldn't be a problem—except this time, I might be right.

Something feels wrong.

There's nothing direct yet. Just the ambient hum of curiosity morphing into suspicion when the whispers stop as I walk back to my office. Then, I catch someone in HR watching me over her coffee like I'm a trending topic in her group chat.

I'm ready to escape and sink into the peace my private space brings. But it's ruined the moment I get to my desk and find a post-it stuck to my keyboard: *Bold move. HR's watching.*

No signature. The handwriting is neat, sharp, definitely not friendly.

I crumple it and toss it without looking. My cheeks burn. Heat prickles under my skin, itchy and alive with the awareness that someone saw something—or heard something. And had the nerve to invade my space.

Worst of all? I have no control over the narrative. Not the version of me that's quietly competent. Not the version that gets to walk out of this office on her own terms.

My favorite mug sits next to my keyboard, the tea I didn't drink gone cold. I stare at it for a beat—this stupid, normal object in a day that stopped making sense hours ago. Then I push back from my desk like the chair is suffocating me.

The bathroom mirror doesn't show a wreck. It shows a woman trying her best not to become one, wearing a mask of lipstick and a defiant smile. Everything curated like armor. Sharp lines. Soft lies. The illusion of calm held together with setting spray and spite.

But my eyes give me away.

They're too sharp. Too tired. Too full of the kind of ache that can't be blotted with powder or smoothed with serum. I don't look ruined. I look like someone who knows she's standing on a fault line and hasn't stepped back.

I breathe. In. Out. Like if I do it right, I'll stop feeling like my skin is two seconds from peeling off.

I splash cold water on my face, blot carefully, and inhale like I can recalibrate my whole nervous system in one breath.

And that's when the email hits.

Subject: URGENT: Executive Oversight Assigned

From: Internal Security Operations

To: Naomi Walker, Lead Cybersecurity Developer

Due to the escalation of the Leviathan breach protocol, executive oversight has been reassigned. Effective immediately, you are to report to G. Hawke on any project involving high-security threat vectors.

My stomach drops.

Of course. Of course the universe would put me right back under the boot I just kicked.

I whisper to my reflection, eyes dry and voice low:

"Of course. The one man who can unravel me is the one man I can't avoid."

My phone buzzes again. A calendar notification.

Meeting Invite: Briefing w/ Exec Oversight | 5:30 PM | Conference Room A13.

I check the time. 5:28.

Fuck.

I straighten my blouse, smooth my skirt, and walk out of the bathroom like it's a battlefield. My pulse taps out war drums in my ears, but my face stays flat, unreadable.

I told him to prove he was worth it.

Let's see what kind of man answers the call.

Into the corridor that feels like a wind tunnel leading to my own execution.

Conference Room A13 is already lit. I open the door—and stop dead.

Gideon is standing at the far end of the table. Alone. Tie loosened. Sleeves rolled. Jaw tight.

And beside him, on the wall-length screen, is a paused video frame.

Security footage.

Of me.

Of us in his penthouse.

My breath catches. My pulse stutters.

"Close the door," Gideon says without turning around.

I do.

And just like that, I don't know if I'm about to be set on fire all over again... this time I'm not sure if I'll like it.

Chapter 9

Exposure Protocol

Gideon

She's standing just inside the door. Silent. Still. But it's not shock that holds her there—it's calculation.

Naomi Walker doesn't rattle easily. Even now, with our sex life paused in hi-def clarity behind me.

The screen glows with frozen proof. My bed. Her body. My hands gripping her hips. Us.

If she's breathing, I can't hear it over the static in my own skull. My pulse is thunder. My restraint? Threadbare.

I don't move. Neither does she.

After Ethan left my office, I couldn't sit still. Couldn't focus. The call from my family still echoed in my skull like a warning bell.

So I turned to what I know. I opened my system logs, fingers flying like I could out-code the anxiety crawling up my spine.

Most of it was noise. Expected. But then—

A flicker. Something misnamed and buried in the executive cache.

Old file structure. New metadata.

I dug deeper.

And what I saw stopped everything.

Security footage. From my penthouse. My bedroom.

Us.

The camera angle was wrong. It wasn't mine. Wasn't supposed to exist.

Not Asylum. Not Leviathan security. Not anything I had eyes on.

Someone tunneled in—through our VPN, our servers. Dropped a payload meant for one viewer. Me.

I should've caught it. Thought I was one step ahead. Turns out they were already inside the house, sipping my scotch and waiting for me to notice the door was open.

When I decrypted the final layer, the message popped like a knife through bone:

Eyes up, Gideon. She's not just yours anymore.

That taste in my mouth? Metal. Like fury chewed through a wire. I could feel it behind my teeth, buzzing, bitter.

They watched us. Watched *her*. In my bed. In my arms.

I should've burned the whole building down.

Instead, I tracked it. No origin stamp. Just a signature of style I know like my own reflection.

Quiet violence. Precision. The kind of message my family sends when they want to remind me: there's no such thing as escape.

This wasn't about Naomi.

This was about control.

And I handed them leverage with both hands the second I touched her.

I couldn't keep this hidden. Not from her. Not after the slap. Not after her message.

So I made a choice. Show her. Or keep her in the dark like they kept me.

She's closer now. A single step deeper into the room, but it shifts my world like a tremor.

I nod once.

"Someone breached our internal systems. Used Leviathan's infrastructure to drop surveillance footage. From my penthouse."

Her voice is low. Sharp. "How long have you known?"

"A few hours."

Her gaze doesn't waver. "Who would do this?"

People with blood under their nails and my name in their mouth.

"People from my past," I say. "The kind I've spent years keeping away from this world. Away from you."

She doesn't blink. But something shifts in her—just enough.

"They want something. And this?" I gesture to the screen. "This is how they twist the knife."

"What do they want?"

I don't answer. Not yet. Not while her eyes still see me as a man—not the legacy I'm chained to.

Her arms cross. Chin lifts.

"I asked for the truth. Not PR statements."

Before I can reply, the screen flickers. New file queued. Same angle. New timestamp.

Two days ago.

Me. Alone. On a call.

Shirtless. Phone to my ear. Talking to Ethan. Arguing.

I don't remember the words. Just the low tone of warning. The mention of my name. The threat to "bring me back."

Naomi inhales sharply. Her eyes cut to mine.

She sees it now.

This wasn't about catching her naked.

It was about watching *me*.

About reminding me: they're always close. Always listening.

"They want me to know they can get through my walls," I say. "That nothing's off limits anymore."

I finally face her fully.

"If you stay in this... they'll come for you too."

She doesn't look away. Doesn't soften.

"I asked you to prove it was worth the fallout," she says, voice quiet.

"Now you're telling me we're already mid-collapse."

She turns to the screen. Hits pause herself. The silence crackles.

Then:

"So tell me, Gideon. Who's really watching us?"

She doesn't wait for my answer. Doesn't need to. She sees it all in my face.

This isn't theoretical. It's war.

And she just got drafted.

Her fingers twitch at her side like she wants to do something—clench, strike, reach.

I should stop this. Tell her to run. Push her out of this building and this nightmare before it sinks its teeth in any deeper.

But instead, I walk to the console. Shut off the screen.

Our reflections linger—hers upright, unflinching. Mine behind her. A ghost in the machine. A man she's still deciding whether to trust.

I step closer.

"I should've told you sooner," I say, voice rough.

She nods once. Then again. Slower. Like she's replaying every moment between us and seeing the gaps for what they are.

"You thought keeping me safe meant keeping me out," she says.

No accusation. Just fact.

I breathe in like it might fix the damage. It doesn't.

"No more secrets."

She tilts her head. "That's a promise. Are you in the habit of keeping those?" "No," I admit. "But I want to be. For you."

The silence stretches. Long enough to hurt.

She turns to face me, and I brace.

But all she does is study me. Not with fear. With the kind of quiet fury that comes from caring too much.

"I don't want to be your weakness," she says.

"You're not," I say. "You're the thing I'd burn everything else down to protect."

She flinches, but doesn't look away.

The door looms behind her. She turns toward it. Hand on the handle. Then pauses. Doesn't look back. Just speaks into the quiet:

"Figure out what you want, Gideon. And then figure out if you're brave enough to keep it."

And then she's gone.

But the war she walked into?

That just found its queen.

The door clicks shut like a trigger.

I don't move. Not for ten seconds. Just stand there with her breath still clinging to the air like perfume and gunpowder.

Then I let it go.

All of it.

The tension drops out of my shoulders like a snapped cable. My jaw aches. My hands shake once—fast, sharp, involuntary. Rage and regret fighting over who gets to live in my bones.

She didn't run. That should matter.

But she left.

And the part of me that's still bleeding from the slap knows: she's not gone because she's scared. She's gone because she's deciding whether I'm worth surviving this for.

I stare at the dark screen. My own reflection stares back. Hollow-eyed. Stripped. No mask. No title. Just a man in a room full of ghosts.

I drag a hand through my hair and hit the console. The file is deleted. Not erased. Just hidden again. Like everything else I've tried to outrun.

I tap the comm on the desk. "Ethan. My office. Now."

His voice crackles through, too casual. "That bad?"

"Worse."

I shut the comm before he can crack another joke.

There's no clean version of what's coming.

Naomi just got pulled into a war I never wanted her to see—and now I have to decide what kind of monster I'm willing to become to keep her safe.

Because the thing my uncle never understood?

Legacy only matters if you live long enough to pass it on.

And I'm not passing her to anyone.

Chapter 10

Simmer State

Naomi

I'm not spiraling. I'm simmering. That's different.

Zoe's name lights up my phone for the fifth time since I left Leviathan. I do the mature, emotionally intelligent thing: I throw it across my couch and pretend it doesn't exist.

ZOE: I swear to god, if you don't respond I'm staging an intervention. It will involve glitter, regret ink, and wine.

It's not that I don't want to talk. I just don't know how to explain the specific brand of hell that is seeing yourself on a surveillance feed mid-orgasm.

Or the part where the man who filmed it wasn't the one holding the camera.

Spoiler: I didn't sleep.

I stared at the ceiling. Then the wall. Then the blinking router light like it owed me money. I scrubbed every device in my apartment twice. Phone, laptop, router, printer, vibrator. Everything.

Because if I've learned anything from the last twenty-four hours, it's this: privacy is a myth. The walls do, in fact, have eyes.

By morning, I'm mascara-smeared, sleep-deprived, and marching into Leviathan on cold brew and spite.

The office smells like toner and blood in the water.

My heels click too loud against the marble. I wear my usual armor: black blazer, crimson lips, and an air of "don't fuck with me" that barely covers the static in my chest.

The break room goes quiet when I pass. A guy from BizOps stares like I'm a fire he'd like to watch spread. My monitor has a new sticky note. Different handwriting. Same smug vibe.

I tear it down and shred it slowly, like I'm dismembering whoever left it. No sign of Gideon. No Slack message. No phantom step behind me. Just that hollow pressure where his presence usually lives, like static in the walls. Like a ghost waiting to be noticed.

I dive into work, chasing logs and running breach diagnostics until my fingers go numb.

Hours pass. Daylight fades into the blue-gray hush of an empty office. The last elevator dings, the floor goes still, and I'm still here—hunched over a terminal, teeth gritted.

ZOE: Hey. If you're dead, blink twice. If you're ghosting your bestie, I'm bringing tough love and judgment.

The penthouse network logs give me nothing for a while. Then, just when I'm about to call it, something blinks.

A packet where there shouldn't be one. Tucked into the logs like a razor blade in a birthday card. Misnamed. Camouflaged. Meant to disappear unless you're someone like me.

I crack it open.

It's not complete. Just enough to recognize a style. A fingerprint, but smudged—like someone wanted to be caught, but only by the right eyes.

Not Leviathan. Not Gideon.

Someone else.

They left this for me.

I isolate the encryption layer. It bites back, delicate and precise—code like calligraphy. Familiar in a way that makes my stomach churn. This wasn't a breach. It was a breadcrumb trail.

And I'm the mouse.

A Slack ping breaks the silence. I glance up.

Vivienne Gray: Dinner. 8PM. Mandatory.

No subject line. No details. Just black text and a digital throat clear.

My stomach knots. I close my laptop. Fix my lipstick with a fingertip. My hands shake, but my mouth still remembers how to smile like it's sharp.

The car ride is quiet. Too quiet. The kind that watches you bleed.

The restaurant gleams with chrome and shadow. Every surface wiped down with malice.

When I walk in, I expect a firing squad with table service. HR. Legal. Maybe one of the VPs with Botox and teeth.

What I get is worse.

Gideon. Alone.

Sleeves rolled, a glass of scotch in one hand, tension in every line of his jaw. He doesn't look at me at first, just the glass.

I don't sit.

"Vivienne sent the message," I say. Not a question. Just the crime.

He gestures to the chair but still doesn't look up. "You stayed."

"That wasn't loyalty. That was survival."

"I'm trying to protect you."

"No. You're trying to protect your version of me. The one who doesn't ask questions."

He finally looks up. Eyes like winter.

"You think I don't want to tell you everything?"

"I think you want control more than honesty."

He doesn't flinch. Doesn't deny it.

"This won't stop, Naomi. Not unless we start playing by their rules. Or destroy the board."

I cross my arms. "Then why am I still walking blind?"

"Because if you see the full picture, you might not stay."

There it is. Cowardice dressed as strategy.

Silence stretches like a tripwire.

Then he exhales. Scrubs a hand over his face.

"There's a facility. Rome. Off-grid. It's where we can run clean. You'd have full access. Uncensored."

My eyebrow arches. "That sounds like a business trip."

He leans forward, jaw tight. "It's not. It's a war zone. But it's the only place I control the map."

My breath hitches. I straighten my spine, smooth my blazer.

"Send the itinerary."

I turn for the door, heels clicking like punctuation.

"I'll let you know if I'm coming."

I don't look back. Not at the drink. Not at him.

Because if I do—if I see the look I know he's wearing—I might lose the thread I'm barely holding.

Might forgive him too soon. Might shatter in the wrong direction.

He's still burning.

But so am I. And mine started lower, quieter. Under the ribs. A slow ache that turned into rage the moment I realized I was never the one holding the match.

I walk until the sound of my heels fades into the rhythm of the street. The city's still alive around me—horns, sirens, that one guy on 8th who plays the saxophone like the world's ending. It smells like hot trash and possibility.

I buy dumplings from a food cart I used to hit after late shifts. The guy remembers me. Calls me Pretty Hacker Lady and throws in an extra soy sauce packet like it's a peace offering from the universe.

I sit on the curb, skirt hiked just enough to not care. Steam curls into my face. I burn my tongue on the first bite.

It's stupid. And real. And mine.

I text Zoe.

ME: Sorry I went MIA. Been in hell. Want to come over? I'll feed you and let you insult my Wi-Fi password again.

She replies before I even lock the screen.

ZOE: If there's booze and dumplings, say less.

I pocket my phone. Let the city breathe around me. Let the heat of the dumpling cut through the cold still living under my skin.

I'm not walking into Rome blind. Not this time.

He controls the map.

But I still draw blood.

Zoe shows up twenty minutes later, all windblown curls and knee-high boots and a bottle of something that probably came from the corner bodega's clearance shelf. She doesn't ask questions right away—just dumps her bag by the door, kicks off her shoes, and throws herself onto my couch like she owns the place.

"Okay," she says, cracking open the bottle and handing it to me like it's communion. "Who do I have to stab?"

"Depends." I mutter. "Do you know anyone fluent in digital espionage and generational trauma?"

Her brows rise. "So... your boss?"

I nod. Then wince. "Yeah. Except apparently he's not the one holding the knife this time. Just the guilt."

Zoe watches me over the rim of her glass. "You look like shit, but like, hot shit. You been crying or rage-hacking?"

"Both. It's a vibe."

She kicks her feet up onto the coffee table, eyes scanning the chaos of takeout containers and laptop cables. "So what's the plan? Do I help you change your identity and disappear, or are we going full cyber revenge fantasy?"

I curl into the armrest, dumpling box balanced on my lap. "I'm going to Rome."

Zoe freezes mid-sip. "Is that code for something or are we actually packing for Europe?"

"He offered full access. Clean servers. Total transparency."

"He lied."

"And I left a handprint to prove it."

She hums. "Fair. So... this trip—is it about work, closure, or hate-sex?"

"Yes."

She cackles. Then sobers. "Just don't let him make you lose your voice, babe. Don't let the apology come with a muzzle."

I nod slowly. Let the words settle.

If I'm going to war, I need more than data.

I need someone who remembers who I was before the storm hit.

Like he knows I need something small to go right.

Someone who still calls me Pretty Hacker Lady even when I can barely call myself anything at all.

I don't know if I'm walking into salvation or a setup. But I need the truth. And I'm done waiting for it.

Chapter 11

Storms and Safe Words

Naomi

Zoe's gone by morning, leaving behind an empty wine bottle, a lipstick-stained mug, and a sticky note on my fridge that reads: "If you die in Rome, I'm keeping your vibrator collection."

I laugh harder than I should.

But the quiet that follows is the kind that doesn't just echo—it interrogates. It paces the room with you. It sits at the end of the bed and stares. It unearths every half-buried thought you were hoping would stay quiet a little longer.

Like: what am I really doing?

Or worse: what are we now? Is he still my Dom? Am I still his? And what the hell does it mean if I miss the way it felt to kneel, even after everything?

The worst part? I miss it. Not him—not entirely. But the weight. The surrender. The moment when the world shrinks down to a voice, a command, a hand in my hair saying, *good girl.*

No decisions. No spiraling. Just sensation. Just now.

But I'm not crawling back into that headspace with my eyes closed and my throat bare. Not again. Not after everything.

Not without knowing the ground rules—and who I am when I kneel. I won't hand over control just to feel small again. If I give him my submission, it's going to be on purpose. On principle. On my terms.

This time he'll earn it.

I pad barefoot through my apartment, the floor cold underfoot, phone in hand. The texts are still there. From Gideon. From the last few days. He hasn't pressed, hasn't begged. Just breadcrumbs.

GIDEON: I'm here when you're ready.

GIDEON: No expectations. Just clarity.

GIDEON: I miss you. Not your lips. Not your knees. Your mind. The part of you that sees through bullshit and still picked me—chose to kneel for me... That's what I miss.

I stare at that last one for a long time.

He could've said body. Could've said submission. But he didn't.

So I text back.

ME: If this is going to work, I need rules.

The reply comes fast.

GIDEON: Yours or mine?

ME: Both.

I leave the phone on the counter. Step into the shower. Steam curls around me as I scrub the sleep from my skin. My hands drift lower. Not for release—but memory. Reclaiming sensation as mine.

My body isn't the problem.

It's the trust.

By the time I'm dressed, my phone buzzes again.

GIDEON: Come to the penthouse. Tonight. No scenes. Just us. We talk. We decide. On equal ground.

I stare at the screen. Then type one word.

ME: Yes.

I pack light. Fingers skim the edge of the sink as I apply my lipstick slow—blood red, deliberate. My reflection stares back steady, sharp. No frills. No armor. Just a woman walking into a conversation that could undo her—or make her whole.

Outside, the car engine hums low—like breath held at the edge of a kiss. I slide into the backseat, heart thudding under my ribs. My hands rest still in my lap, but every nerve hums. I don't check my phone. Don't check my face.

By the time we pull up, the sky's gone that soft violet that makes city glass blush. I step out into the kind of cold that wakes you all the way up. I hesitate for one breath. Then move.

The elevator swallows me whole. It climbs steady. My reflection in the brushed steel doors flickers with each floor.

Pulse in my wrists. Pulse in my knees. Pulse everywhere.

My mouth is dry, my hands too steady. That's how I know I'm lying to myself. Fear isn't always loud—sometimes it's coiled beneath your ribs, waiting for you to notice.

When the doors open, it's not music or candlelight I notice first—it's the stillness.

And him. No music. No toys. No leather.

Just Gideon. Standing barefoot in black slacks and a gray T-shirt, sleeves hugging those forearms like sin.

He says nothing at first. Just watches me walk in.

I stop a few feet from him. Cross my arms.

"We don't play until we talk. Clear?"

His nod is slow. "Crystal."

I toe off my heels. Let the silence hang just long enough to make him wonder what version of me he's getting.

"I need to know it's not about power," I say. "Not your title. Not your past. Not what you think I can't handle."

He steps closer. Doesn't touch. Just lowers his voice.

"Then tell me what you want. And I'll give you that. Nothing more."

I lift my chin. "I want to know every line before I cross it. I want the right to stop, to slow, to say yes so loud it leaves a mark. And I want aftercare that includes eye contact and not a goddamn NDA."

He takes a breath—measured, but not calm. Like he's weighing the exact shape of truth that won't send me bolting.

"Naomi, I never wanted you silent. I wanted you safe. But I see now—silence isn't safety for you. It's a muzzle with gold trim. Comfortable, silent, suffocating."

"Exactly," I whisper.

The air thickens. I can taste it—like ozone before a storm.

Then I say it. The thing neither of us has dared since the club.

"I want to submit. But on my terms."

Something changes in his eyes. Not darker. Not lighter. Just *clearer*. Like the storm in him has direction now.

"Then give me your terms. And I'll give you the edge you need to fall."

My pulse pounds.

I step into him. Press a palm flat to his chest.

"One scene," I say. "Tonight. My rules. My safe word. You break them, I walk."

He dips his head, voice rough.

"And if I don't?"

I smile, slow and lethal.

"Then maybe you earn the right to hurt me the way I like."

His breath catches.

And just like that—we're back in the game.

I don't move at first. I let the weight of what I just said settle between us like smoke. Let him feel it—my control, my consent, the steel under the softness.

His jaw flexes, barely. The only tell. He's waiting for me to set the first rule.

Good.

I step past him, deliberately brushing his arm. He doesn't grab, doesn't guide. Just follows, soundless, as I walk the length of the suite—slow, measured, like I'm circling a cage I used to call home.

"I want the room warm," I say, toeing the thermostat up two clicks. "And the lighting low. No red. Red's mine."

A pause. I don't look at him when I say it. "You'll speak when I ask. Not before."

Behind me, I hear the quiet exhale of a man reeling it in. Reeling it *all* in.

"I choose the implements," I add. "Nothing I didn't touch first."

He nods once, the way someone nods at a force of nature bearing down.

I turn, walk straight to the cabinet I've only seen from the safety of memory. My fingers skim leather, metal, suede. The flogger with the braided tails. The soft-lined cuffs. I lift a blindfold but toss it back—*not tonight.*

When I turn around, he's still waiting—hands behind his back, head slightly bowed, chest rising just a little faster than before.

"Strip," I say. "But keep the cuffs nearby."

His eyes flicker, just for a second. And then he obeys.

And that's when it hits me—not lust, not fear, but *clarity*.

I want this. All of it. The game, the power, the slow unravel.

Want him watching me like that—like I'm the storm and the safe house.

Behind me, I hear him shift, and then—his voice, low and dry, with that rare flicker of humor he uses like a blade.

"You're a natural at this," he says. "You sure you're not a switch? Not just a bratty submissive with good lighting?"

I glance over my shoulder. He's smirking, but it's reverent, not smug.

I smirk right back. "Careful. You keep talking, I might gag you and call it mindfulness."

He laughs—quiet, rough—and fuck, it's almost a moan.

Good.

I want him on edge. I want to press and pull. I want to be devoured, but on my own fucking terms.

Chapter 12

Give and Take

Gideon

She told me to wait.

So I do.

Standing still, hands loose behind my back, barefoot on cold stone while candlelight carves the room into shadow and suggestion. I don't move or speak. Not because I'm trying to be obedient—because I want her to feel it.

The tension. The silence. The power shift between us—not taken, but handed over.

The old me would've met her at the door. Directed. Controlled. Offered safety through structure. But Naomi doesn't need a leash.

She needs to know I'm still hers even when I'm not holding the reins.

The elevator dings. My pulse doesn't quicken. It's already racing.

And when she steps out—barefoot, blazer off, lipstick like a threat—I nearly drop to my knees.

She's calm. But it's the kind of calm that stalks, not rests. The kind that owns the room just by breathing in it.

I stay silent. She doesn't ask me to speak.

She paces once, fingers trailing over the cabinet edge, eyes skimming the wall of implements like she's reacquainting herself with a language she already speaks fluently.

Then: "Flogger. Leather. Not the braided one. Too much bite for tonight."

I exhale through my nose. Slow. She caught that hesitation. Good.

"Kneel," she says.

My knees hit the floor like they remember her gravity.

She circles me. Not fast. Not hesitant. Just aware. As if she's reading me through scent and silence. I let her. I want her to.

A finger drags along the back of my neck. Not possessive. Not gentle. Just there. Enough to say: I see you. And I'm deciding what to do with you.

Then she leans in, breath hot by my ear.

"Tonight, we're trading places. That clear?"

"Yes, Naomi."

Her nails graze my scalp. "Try again."

I swallow.

"Yes, ma'am."

And fuck if I don't feel the world narrow to that one word. That one voice.

She pauses behind me, and I swear the air itself bows.

Not because she demands it.

Because she deserves it.

She's not just dominant. She's cosmic. Like gravity with a pulse. Like rage dressed in velvet. Sacred in the way fire is—beautiful right before it burns you down.

Maybe I've been waiting for this longer than I knew—to kneel, not just for a woman, but for a goddess.

"Look at me," she says.

I do.

And I'd burn temples for her. Build them too. Anything to keep that fire in her eyes fixed on me.

"Say it," she commands.

And somehow—I know exactly what she wants. Not because we planned this. Not because it's protocol. But because she's standing over me like a storm with intent, and the only word that feels right burns in my throat.

"My goddess," I murmur—like it's not just kink, but confession. Like it's a truth my body knew before my mouth ever dared speak it.

She smiles—slow and lethal.

"Good boy." The words land like a seal, not a leash.

The session hasn't started yet.

But I'm already undone.

She steps in front of me, slow and deliberate. The hem of her dress whispers against my knee, and still I don't look away from her face.

I want her eyes on me when she makes her move.

She doesn't touch me. Not yet. Just lifts the flogger she chose with care—black leather, soft enough to seduce, heavy enough to mark.

"Up," she says.

I rise.

She circles me again, testing the weight of the tails in her palm, like a priestess preparing for ritual. No hesitation. No questions. She knows exactly what she wants to give me—and take from me.

"You want a safe word?" she asks, voice flat but not unkind.

"Already have one."

Her brow lifts.

"You."

Her smirk is cruel in all the right ways. "Cute. But that only works if I'm in the mood to stop."

I hold her gaze. "Then don't."

Something in her expression shifts—not softer, but deeper. Like she's storing that moment away for later.

"Turn around," she says. "Hands behind your back."

I obey. The leather cuffs snap into place with quick, practiced movements. She's not tentative with me. And God, I love her for that.

The first strike lands like a kiss through fire. Not pain. Not yet. Just promise.

My breath punches out of me. Not because it hurts. Because it's her.

"I want every sound," she says from behind me. "No stifling. No silence. If I'm doing this, I'm doing it loud."

And just like that, my world starts to blur.

Another lash. A little harder.

"You're not being punished because you broke a rule," she says, her voice steady. "You're being punished because you kept your mouth shut when you should've told me the truth. Because you thought control meant silence."

The next strike lands sharper. Across the top of my thighs.

"Because you forgot I'm not here to be protected. I'm here to be trusted."

The words hit harder than the leather.

Because she's right.

Because every strike is a mirror, and I'm being made to look.

The next one lands lower. Thudding against muscle and memory.

"I can't afford your secrets," she says. "Not when they put me in someone else's crosshairs."

I nod, jaw tight.

"No nodding," she snaps. "I said I want sounds."

A choked noise escapes me—half groan, half apology.

"Better," she murmurs. "Now keep your legs wide. Stay open."

The flogger drags down my spine like a slow exhale, then disappears. My skin hums in its absence. Every nerve tuned to her.

She steps close. I feel her breath before I feel her hands.

"Do you even know what this is costing me?" she whispers at the base of my neck. "Letting you back in. Letting myself want this again."

I want to answer, but she doesn't want words.

She wants honesty in muscle. In moan. In stillness.

So I give her that.

Another strike. Faster this time. Closer to the edge of pain. I grunt, hips jerking.

"Good," she breathes. "Let it out."

Then her palm—bare, hot, grounding—presses to the small of my back. Not punishment. Contact. Claim.

"This isn't just about you learning to trust me," she says. "It's about me watching you do it. Loud. Vulnerable. No armor."

She walks around to face me, flogger dangling from her fingers like a question.

Her eyes search mine.

"You still want this?" she asks, quiet now.

"I want you," I rasp. "Any way you'll have me."

Naomi tilts her head.

"Then say it again."

I know what she means.

I drop my eyes. Let go of everything.

"My goddess."

Her hand cups my cheek, and for the first time tonight, her touch is tender.

"Then kneel for me properly," she says. "Not because I said so. Because you need to."

And I do.

I kneel.

And this time, it feels like prayer.

She moves behind me again. No urgency. Just gravity that rewrites planets. The flogger rests against my lower back, not swinging now—just heavy, like it knows what's next.

Then her fingers are at the cuffs. Careful. Precise. The slow drag of leather loosening feels like permission and punishment all at once.

"Bed," she says. "Face down. I want you pliant. Quiet. Open."

I move. Not like I'm obeying—like I've been waiting to.

The mattress catches me like a secret. The sheets are cool against my skin, and then she's there—hands on my shoulders, then my back, then lower.

Palms to soften. Nails to remind. Teeth to claim.

Each touch a sentence. Each silence a paragraph. She's not writing on my body—she's editing me.

Until there's nothing left but breath and ache and the sound of her above me.

And then she shifts. Knees on either side of my thighs. Her weight settling onto me—not crushing, but claiming.

"Hands above your head," she says.

I stretch out, spine lengthening, chest pressed to the bed. She pulls my wrists together, binds them with the cuff strap she never let go of.

Then—skin.

Her thighs bracketing mine. The hot slide of her slick against the base of my spine. She grinds once, slow. My hips jerk.

"Still?" she asks.

"Trying," I grit out.

A low, satisfied hum.

Her fingers curl into my hair and pull my head back—not rough, not kind. Just hers.

She bends low and murmurs, "I'm going to ride you now. Quick. Deep. No talking. Just take it."

And I do.

She lines us up with maddening control, then sinks down in one smooth stroke that knocks the breath from my lungs. Her body tight around me. Her nails in my shoulders. Her rhythm brutal and gorgeous and just a little bit cruel—like she's taking back every part of herself that someone tried to shame.

Every snap of her hips is a reminder: she owns this. Owns me. And I never want it back.

When she breaks—loud, ragged, relentless—I follow, undone beneath her, the world narrowing to the heat of her thighs and the taste of her name in my mouth.

Only then does she untie me.

When she gathers me close, there's no tension left to hold.

And that's when I let go.

Not of control. Of the apology I never gave her. Of the shield I wore even while kneeling.

We lie there for a while. Breath on skin. Sweat cooling. My hands open, finally empty.

She shifts against me—pulls back just enough to look down.

Her voice is low, steady. "I want to give you control again."

I blink up at her. There's no dramatics in her face. No softness either.

"Don't make me regret it."

I sit up on my elbows, chest still rising too fast. She's right there, watching, steady as a pulse.

"I won't," I say. Not like a promise. Like a vow. "Not this time."

She doesn't blink. So I reach for her face, slow, like she's breakable. Not from fragility—because she's full to the brim and any wrong move might spill everything.

My fingers trace her jaw. Her cheekbone. Her mouth.

"I didn't know how to let go," I admit. "Not then. But I'm learning."

"Okay—I'll go to Rome. Call it a distraction. Call it curiosity. But I want answers—and I'm not letting you hunt them alone."

I pause, heart hammering against the edge of truth.

She doesn't say anything else. But she leans in—just a breath closer.

That's enough for now.

Chapter 13

The Echo of Control

Naomi

The moment I step through the sleek glass doors of Leviathan Tech, it feels like stepping back into a different lifetime. The buzz of keyboards, the soft murmur of voices, the cool hum of climate-controlled air—it's all so familiar, yet I no longer belong to it. Not really. My body still thrums with the memory of Gideon's mouth on my skin, his voice in my ear, the possessive bruises he painted down my neck like a trail only he's allowed to follow. I slide into my workstation with trembling fingers, adrenaline and aftershocks coiling low in my belly.

The code on my screen blurs. Every keystroke feels too loud, every breath too shallow. I can't shake the phantom of his touch—rough, reverent, undoing me with ruthless precision. I should be horrified. I should be disgusted with myself for what I let him do last night. But I'm not. I'm vibrating with wicked exhilaration, with the thrill of knowing I'm marked in ways no one around me can see.

A message pings onto my screen.

Zoe: bitch i *know* that glow is not moisturizer. what did he do??

I huff a laugh, biting down on a grin. Trust Zoe to zero in on the filth beneath my composure. I type back:

Me: you ever get broken so good you can't sit without remembering every second?

Zoe: ⊠ god i love that for you. okay now spill or i swear i'll hack your camera

I promise her drinks later—no details over office chat, not with Leviathan's security protocols. As I hit send, my eye catches something unusual in my system logs. A diagnostic scan that shouldn't be running. It's masked well, hidden under routine server maintenance, but the trail is just sloppy enough to leave a signature: RedStitch_Logs.

My pulse stutters. That's not ours.

Before I can dig deeper, a shadow falls across my desk. I look up—Mia. Her smile is tight, wrong, a predator's smile dressed in gloss. "Rough night?" she asks, syrup-sweet. Her gaze lingers just a second too long on the faint bruise beneath my collar.

I sit up straighter, blood cooling. "Just tired."

"Mm," she hums, then glances down at my open terminal. Her eyes sharpen. "Be careful what you let people see. You never know who's watching." She turns on her heel and disappears down the hallway without waiting for a response.

For a beat, I sit frozen. Her words echo long after she's gone. It feels like a threat. Or a warning. Or both.

Then the air shifts behind me—and before I can turn, a large hand wraps around my wrist, pinning it gently but firmly to the desk.

"Don't even think about it," Gideon's voice rasps, low and lethal in my ear. I stiffen, breath catching. "Touching yourself in the office? Naughty little code witch."

My thighs clench involuntarily, a whimper escaping. I should push him away. I should demand answers—for the strange log, for Mia's cryptic warning—but instead, I sag into his heat like it's salvation.

"Anyone could see," I whisper, dizzy with want.

His grip tightens. "Let them."

And then he's bending me forward, the cool air licking beneath my skirt, one hand sliding between my thighs. My mind screams *reckless*, but my body, traitorous and greedy, arches into his touch.

"Still soaked," he murmurs, like it's proof of loyalty. "My filthy, perfect girl."

The high stakes, the voyeuristic threat, the dangerous thrill—it all crests at once, and I shatter. Right there at my desk, against all reason, I surrender.

Just as the aftershocks ripple through me, a presence slices through the haze.

"What the actual fuck?"

That voice slices through the haze like a whip crack, shocking the air right out of my lungs.

My head jerks up—and there she is. Mia. Standing a few paces away, slack-jawed, her glossy, curated mask slipping into something feral. Shock. Rage. Disgust. It ripples across her face like a glitch in a perfect UI.

Shit.

Panic detonates in my chest, but I can't move—not with Gideon still anchored behind me, one hand buried between my thighs like he owns every inch. I try to twist away with a strangled whimper, but he only tightens his grip, shoving me deeper into the desk like he's sealing a deal.

Tears prick at the corners of my eyes, hot and humiliated. How is he still so calm? So completely in control, like we aren't seconds away from chaos?

He doesn't even spare her a glance. Just that low, velvet drawl—dark amusement wrapped around steel. "How gracious of you to interrupt."

His fingers flex against the soaked silk of my panties, slow and deliberate, dragging a helpless moan from my throat. Shame and desire crash together inside me, twisted and hot. I'm still pulsing from release, and now—now—I'm being watched. Witnessed.

And somehow, it only makes everything worse. And better.

I see it happen—the realization hit her, the full picture forming in her pretty, horrified face. The flash of judgment, of rage. She's not just shocked. She's calculating.

A beat of silence, then she spits the words like venom.

"I knew you were twisted, Hawke. But in the office? With her?"

She flings a hand in my direction like I'm filth. Contamination.

Gideon doesn't even blink. He presses a kiss to my nape, open-mouthed and unhurried, right over the frantic thrum of my pulse.

"Careful," he murmurs, voice low and lined with warning. "You're edging into insubordination."

Another stroke. My knees nearly buckle.

Mia's expression curdles into something unspoken. But whatever plan she had dissolves under the weight of him—of us. She huffs, turns on her heel, and stalks off in a storm of designer rage, her heels a war drum against the floor.

But even as she disappears, my system log flashes behind my eyes—RedStitch. Mia's theatrics don't feel like guilt. They feel like bait. And something about that signature still feels...wrong. Too clean. Too polished. Like someone wants me looking in the wrong direction.

And just like that, the moment detonates in silence.

I sag against the desk, breath shattered, heart trying to beat its way out of my chest. There's a ringing in my ears, and I don't know if it's shame or arousal or the sound of everything inside me cracking open. I should feel mortified. I should feel afraid. But all I feel is his breath behind me and the aching space he hasn't touched yet. What the hell just happened?

He touched me. Owned me. In front of her.

And I didn't stop him.

Gideon watches me unravel, eyes half-lidded, devouring. My insides are still trembling, aching with everything he gave—and everything he didn't.

Surely, surely he wouldn't—

But then I feel it. That eerie stillness in him—the kind that only comes before chaos. His gaze burns through me, throat working, jaw clenched like he's holding back something feral.

And then he moves.

Of course he does.

He lunges before I can even blink, dragging me up against him like I'm the answer to a question he can't stop asking. His mouth crashes onto mine—no warning, no pretense. Just heat. Just hunger. Just him.

It's not gentle. It's not sweet. It's filthy. Wild. Like he needs to mark me again before the world peels us apart. His tongue forces its way in, claiming, ruining, tasting like sin and control and everything I should be running from.

But I don't run. I break.

A helpless sound claws out of me, and my hands are in his jacket, fisting, clinging. My whole body is molten and weightless and wrecked, and he's kissing me like he'd burn the world down to keep me tasting like this.

When he finally rips away, I'm breathless—gasping, dizzy, soaked in adrenaline and want. My chest is heaving. My thighs are trembling. His eyes? Black. Bottomless. Like he wants to consume me from the inside out.

"My goddess," he breathes. His voice is wrecked. His hands are shaking. "My filthy-sweet, fucking perfect girl."

And that's it.

The last thread of sanity in me just *snaps*. Gone.

There's no me without him anymore. Just this. Just us. Just the madness we keep feeding like it's holy.

I tilt my head back, baring my throat like an offering. Daring him to keep going. To ruin me completely.

Let the fallout come. Let the whole damn sky crack open. I'd still crawl back for more.

Chapter 14

Into The Fire

Gideon

Naomi.

My sweet syntax girl. My divine unraveling.

She's in my blood now—scratching down my spine, laced into every pulse. Each mile I put between us is like being flayed alive, a thousand cuts of absence. Logic says space is smart. Control says I should wait. But I've never been good at obeying my own rules.

Especially not when it comes to her.

Since the moment she crashed into my life—all sharp defiance and trembling need—nothing's felt right unless she's in my orbit. She's the contradiction I crave: soft curves and hard boundaries, surrender laced with fire. I don't just want to fuck her—I want to *undo* her. Break her wide open and make a home in whatever's left.

But obsession doesn't exist in a vacuum. There are always consequences. People watching. Waiting.

As I pull into the garage of my building, I sit in the idling silence a beat longer than necessary. The London meeting was meant to be a formality. Roman warned me—*You're being too visible. The Hawthornes don't like unpredictability. They'll test you.* And they are. They have been. From boardroom sabotage to whispers about my private life, the old guard is circling. They want compliance. Legacy. Control.

And they sure as hell don't want Naomi Walker.

I should play it safe. Let her go. But when has anything about this been safe?

The car screeches to a halt in front of my building. I leave it running and stalk through the marble and glass lobby, snapping orders into my headset. "Royce, have the jet ready in an hour. Tuscany. I want Amelia to pack the usual, plus the black rope, the antique cuffs, the sensory hood. And the pinot from my father's private cellar."

A pause. "For Tuscany, sir? Are we extending the timeline?"

"Indefinitely," I bite out. "And cancel the security detail. I want full privacy."

Royce doesn't argue, but I can feel the tension on the line. He knows this is a diversion from the plan. A risk. He also knows better than to question me.

I take the elevator up, the mirrored walls throwing my reflection back like a warning. Hair damp from rain. Jaw clenched. Eyes dark from too many sleepless nights thinking about her—about what I want to do to her, about what it means that I can't stop.

As I storm into the penthouse, the weight of two conflicting worlds drags behind every step. One foot still buried in the family empire—dark ties, obligations I've tried to outrun. The other tangled in a woman whose body and mind speak a language so deep, it's rewired my entire system.

Roman and Remi have called three times today. I ignored every ring. I know what they'll say—warnings dressed up as pleasantries. Advice disguised as orders.

Get her out of your system, Gideon. Don't make this more than it is.

But it's already more. It's *everything.*

I rip off my jacket and shirt as I stalk into my closet. The beast inside me paces, rabid. I want her trembling. I want her open. I want her wrapped in silk and moaning my name with every breath.

The phone is in my hand before I realize I've moved.

She picks up on the second ring, breath catching like she already knows what's coming.

"Naomi."

The word lands like a lit match. She sucks in a breath.

"Gideon—what—?"

"You have sixteen minutes to pack a bag."

"What? Where—"

"Tuscany. With me. I'm not asking. You'll be ready. You'll be waiting."

"You can't just—"

"I can. And I am. Wrap yourself in something indecent. Show me the fire you try to bury beneath cardigans and code. I want you wet and ready when I walk through that door."

The silence crackles. Then: "Yes, Sir."

That's it. My last shred of restraint snaps.

I don't knock. The lock gives under my hand like it's supposed to. Like it *wants* to. Her apartment smells like coffee, lavender, and something messier underneath. Her.

She's in the bedroom. Half-dressed, flushed, scandalized. Beautiful.

"You can't just barge in here!" she yells, eyes sparking.

I drink her in. Damp hair, bare thighs, lace doing nothing to hide how ready she is for me.

"I was hoping you wouldn't be dressed."

She clutches a sweater to her chest like armor, but the way her legs press together gives her away. I cross the room in three strides, grab her wrists, and pull her in. She molds against me like she's meant to be there.

"You were supposed to be ready." I nip her neck, drawing a gasp. "What's the holdup? Too distracted fingering yourself to your little romance novels?"

She flushes. "I wasn't—"

"Liar," I growl, sliding my thigh between hers and grinding up. "You soaked this lace pretending it was me."

She whimpers, biting her lip. I nearly lose it.

But not yet. I promised her more than a fuck. I promised her *everything.*

I force myself to step back. To breathe. To let her pack.

"Finish getting ready," I say, voice rough. "The sooner you're done, the sooner I can peel that scrap off you and remind your body who it belongs to."

"Yes, Sir," she whispers.

She moves around the room like a siren in silk, hips swaying, cheeks flushed. She throws in lingerie, strappy heels, and a black dress that's barely legal. I watch her zip the suitcase shut, slow and deliberate.

The sound echoes like a starter pistol.

I'm on her in a second, lifting her off the floor, her laugh warm against my throat.

"Ready to be ruined, Sweet Red?"

She wraps her legs around me, breath catching. "Always."

And just like that, we're off. Toward the jet. Toward Tuscany.

The wine is loaded. The villa prepped. The bed turned down, ropes coiled, anticipation like smoke in the air. And the cuffs—waiting in the drawer beside the bed with her name written in every knot.

Toward whatever beautiful chaos comes next.

And I won't stop until she's mine in every possible way.

Not just owned. Not just broken.

Worshipped.

The jet hums beneath us like a living beast, thrumming with possibility. She sits across from me in sin-black silk, thighs crossed, eyes wide with everything she can't yet say.

I don't touch her.

Not yet.

Not until we're over the water. Not until the cabin lights dim and privacy becomes law.

She thinks I'm calm. That I'm giving her space.

But the restraint is pure strategy. When I finally touch her—when I *take* her—there won't be a doubt left who she belongs to.

I raise my glass. "To Tuscany."

She clinks hers, hand trembling. "To whatever happens next."

I smile, slow and savage.

"Oh, Red. You have *no* idea what's coming."

The phone buzzes on the armrest beside me. Remi.

I debate ignoring it. I don't.

His voice is smooth, familiar, carrying that Hawthorne humor we've used for years to survive this mess.

"So. Tuscany, huh? Couldn't resist coming back to the mothership?"

I snort. "If by mothership you mean avoiding the old men's weekly coup attempt, then sure."

"Just be careful, cousin. You know the uncles love a good power vacuum. And Roman's already taking bets on how long you last."

I grin despite myself. "Tell Roman to go fuck himself."

"I'll add it to my morning agenda."

He pauses, voice lowering a fraction.

“Seriously though... bringing her in this deep?”

“I know what I’m doing.”

“You always say that. Right before someone starts bleeding.”

“As long as I’m not the one doing it.”

“Good. Because you know if you fall, we’ll be there pulling you back out.”

The call ends, but the weight of it lingers long after the silence returns.

Chapter 15

Altitude And Attitude Adjustments

Naomi

The jet is too quiet.

Not in a bad way. In the way that makes your skin prickle with anticipation. The kind of silence that isn't empty but full of unsaid things—sex-slick tension and promises tied in velvet rope.

I'm not used to this kind of opulence. But more than that, I'm not used to being this version of myself—half-naked in a private plane, drenched in the aftermath of Gideon Hawke's attention, strung so tight I could unravel from one well-placed word.

He's sitting across from me like he owns the fucking sky.

Jacket discarded, shirt unbuttoned just enough to tempt ruin. Legs sprawled like the plane belongs to his thighs. And maybe it does. Hell, maybe I do.

The weight of his stare crawls over my skin, sliding under my hemline like a phantom hand. I shift in the buttery leather seat, pretending I'm not soaked through. Pretending I can still play this cool. But the way his mouth curves—smug, devastating—tells me he sees right through me.

"Relax, Sweet Red," he murmurs. "You look like you're about to be devoured."

My laugh is breathy. "You mean I'm not?"

His smirk grows, but there's something behind it—feral. Possessive. He tilts his glass and watches me over the rim. "You haven't even tasted the beginning of what I have planned for you."

I press my thighs together. A feeble defense. There's no holding this line. Not when he's already under my skin and between my ribs.

"You always talk like that," I murmur, voice barely steady. "Like I'm already yours."

"You are," he says simply. No hesitation. No question. Just brutal certainty.

I should argue. Remind him I'm not property, not a kink project for him to mold into perfection. But that's not what he's doing, is it? That's not what *this* is.

This is Gideon Hawke—dangerous, dominant, and raw—handing me the key to every dark desire I've been too scared to unlock. He doesn't want to change me. He wants to strip me down to the bones of my craving and build me into something feral and free.

The worst part? I want it too.

"So what happens when we land?" I ask, trying to sound casual.

He sets the glass down and leans forward, elbows braced on his powerful thighs. "Then I stop being polite."

Goosebumps scatter across my skin like he struck a match to my spine.

"Polite is a strong word for what just happened on that couch," I whisper.

His smile is pure sin. "That was restraint."

I should be terrified. Maybe I am. But it's the kind of fear that feels like hunger. Like being on the edge of a cliff and knowing you're about to jump—not because you want to fall, but because you *need* to fly.

He doesn't move, doesn't reach for me. Just waits. Watches. Like a predator giving me the illusion of choice before he pounces.

I lean forward anyway, pulse skittering like code under my skin. "And if I said I'm ready?"

His pupils blow wide. "Then you'll learn what it really means to be *mine.*"

The jet dips slightly as we bank, a reminder that the world is still turning below us. But up here, in this charged, suspended space between cities and skin, the only thing that matters is this pull between us—gravity rewritten, logic gone.

He raises a brow. "Last chance to back out, little Red."

I shake my head slowly, deliberately. "I'm not running anymore."

His smile turns molten. "Good."

I adjust my position, squirming under the aftershock of his words, the weight of his stare. It's too much and not enough all at once. My pulse riots. My panties? Forget it. I need a reset—or at least sixty seconds of cool air and sanity.

I shift again in the seat, trying to collect my scattered thoughts, but it's no use. The air between us hums, and I know if I look at him for one more second, I'll climb into his lap and beg.

So I stand, muttering something vague about touching up my lipstick, and grab my phone. As I turn down the narrow hallway toward the bathroom, I feel his eyes on me. Not following. Just waiting. Patient as sin.

Inside the tiny, gold-trimmed space, I splash cold water on my cheeks and brace my hands on the counter. My reflection is flushed, pupils blown, hair wild from his fingers. A faint mark blooms at my collarbone—a souvenir from his mouth. I look like someone who's been ruined mid-air. Because I have.

The marble counter is cool under my fingertips, the air thick with the spice of his cologne lingering on my skin. For one breathless moment, I let myself spiral.

I could say no. I could walk back to my seat, buckle up, and pretend this isn't the most unhinged, unspeakably hot chapter of my life. But then he wouldn't touch me like I'm a cathedral and a curse. Then I wouldn't feel this beautiful, terrifying surrender. And I want that. I want all of it.

I fumble for my phone, needing something to tether me to reality. The group chat lights up before I even unlock it.

Zoe: if ur not currently mile-highing that man, i swear to god

Jor: give her a second, she's probably tied to a ceiling

Jade: ⊠⊠⊠

Zoe: NAOMI.

I nearly type *"he growled and my knees gave out"*, but delete it.

Me: *He's dangerous. In like, I-might-lose-my-soul-and-say-thank-you way.*

Jor: ugh i love that for you

Zoe: drop a pin. not for safety, just so i can haunt the location later.

Jade: remember your safe word, bestie ⊠

A laugh bubbles out—sharp, sweet, an exhale of tension I didn't realize I'd been choking on. These women? They're my oxygen.

The screen lights again.

GIDEON: You've got sixty seconds before I kick this door in.

My stomach drops. In the best way. In the soaked-through, thighs-clench, heart-racing way.

GIDEON: *Tick tock, Sweet Red.*

I gasp, clutching the sink like it might stop me from melting through the floor. The girls are still blowing up the chat, but I'm already sliding the phone into my pocket and adjusting my dress.

Time's up.

I open the door slowly, adjusting my dress like it might hide the flush in my cheeks or the bite marks blooming at my collarbone.

Gideon's already on his feet.

Not leaning, not lounging—waiting.

That kind of stillness that says: *I've been patient. Now it's your turn to squirm.*

His gaze rakes over me, deliberate. "Feeling better?"

"Define better," I rasp, leaning one shoulder against the frame like I'm not two seconds from combusting. "The group chat thinks I'm tied to the ceiling."

His mouth twitches. "A flattering assumption."

"Also accurate."

He steps closer—just once. No rush. My breath stutters as he brushes a knuckle down my arm.

"I gave you a minute to catch your breath," he murmurs. "That was generous."

I swallow hard. "And now that I've caught it?"

"Then I'll take it from you, again. Every last gasp."

I don't even realize I've stepped toward him until the space between us vanishes—like I was pulled into his gravity.

His fingers ghost down my spine, and my back arches instinctively.

"Still squirming," he observes. "Still wet for me."

My lips part in a gasp. "You're very confident."

"I've earned it."

The worst part is—he has.

But I can't let him know just how deep he's sunk his claws. Not yet. So I tilt my chin and summon what's left of my composure.

"You said you'd stop being polite once we landed," I say. "We're still airborne. What's your excuse now?"

His hand fists in the hem of my dress, dragging it slowly upward. "Think of this as...final boarding call for your virtue."

I snort, a laugh slipping through even as my thighs clench. "Please. That train left the station somewhere over the Atlantic."

He hums, pleased. "Good girl."

My knees wobble.

"Turn around," he says quietly. "Hands on the wall."

I blink. "Excuse me?"

"You heard me, Naomi."

The way he says my name—it's not a request. It's prophecy.

But I don't move.

Not until I say it. Not until I *choose* it.

"You sure you're ready?" I whisper. "Because once I give you everything, I don't know how to take it back."

His jaw flexes. Something flares in his gaze—dangerous and wild and worshipful all at once.

"I don't want it back," he says. "I want it *ruined.*"

My breath leaves me in a rush.

Okay, then.

I turn. Place my palms flat against the wall beside the drink cart, trembling all over. The low thrum of the engines is nothing compared to the roar in my ears. The chill of the cabin bumps against the heat curling low in my belly, and I swear I can feel him watching every breath.

Behind me, I feel the shift in air before I feel his hands.

One slides up my thigh, slow and reverent, until he's cupping the soaked silk between my legs.

The other wraps lightly around my throat, not squeezing, just reminding.

I bite my lip, arching into the touch.

He lowers his mouth to my ear, voice gravel and sin.

"You should thank your friends," he murmurs. "That little bathroom break bought you just enough time to become my next in-flight entertainment."

And then he slips a finger beneath the fabric and drags it down, down, down—

I moan, forehead thunking against the wall.

This man is going to destroy me.

And I'm going to beg for more.

Chapter 16

Break Me Gently

Naomi

The jet touches down in Rome just before golden hour—because of course it does. As if this whole unhinged chapter of my life couldn't get more cinematic. The city greets us with a humid kiss, all gilded light and distant bells and the kind of old-world romance that makes your knees go soft.

I'm buzzing. Not just from the altitude or the orgasm he wrung out of me at thirty thousand feet—but from *him*. From the intensity of being looked at like I'm the only thing tethering him to the earth. But now, I can't help but wonder—what happens when the tether starts to fray?

Gideon holds my hand like he owns it. Like I'm not capable of walking through this airport unless he decides I can. There's a black car waiting at the curb, the driver already ducking into a crisp bow as we approach. And the second the doors close behind us, that subtle pressure of his palm slides to the nape of my neck. He doesn't say a word. He doesn't have to.

By the time the gates swing open, revealing a villa carved from marble and fantasy, I've already sweat through my dress. The scent of cypress and ancient stone clings to the warm Roman air, a sensory punch of history and luxury that makes my skin buzz. Rome doesn't just exist—it *performs*, stretching its sun-drenched limbs like it knows it's being watched. Ivy creeps up stone walls. A fountain gurgles beside a path of ancient stone. I'm still staring when he leads me through the foyer with a murmured, "We'll only be here a few days."

Only a few days? I almost ask. But then he's guiding me upstairs, his palm warm and firm against my lower back.

The bedroom he leads me into is drenched in gold and shadow. I don't even get a chance to admire the intricate molding or the sprawling view before he halts behind me.

"Strip."

The word drops like a stone in a still pool. No preamble, no hesitation. I know that tone. I know what it means. My breath catches and my fingers move on instinct, lowering the zipper of my sundress until it slides over my hips in a whisper of fabric.

His tie becomes a blindfold. Silk rope binds my wrists. And his voice, that low velvet-dagger whisper, talks me through every second of being worshipped like I'm divine.

Later, after I've floated back down to Earth and he's unbound me with a gentleness that makes my throat ache, I curl into his side. His fingers linger for a moment too long on the rope marks, as if memorizing them. I catch the ghost of hesitation in his breath before it smooths out, a performance I wouldn't have noticed before. He doesn't speak. Doesn't sleep. Just breathes. Steady. Shallow.

I press my ear to his chest, listening to the thunder of his heartbeat. Still too fast. It's the only wild thing he doesn't try to control—and somehow, that's more intimate than anything he's said aloud.

The next morning, sun spills through gauzy curtains, and I wake to an empty bed. I find him on the terrace already dressed, sipping an espresso like he didn't keep me spread-eagled and ruined on thousand-thread-count sheets just hours earlier. He nods at me, all crisp shirt and sharp jawline, and gestures toward the table set for two.

We wander through winding alleys later that afternoon. Gelato drips over my fingers as he kisses my temple in public. His hand tightens on my waist every time I get too bold with my sass. He buys me a book in a language I can't read and makes me promise to translate it one day. We linger over wine and candlelight on a rooftop restaurant, and when I tease him too much over dinner, he pulls me into a dark alley near the Pantheon and tells me I was made to kneel.

So I do. Right there. With cobblestones under my knees and history echoing around us.

When we stumble back into the villa, flushed and breathless, I almost forget the part where he vanishes again after I fall asleep.

Almost.

Except I wake up around two a.m. The sheets are cool beside me. I follow the dim glow of light seeping from beneath the kitchen door, moving barefoot down the long hallway. I pause just short of the threshold.

Gideon stands shirtless in the shadows, lit only by the fridge light. His silhouette is all sharp edges and coiled restraint, a marble statue built for war. His voice curls through the air like smoke—measured, icy, threaded with steel. A phone cradled to his ear. His voice low. Sharp. Italian curling off his tongue like something dangerous. When he says *famiglia*, it's not soft. His accent hardens, slicing through the hush like a blade. The word sounds older than him—older than this kitchen—something passed down like a curse or a crown. My name slips in there. So does *famiglia.*

A scent hits me—gunmetal and ash. Colder than his usual warm spice. It sticks in the air like a warning, the kind that makes prey go still.

He doesn't notice me until I shift, the floor creaking beneath my weight.

His tone changes instantly. He ends the call without so much as a glance.

"I couldn't sleep," I say quietly.

"Me neither."

He brushes past me on the way out, not offering more.

Back in the bedroom, I lie awake and scroll.

The group chat is unhinged.

ZOE: do italians eat ass with more passion or am i projecting?

JOR: she's probably negotiating her way out of a blindfold with safe word flashcards

JADE: she's either getting dicked down or buried in silk ropes, I will settle for nothing less.

ZOE: RED. WAKE. UP.

ME: He eats the peach like groceries Zoe! He fucks me like a pornstar. Then praises me like he's speaking in symphonies.

ZOE: The Mozart of dirty talk. Universe, I see what you're doing for others.

JOR: girl this is either your villain origin story or your wedding announcement, no in-between

JADE: stay sexy and paranoid. also send nudes.

I snort, but it doesn't quite stick. Something in my chest is hollowing out and I don't know why.

The next evening, we're back on the terrace. Rome sprawls beneath us, glittering and oblivious. Gideon pours wine with elegant fingers, his eyes distant as I talk. I trail off mid-sentence when I realize he's not listening.

He notices. Tries to cover it with a kiss. A touch. A possessive murmur against my neck.

It doesn't work.

I let him take me against the terrace railing anyway.

And when I come apart, screaming his name into the Roman night, it's not escape I feel. It's something else entirely.

Something closing in.

Something waiting.

And silk rope won't be enough to keep it out.

I stay pressed against the railing longer than I should, the echo of his name still hanging in the humid air. Gideon's arms cage me in, lips dragging lazy kisses down my shoulder like punctuation marks to the scene we just wrote against the stars.

But even drunk on endorphins, I can feel the space yawning open again. A gap between us that can't be tied shut with rope or orgasms.

I turn in his arms, breath still ragged. "That call you took last night... the one in the kitchen. Who were you talking to?"

His lashes lower. The soft intimacy of the moment recedes like a tide. "Business."

"*Famiglia* isn't just business, though, is it?" I press, gently. "You said my name."

For a flicker, something sparks in his eyes—dangerous, beautiful, wounded. But it's gone just as fast, replaced by that velvety smirk that usually melts my spine.

"I say your name all the time, Naomi. Usually when I'm making you beg."

I force a laugh, but it tastes like iron. He leans in, pressing a final kiss to my temple, and murmurs something about needing to make a few calls.

When the door clicks shut behind him, I stand there in nothing but a silk robe and confusion. The sky over Rome is bleeding gold, and I feel like I'm slowly drowning in it.

I wander back inside, bare feet brushing against cold marble. In the bedroom, his scent lingers—spice and cedar, leather and ozone. But underneath it now, faint and chilling, is the ghost of something colder.

I slip one of his crisp white shirts off the hanger and pull it on, the sleeves too long, the collar swallowing my neck. But it grounds me, somehow.

The little Italian novel he bought me sits on the nightstand. I thumb through the pages, stopping at a line printed in delicate script: *Ti spezzerò dolcemente.* I type it into my phone.

I will break you gently.

The words sit heavy in my chest, like truth dressed up in poetry.

When I lift my gaze to the mirror, I look like someone else. Hair wild. Eyes wide. Dressed in a man's shirt, in a borrowed city, in a story I don't fully understand.

Rome whispers outside the window—cathedrals and sin, sirens and secrets. I pad to the glass and lean my forehead against it, watching the lights flicker to life across ancient rooftops.

I wanted to be the heroine. The main character. The bold bitch who gets swept away and owns it.

But right now, I don't feel like the lead.

I feel like the plot twist.

Chapter 17

The Stars Between Us

Gideon

The Tuscan sun dips low on the horizon, painting the sky in molten fire. I lead Naomi onto the villa's candlelit terrace, every sense sharpening. The air is drenched in jasmine and ripe grapes, warm and decadent, and she's right beside me—a vision in a backless silk dress, curls bouncing with every step.

She glances up, brows lifting. "What is all this?"

"This—" I gesture to the twinkling lights, the linen-draped table, the champagne chilling in a bucket of ice "—is me romancing the hell out of you."

She smirks, skeptical but intrigued. "You trying to buy your way out of something, Hawke?"

"I'm trying to wine and dine you until you can't see straight," I reply, pulling out her chair. "Until your only thoughts are of how good it feels to be worshipped."

A flush steals up her neck. I've barely touched her, and still—I feel the spark, the awareness between us like an electric thread.

We toast. We laugh. We eat.

I lay the trap halfway through dessert.

"Let's play a game."

Naomi licks a smear of ganache from her spoon and eyes me warily. "What kind of game?"

"An exchange of truths. Raw ones. No armor. Just us."

Her gaze narrows. Then she downs the rest of her champagne and says, "You first."

It startles a laugh out of me. I pour her something stronger—Macallan 25, the kind you save for confessions.

"Alright," I murmur. "What's your biggest fear?"

She hesitates. The terrace flickers with lanternlight. Her silhouette shimmers, delicate but unyielding.

"That I'll never be enough. That I'm too much in all the wrong ways. And that eventually, the people I love will realize it and leave."

I feel the blow like a fist. Because I know that voice in her head. I've lived with it my whole life.

"You're not just enough, Naomi. You're everything."

She doesn't believe me yet. But I'll show her.

We trade questions like lifelines.

I tell her about my mother. About how I watched her disappear piece by piece long before her body ever gave out. How she smiled less, spoke less. How the light behind her eyes dimmed under the weight of expectations she never fully agreed to carry.

"She married into something she didn't understand," I murmur. "Or maybe she did. But she thought she could survive it."

Naomi's thumb rubs slow circles over my knuckles. Silent, patient.

"My father followed Vito's every word. Obedience disguised as loyalty. My mother..." My throat tightens. "She was different. She wanted freedom. And the more she tried to breathe, the more the family made sure she couldn't."

Naomi whispers, "That wasn't your burden."

"I was a kid." My voice fractures. "I thought if I was smarter. Stronger. Good enough. She'd stay. She'd fight. But she was already drowning by the time I understood what was happening."

Her fingers tighten around mine. "You were never meant to save her."

I nod, but the guilt doesn't ease. "I couldn't protect her. So now I try to control everything else. Because if I fail again, it won't just break me—it'll destroy everything I touch."

Naomi reaches for my hand. "It wasn't your fault."

But it still feels like it. Some scars stay warm even after the fire dies.

She leads me into the garden afterward, murmuring about stargazing. And there, nestled in a nest of cushions under vines and lanterns and the vast, ancient sky—she gives me a moment I never knew I needed.

I lie beside her, quieted. Listening to the wind. To the way her breath hitches when I trace the freckles on her arm like constellations.

I tell her about Orion, about the myths my mother believed in. About how she always said I'd fall for someone who would wreck me in the best way.

"Looks like she was right," I say, brushing my thumb over Naomi's bottom lip.

Naomi snorts, dissolving into giggles.

God, I love her.

"That," I tell her, raining kisses across her nose and cheeks, "is my favorite thing. The snort. The way you let go. The real you."

She tries to hide her face. I don't let her.

We make love under the stars. Not rough or hurried or dark—but slow. Worshipful. Like I can touch her enough to rewrite every cruel word she's ever internalized. Like I can map her body and discover a universe.

She tells me she wants all my pieces. The good, the broken, the ugly. The truth.

So I give it to her.

"I love you."

There's a heartbeat of silence. Then she whispers, "Finally," and kisses me like she wants to steal the breath from my lungs.

Later, when she drifts off against my chest, fingers curled in my shirt, I stare up at the sky and think of the masquerade tomorrow. Of the performance I'll have to give. The legacy that threatens to pull me back in.

But for tonight, I'm hers. No masks. No roles. Just a man in love with a woman too good for the world I come from.

Let the stars bear witness.

The ballroom gleams like a weapon. Polished marble, low golden lighting, the clink of crystal echoing as the staff place the final flutes of champagne on mirrored trays. Outside, the sun slouches low across Rome's skyline, gilding everything in a blood-warm hue.

Rome moves differently than New York. Slower, more decadent. It breathes history into your bones, and tonight, it feels like the walls themselves are watching.

I stand alone under the chandeliers, rolling the chain of my pocket watch between my fingers. I haven't carried it in years, not since I inherited it. I don't even check the time—just keep winding it around my knuckles, over and over. A loop. A tell. A meditation I haven't earned.

Remi spots it the moment he walks in.

"Well, shit," he mutters, flicking an invisible speck from the lapel of his velvet blazer. "He's rolling the heirloom. That's new."

"Very vintage," Roman deadpans, following behind with a half-smile and eyes sharp as razors. "What's the matter, cousin? Gilded cage closing in?"

"I didn't invite you here to wax poetic about my jewelry."

"No," Roman says, pacing a slow circle around the ballroom, hands in his pockets. "You invited us to this mafia debutante ball because Father dearest wants to show off his prized bastard and keep the alliance rumor mill churning."

Remi leans against a column, uncorks a miniature bottle of grappa from somewhere inside his jacket. Offers it. I decline with a glance. He smirks and downs it anyway.

"So," Remi drawls, voice light but eyes deadly serious, "is she coming?"

"She'll be ready."

"Is she ready, though? For all of this?" Roman asks, tone deceptively soft. "For famiglia?"

The word scrapes across my spine. I roll the watch chain tighter.

"Don't say that around her."

"What, famiglia?" Remi quirks a brow. "Jesus, Gid. You think we brought a blood-soaked banner with us? We're not here to spook your little goddess. We like her."

Roman steps in closer, his voice low. "But you're not being honest with her."

That stings more than I want to admit. I look away first.

Remi tosses me a look. "You didn't tell her about the marriage alliance, huh? Or Dante? Or that this whole event is a ceremonial dog and pony show for legacy vultures who'd sell their children for a stake in the Hawthorne-Corleone pipeline."

"You two came here to make a scene or help me avoid one?"

"We came to make sure you don't get eaten alive," Roman says flatly. "Or worse, get her eaten alive."

I scoff, but it rings hollow. Then my phone buzzes.

My father.

Of course.

I take the call, stepping into the shadows beside a marble pillar. The voice on the other end is cold steel wrapped in velvet. Smooth threats, laced with obligation. He talks alliances, power consolidation, my cousin Dante Corleone's rise in Accent City, and how I'm "expected to maintain appearances."

I tell him I'm not marrying into blood debt.

He replies, "Then make sure your distraction is convincing enough to buy us time."

The line goes dead. I almost crush the phone in my hand.

When I turn back, Roman's already watching. Seeing too much. Always.

"You're unraveling."

"I'm fine."

Remi tosses a grape in the air and catches it in his mouth. "You're in love with her."

I look up, slowly.

Roman smirks. "He didn't deny it."

"She's not a shield," Remi adds. "She's a mirror. Don't flinch when you start seeing things you buried."

When I return to the villa, Rome's scent clings to me—warm stone and citrus, motor oil and basil. The villa itself is silent save for the soft click of Naomi's heels echoing down the hall.

She's in front of the vanity, legs crossed, dress slung low off one shoulder. Her lips are soft from biting them. There's a flush in her cheeks that has nothing to do with heat.

She laughs at something on her phone. The sound nearly undoes me. It's too human, too easy. Too much.

I cross the room in silence, slipping behind her, fingers brushing the nape of her neck. Her skin is warm silk, and she shivers beneath my touch.

"Tonight," I murmur, letting the command settle into the curve of her spine, "you don't wear panties."

She startles slightly, catching my gaze in the mirror.

"You maintain eye contact at all times. You listen only to me. Obey without hesitation. Subtle, deliberate. No one else needs to know. But I will. Every time."

Her pupils dilate. Her breath shallows. I watch her toes curl against the carpet.

"Why?"

"Because I need something tonight that belongs only to us."

She nods. No hesitation.

But when she turns to kiss me, I hesitate. Just for a breath. Long enough to hear my father's voice echo in my skull: *Make sure your distraction is convincing enough to buy us time.*

Naomi doesn't miss it. Her eyes search mine like a question I can't afford to answer. Not yet.

I pull her closer anyway. Kiss her temple instead.

"You'll be safe tonight. No matter what. You have my word."

She holds my gaze a moment longer, then slips from the room. The scent of her lingers—jasmine and something darker. Something that always calls me back.

When she's gone, I stay at the mirror. The chain slides through my fingers like penance.

Remi's voice lives in the silence: *She's a mirror.*

And for the first time in years, I can't meet my own reflection.

Chapter 18

A Taste of Tomorrow

Gideon

Naomi's voice drifts through the open balcony doors, low and commanding, smooth as scotch over ice. The Roman breeze carries it into the suite, teasing the edges of the linen curtains, stirring the scent of fresh bread and citrus from the street below. She's perched at the patio table, one leg curled beneath her, silk robe gaping just enough to distract if I weren't already enthralled by the other show she's giving—flawless execution under pressure.

"Check the backup DNS tables," she instructs, her fingers flying over the keys with the elegance of a concert pianist. "If it's what I think it is, we've got a piggyback intrusion riding a masked redirect. Flag it, patch it, and don't touch the live client until I've reviewed the logs."

Her voice doesn't rise. It slices. Precise. Lethal. She pauses to listen as someone on the other end tries to explain the audit trail. Her nostrils flare. Her eyes narrow.

"No," she says. "You're missing the pivot point. Look at the false heartbeat in the log. You'll see the clone process kicking off three minutes before anyone touched the internal build."

A beat.

"That's right. You found it. Now make it disappear like it was never there."

Behind it all, the soft click of the keyboard forms a counter-rhythm to the distant rumble of Rome's late-morning traffic. A bell tolls from some distant tower. I sip my espresso from the doorway, letting the bitter heat anchor me as I watch her. When she finally closes the laptop and leans back, there's a flush on her cheeks and a satisfied gleam in her eye—the look of someone who just won a war most people didn't know was happening.

"You just saved us a six-figure disaster," I say.

Naomi lifts her cup, eyes on mine. "That's why they pay me the big bucks."

She takes a sip and stands, stretching slow and unapologetically. The robe parts further along her thigh, and my gaze follows instinctively, but it's not the sight of her skin that wrecks me—it's the power in her stance. Like she owns the moment. Like she owns me.

"You done playing voyeur, or do you plan to keep lurking and brooding all morning?" she teases, walking toward me, her grin just this side of smug.

"I plan," I say, offering my hand, "to take you somewhere."

Naomi raises a brow, placing her hand in mine. "Lead the way, Mr. Hawke."

By late morning, we're rolling out of the city in a sleek black car, the hum of the engine and Naomi's tapping fingers blending with the rhythmic lull of countryside roads. She props one leg up on the seat, watching the chaos of Rome melt behind us, replaced by undulating olive groves and vineyard-stained slopes. Golden light spills over the countryside like liquid wealth.

We pass weathered stone houses, laundry flapping like flags of surrender. Beehives tucked beneath fig trees. Somewhere, children shout in Italian as a soccer ball thuds against pavement. The scent of warm earth and herbs drifts in through the half-lowered windows.

As the car winds up a narrow lane and through wrought iron gates, the villa reveals itself like a secret waiting to be whispered. It sits surrounded by lavender in full bloom, glowing in the soft press of afternoon light.

Naomi's fingers tighten slightly around mine as we step out onto the gravel drive. Her gaze finds the twinkling fairy lights first, then trails down to the table set beneath them. White linen, glinting silverware, a bottle of champagne in a sweating bucket of ice. The air smells of lemons and rosemary.

"You're going to make me blush," she says, low, almost reverent.

"I'm going to romance the hell out of you," I reply, brushing a kiss to her knuckles.

Her laughter bubbles up unexpectedly, rich and unguarded, and I know I've already won the moment.

A short while later, after a quick freshen-up and a change into clothes more suited to seduction and slow meals, we're seated at the table under the soft glow of golden hour. We're served in courses by a chef who knows how to vanish when needed. Grilled peaches with mascarpone and basil. Seared duck with a glaze that tastes like the end of summer. Warm bread broken between us, dipped into oil that sings with fresh-pressed olives. Naomi moans after her first bite. I consider proposing on the spot.

A cicada chirrs somewhere nearby. Naomi leans back in her chair, a queen surveying her kingdom. The flickering candlelight dances in her eyes.

We talk. About nothing and everything. The ridiculousness of that tour guide this morning, her take on the new encryption protocols, my inability to stop checking the perimeter cameras even in paradise. She eyes the second bottle I brought—Macallan 25, because her scotch tolerance is as impressive as her server uptime. I pour her a finger.

"Let's play a game," I say, topping off my own glass.

Naomi leans back, arching a brow. "If this ends with me naked in the garden, just say that upfront."

I chuckle. "Secrets. One for one. What are you afraid of?"

She doesn't answer right away. The mask she wears so well softens, falters. Her lips part, and her eyes lose some of their flint.

"That I'll never be enough," she says softly. "Or too much. That I'll burn bright and still leave people cold."

The words settle between us like ash. My heart aches with the honesty of it.

"Sweet Red," I say, reaching for her hand. Her pulse thrums beneath my thumb. "You're not too much. You're exactly the fire I never knew I needed."

She swallows, and I can tell she wants to believe me.

"My turn," she says. "What's your biggest regret?"

I take a slow drink. The scotch burns going down, but not enough to dull what I know is coming.

"Letting my mother die thinking I didn't love her enough to save her."

The air shifts. Candlelight flickers in the silence. Naomi reaches for my face, her palm warm against my skin.

"You did what you could," she murmurs. "You loved her. That's not failure."

I shake my head, but the gesture's weak. Her eyes stay on mine, steady and unwavering.

Naomi smiles this time, steady and sure. "Good. You're getting better at saying it." She rises first, tugging me by the hand past the terrace. The gravel crunches beneath our feet as we enter the gardens. The scent of rosemary, damp earth, and jasmine thickens, a fragrant tide pulling us deeper into the night.

Around a bend, beneath an arch of bougainvillea, lies a nest of blankets and lanterns glowing like bottled starlight. Naomi turns to me with a smirk.

"I had help from the staff," she says. "Figured if you're going to romance me, I'd return the favor."

We collapse into the cushions together, the sky overhead unraveling into velvet darkness stitched with stars. Naomi curls against my chest, her breath soft against my skin.

"When I was a kid," I murmur, "my mom used to take me onto the roof of our building. She'd show me the constellations. Orion. The Pleiades. She said I'd fall in love with a woman who would challenge me every day of my life."

Naomi tilts her face toward mine. "Sounds like she knew what she was talking about."

"She always did."

Our lips find each other with the inevitability of gravity. The kiss deepens, slow and reverent. And when we make love beneath the stars, it's not hunger that drives me—it's worship.

Every stretch mark, every freckle, every laugh-snort and whispered gasp is holy. She's not a woman to me in that moment—she's the entire galaxy unfolding beneath my hands.

Later, when she's sleeping with her leg thrown over mine and her breath warming my collarbone, I reach for my phone. Just a glance.

The message glares like an omen.

Vito: Claudia arrives tomorrow. Handle it.

I stare at the screen, the buzz of the night pressing too close. I delete the message without blinking.

The jasmine feels heavier now. Cloying. I press a kiss to Naomi's crown and draw her tighter to my chest.

"I should've told you," I whisper into the dark.

But I didn't.

Because I wanted one more night before I ruined everything.

Naomi sleeps beside me, her body curved into mine like a comma at the end of a long sentence. Her lips are parted, lashes fanning against warm cheeks, and her breath slips out in soft, steady waves that anchor me more than I want to admit.

She's radiant like this—unguarded, boneless, drenched in the kind of trust I don't deserve. In sleep, Naomi is stripped of her fire and intellect, all sharp edges dulled to softness. And still, she wrecks me. Maybe even more so.

I prop myself up on one elbow and stare, letting my eyes drink her in like a man crawling out of the desert. The wild halo of curls spills across the pillow, a defiant crown even in rest. A rich mahogany strand drapes across her cheek. I reach out, brushing it away with a reverence usually reserved for sacred things.

My Sweet Red. Giver of lectures on hair bonnets. Keeper of secrets I've barely scratched. Champion of server fires and Sunday gospel playlists. She's all grit and grace, and I've never wanted anything more.

The memory of last night lingers on her skin—the echo of our laughter, the way she gripped my shoulders when I worshipped every inch of her. It's becoming an addiction. The taste of her. The sound of her gasping my name in that honey-slick voice, undone and radiant.

I press a hand to my face, forcing a steady breath.

Christ, Hawke. Get a grip.

You'd think three days of nonstop indulgence would take the edge off. But the hunger only sharpens. She feeds something feral in me. Something I've kept leashed for too long.

I slip carefully from the sheets, letting the absence of my weight barely disturb her. Crossing the room, I fish out my camera from its leather case, the familiar weight grounding me. For years, photography was control. Composition. A way to frame the chaos and make sense of it. But now?

Now, I want to capture chaos.

Naomi, tangled in white sheets. Naomi, half-draped in sun, a constellation of stretch marks glowing like stardust on her skin. Naomi, bare-faced and battle-worn from the night before, still the most beautiful thing I've ever seen.

I raise the camera and find the shot. Light floods the frame, haloing her curves. I exhale slowly.

Click.

Shit.

I forgot to mute the shutter.

Naomi stirs. One hand flutters over the pillow before her eyes blink open, slow and disoriented. Her gaze finds me instantly. Finds the camera.

A beat.

Then she smirks. "Mr. Hawke... were you photographing me in my sleep?"

That voice. Husky and amused, curling around my gut like smoke.

I lower the camera and offer my most unapologetic smile. "Just immortalizing a vision. For artistic purposes, of course."

Her brow arches. "Uh huh. Very respectful. Very professional. Totally not giving creepy husband energy."

"I'd argue devotion, not creepiness." I cross the room, kneel beside the bed, and tuck a curl behind her ear. "Besides, it's for personal use only. My own little shrine."

Naomi hums, stretching lazily, the movement pulling the sheet dangerously low. "So I'm your muse now?"

"You've always been my muse."

She looks away, suddenly shy. It's rare, and it makes something ancient and protective rear up inside me.

"I'm serious," I say. "No landscape. No city skyline. Nothing I've ever shot compares to this. To you."

Naomi rolls her eyes but the blush crawling up her neck betrays her. "You're dangerously good at this, you know."

"Book boyfriend made flesh," I murmur, stealing a kiss.

That gets a snort-laugh out of her, which immediately turns into a groan of protest as I yank the sheets back and toss her robe toward the closet.

"Get up. We've got places to be."

She blinks. "Wait, what? I thought we were having a slow morning. Cuddles. Coffee. More sex."

I smirk, already pulling on a crisp linen shirt. "Oh, we're still doing all that. Just... later. After brunch. And a shopping spree."

Naomi sits up slowly, the sheet falling to her waist, revealing bare shoulders and bite-marks I'm already proud of. "Shopping spree?"

"You need a few more souvenirs. I plan to spoil you thoroughly. Think Pretty Woman, but with better taste."

She narrows her eyes. "Gideon..."

I cross to her, pressing a kiss to her temple. "Ah ah. No arguments. What's mine is yours. Come be worshipped in silk."

By mid-morning, we're seated on a sunny terrace of a small bookstore-turned-café, sipping prosecco while the scent of old pages and warm croissants wraps around us. Naomi moans around a forkful of tart, and I swear the waiter blushes.

"You keep doing that," I murmur, "and I'll have to drag you into the stacks."

"Don't threaten me with a good time."

We eat until full, and then shop until her protests grow weak with delight. Naomi tries on flowy dresses in soft hues, the kind that hug her curves and billow around her knees. I help her out of each one under the guise of assistance, fingers grazing where they shouldn't. She swats me away every time—with diminishing sincerity.

By the time we hit the last boutique, our arms are full of silk and lace. I pull her into the final changing room, and this time, she doesn't resist.

The air between us tightens.

I back her up against the wall, my hands sliding under her hem, finding bare skin.

Naomi gasps as my fingers dance over the lace at her thighs. "You're insatiable," she whispers.

"Only for you."

I show her just how true that is—with my hands, my mouth, my body pressed tight against hers until her sighs drown out the hum of the world.

Later, I carry her back to the car, her laughter tucked against my neck. She naps on the ride back, spent and flushed, draped in a cashmere throw. The sun paints her in amber and bronze. She's a work of art, and she's mine.

The thought returns unbidden—

Naomi, in white lace. Naomi, belly round with our child. Naomi, wrinkled and soft beside me as the sun sets on a life we built.

Shit. I want it all. Marriage. Babies. Forever.

I glance over at her, asleep in the passenger seat. My heart clenches.

Then the buzz of my phone slices through the silence.

You've been warned, Gideon. Claudia lands at 6. Don't disappoint.

My jaw clenches. I delete the message without a second glance.

Naomi stirs, murmurs something about chocolate gelato in her sleep. I smile.

"I'll protect this," I whisper. "Even if it kills me."

Chapter 19

Moonlight And Honey

Naomi

Sun kisses my skin like a blessing as we gallop through the rolling Tuscan hills, wind tangling my hair into wild ribbons. The rhythmic thud of hooves against dry earth drums through my body, syncing with the wild, soaring beat of my heart. The air smells of sun-baked hay, cypress resin, and something sweet—grape must, maybe, or wildflowers crushed beneath our path.

Gideon rides slightly ahead, a vision of coiled power and casual elegance. His black shirt flutters open at the throat, hair tousled from the wind, and when he glances back at me with that crooked smile, I swear I forget how to breathe. Those glacier-blue eyes, usually so guarded, glint with a rare, unburdened joy.

Out here, under this sprawling sky, I'm not Naomi the code-slinger or Naomi the cautious submissive fumbling through a new world. I'm nothing except a woman—alive, open, and gloriously free. With him, I get to lay down the weight I've carried for years and just exist.

We crest a gentle rise, and the land spills open below us in a quilt of gold and green. Cypress trees stripe the hillsides, and nestled in a sun-warmed valley is a vineyard that looks like it was painted into reality—rows of grapevines curling in tidy lines, a weathered farmhouse in the distance, and a round wooden vat just waiting for mischief.

As we approach, the scent shifts—sharper now, fermented fruit and turned soil. A wiry old man with bronzed skin and eyes crinkled from decades of sun waves us down with exuberant Italian and beckons us closer. Gideon responds easily, his voice melting into the cadence of the language as though it's second nature.

He dismounts first, tying off his reins with an easy confidence, then turns and strides toward me with that barely leashed intensity.

"Allow me," he murmurs, offering both hands. I slide down into his arms, landing against his chest with a soft thud. His hands linger at my waist, warm and possessive, the press of his body a silent promise.

My cheeks flush, but I don't pull away. Instead, I soak it in—the heat of him, the rough brush of stubble against my temple, the faint cologne laced with sweat and leather. A heady mix.

The vineyard owner chuckles and points toward the wooden vat. Gideon grins, peels off his shirt in one smooth motion, and it's unfair. His chest gleams under the sun, each line of muscle cut from marble, dusted with a light trail of hair that vanishes beneath his waistband.

"Enjoying the view?" he teases, catching my hungry stare.

"Tuscany has some breathtaking...vistas," I reply, my voice a touch too breathy.

He stalks behind me and lifts the hem of my sundress, methodically tucking it into the edges of my bikini briefs. His fingers graze bare thigh and I shiver.

"That's better. Now I can enjoy the view too," he growls against my ear, voice wrapped in silk and threat.

We step into the vat. Cold grapes squish beneath our feet, sending juice splattering up our calves. I squeal, and he throws his head back laughing—an uninhibited, boyish sound I rarely hear.

He twirls me, grabs my hips, and we begin a stomping dance. Juice spurts in all directions, and I give as good as I get, flicking purple droplets at him until he lunges, scooping me into a spin that leaves us both gasping. His hands are everywhere—my waist, my back, my thighs—firm and unapologetic.

The old man sits beneath an olive tree and watches with patient amusement, sipping from a chipped ceramic cup. He might as well be sipping ambrosia, for how perfect this moment feels.

Eventually, dizzy and sticky, we collapse onto a blanket beneath the olive tree. Spread before us: warm crusty bread, ribbons of prosciutto, creamy cheese drizzled with olive oil, dark figs, and sweet golden grapes.

We eat with our fingers, laughing between bites. I swipe honey from his chin. He licks wine from the corner of my mouth. I catch myself staring—not at his body, though God knows it's glorious—but at the way he watches me like I'm something sacred. A rare artifact.

"This feels unreal," I murmur, lying back and watching the olive branches sway above.

He mirrors me, resting on one elbow, then twines our fingers together. "No. This is the most real thing I've ever known."

His words knock something loose inside me. A tight knot of fear, of old defenses, begins to unravel.

My phone buzzes, breaking the spell. Zoe.

"Brace yourself," I warn him.

"Bitch," Zoe shrieks when I answer. "Are you *really* grape-stomping with your fine-ass dream man? Did I see horseback riding too? What the actual fuck, Naomi?"

I laugh until my cheeks hurt. "Yes. All of it. Plus a wine picnic with a man named Lorenzo who might be a retired Roman god."

"Stop. I swear, if I weren't so thrilled, I'd hate you."

"He makes everything feel possible. Like I can finally just... be."

Zoe goes quiet for a beat. Then softly, "Good. You deserve this. Just promise you won't forget us regular folk while you're living your grape goddess fantasy."

"Never."

She snorts. "Also? Two new toys. From Asylum. One of them has ruin-your-life thighs. I think I might be in trouble."

"Zoe, please don't get murdered."

"If I do, bury me in latex. Also—wait—did I mention he might be a sadist?"

Before I can respond, the phone is gently plucked from my hand.

"Sorry, Zoe," Gideon's voice drawls. "I've got a goddess to worship. You understand."

Click.

I blink down at my now-dark screen.

"You really are a menace," I murmur.

He grins, offering his hand. "And yet, you adore me."

I do.

More than I expected. More than I should.

And as we walk back beneath a sky deepening into lavender and rose, the air thick with ripe fruit and sunset gold, something settles in my chest. Heavy. Certain.

This isn't just a beautiful day.

It's the prologue of everything.

We return to the villa just as the sun dips below the hills, casting everything in a syrupy golden light. I'm flushed from the wine, sticky with grape juice, and somehow still floating. The air smells like rosemary and heat, and the gravel crunches underfoot as Gideon leads me toward the outdoor shower.

He strips me slowly, reverently, like he's unwrapping a gift he already owns but never takes for granted. The breeze kisses my bare skin, and I shiver—not from cold, but anticipation.

The water runs cool at first, sharp enough to make me gasp. But then it warms, sluicing over my shoulders, down my legs, washing away the mess of the day but none of the sweetness. Gideon's hands follow the spray, slick and sure, smoothing soap over my skin in long, patient strokes.

It should feel indulgent, being bathed like this. But it doesn't. It feels sacred.

When he lifts my hair to rinse my neck, I tilt my head back into him, eyes closed, body soft. He murmurs something into my skin I don't catch. I don't need to. His hands speak louder.

Afterward, he wraps me in one of his linen shirts—still warm from the sun—and carries me inside like I weigh nothing at all.

Dinner waits on the terrace. Roasted peaches with burrata, slices of prosciutto that melt on my tongue, and a bottle of crisp white wine that tastes like chilled sunlight. We eat with our fingers, laughing between bites, stealing kisses between sips.

And somewhere between the sweetness of fruit and the salt of his mouth, I realize I've never felt so... fed. In every sense of the word.

I curl my legs beneath me on the cushioned bench, letting my body lean into his. "When I was a kid, I used to dream about Italy," I say. "But not like this. I just wanted to disappear somewhere beautiful."

Gideon doesn't speak right away. His hand finds mine beneath the table and squeezes gently.

"Now?" I murmur.

"Now I think I want to be found."

His gaze sharpens, but he doesn't interrupt. He lets the words come out in a slow, halting trickle.

"I spent so long trying to earn everything. Approval. Belonging. Desire. I kept waiting for the world to say I was good enough. And then you... you just looked at me like I already was."

Gideon lifts my hand to his mouth and kisses the inside of my wrist. "You are."

The words are simple. But they land in me like a faultline shifting—quiet, but irreversible.

I don't know if I cry. I just know I reach for him and he's already there, catching my mouth with his, kissing me with a kind of slow, aching hunger that makes my chest swell tight.

He doesn't rush.

He lifts me onto the table, hands steady at my hips, and pushes the shirt off my shoulders until it pools around my waist. I arch into his mouth as he kisses down my chest, his tongue warm and soft around each aching peak. Every touch feels deliberate—measured. Like he's mapping me, revering me.

When he kneels, when his mouth finds me and his tongue slides deep, I forget how to breathe. My thighs tremble around his head and I thread my fingers through his hair like a lifeline.

The pleasure builds slowly, steadily, but it's not just heat—it's *trust*. Every stroke of his tongue says, I see you. Every curl of his fingers says, You're safe.

And when I come—when I break apart under the stars and cry his name—it's not just my body that surrenders.

It's all of me.

His kiss turns feral—no longer gentle, no longer seeking. It *devours*. Like he's starved and I'm the only thing that could possibly save him.

I barely manage a breath before his hands grip my thighs, and suddenly I'm weightless. Lifted like I'm not even real, like I'm light as air in his arms. My back hits the wall with a jolt, cool plaster kissing the heat of my skin. My legs lock around his waist instinctively, my body reacting before my brain can catch up.

He's there—thick and hard and pressed right against my entrance, the swollen head of his cock nudging at me, hot and slick and *right there.*

"Gideon"

"I warned you." His voice is a low snarl in my ear, all gravel and possession. "You teased me all day, Red. Now you take what you've earned."

Then he thrusts.

Hard. Deep. One brutal stroke that punches the air from my lungs and shreds what's left of my restraint. The stretch burns, delicious and devastating. I cry out, not from pain—*never* pain—but from the overwhelming fullness of him claiming me like he owns me.

He fucks me against the wall like the world could end tonight.

Each slam of his hips bounces me against the surface, the sting of impact chased by waves of molten pleasure. My fingers claw into his shoulders, desperate to hold on, to *anchor* myself against the flood. He eats the sounds I make—every moan, every curse, every breathless beg—devouring them like sustenance.

"You don't get to walk straight after this," he growls, lips brushing my jaw, my neck, my collarbone. "Don't get to forget who wrecked you. You'll feel me *every time you sit down*. Every step. Every thought."

My entire body convulses at the words. His cock drags over something deep and perfect inside me and my head thuds back against the wall, eyes squeezed shut, mouth open in a silent scream. My climax doesn't ask permission. It *consumes me.* A jagged, explosive rush that tears through me and leaves me shaking in his arms.

But he doesn't stop.

He doesn't even slow down.

Gideon grinds deep, lips trailing up to bite at my throat, teeth sinking just enough to make my pulse stutter. The scrape of his stubble, the sweat beading between us, the scent of sex and citrus and heat—it's all too much. I can't breathe. I don't want to.

And then, without warning, he pulls out.

I whimper at the loss, dazed and wrung out, but he's already shifting me, cradling me like I'm the only thing he gives a damn about. I cling to him, legs still wrapped tight, thighs sticky with my release. My heart stutters as he walks us through the villa.

The air is cooler now, scented with lavender and woodsmoke and dusk.

"Where—?"

"Outside." One word, low and dangerous.

He kicks open the balcony doors and moonlight spills over us like silver silk. The stone under my feet is still warm from the sun. The vineyard sprawls out below, a sea of shadows and starlight.

Gideon sets me down on the marble balustrade, forcing my thighs wide. I grip the stone rail behind me, bracing. The night air ghosts over my slick, throbbing skin, but I barely register the chill. I'm *wired*. Wrecked. Desperate.

He stands between my legs, eyes burning into me. One hand wraps around his cock, stroking slow, lazy, like he has all the time in the world.

But there's nothing lazy about the way he grabs my hips and slides back inside with a sound that's more growl than groan. I gasp, head falling back, stars spinning above me.

This time, he moves *slow*.

Every thrust is deliberate, unhurried, *lethal*. His hands hold my face, his lips press against my forehead, my cheek, my mouth. The contrast from moments ago is dizzying—rage turned reverence, dominance turned devotion.

"I want the whole world to see this," he whispers, fucking me so deeply I swear I can feel him in my throat. "See what it means to be *mine*."

I grip the edge of the rail, knuckles white, trying to keep from unraveling again. My body hums—raw, overstimulated, feral with need. Every drag of his cock feels like poetry. Like punishment. Like prayer.

His thumb finds my clit, circling slowly. He watches my every twitch, every gasp, his own mouth slack with awe.

I'm going to fall apart again.

I *want* to fall apart.

"Come for me, Sweet Red," he murmurs, pressing his forehead to mine. "Soak me in moonlight. Let them all see how beautiful you are when you give in."

And I break.

With a scream that shatters the stillness, I come undone around him again—harder this time, rawer. My muscles seize, clenching around him with wild, fluttering pulses that pull him deeper.

He groans—loud, guttural—and thrusts once, twice more before spilling inside me, hips grinding as he empties himself with a hoarse whisper of my name.

My body shudders, boneless, spent. His arms wrap around me, holding me there on the edge of the world.

And everything is still.

Just breath. Skin. The steady thud of his heart against mine.

He presses his lips to my temple, lingering there, like he's carving the moment into memory.

"You're it, Naomi," he breathes. "You're everything."

And under the open sky, sweat-slick and claimed and entirely, *blissfully* undone—I believe him.

The night wraps around us like a velvet hush, the only sound our ragged breaths and the gentle rustle of vineyard leaves catching the breeze below.

Gideon doesn't move. Doesn't speak. He just holds me there on the stone, his body still joined with mine, arms coiled tightly around my back like he's afraid I'll disappear. His forehead rests against mine, and I can feel the slight tremble in his arms—not from exertion, but something deeper. Something *breaking open*.

I card my fingers through his damp hair, feel the tension slowly bleed from his muscles as he exhales.

"I've never..." My voice is a whisper, barely real. "No one's ever made me feel like this."

He lifts his head, eyes dark and glassy, his thumb stroking under my jaw like he's grounding himself. "You're not just something I want, Naomi. You're the only thing I *need*."

Something inside me twists. Not fear this time, not even uncertainty—just the raw ache of being *seen*. And wanted. Not for being pretty or polite or palatable. But for being *me*. Loud and messy and full of edges.

"I don't know how to be someone's need," I admit. "I barely know how to be someone's want."

His hand cradles my face with infinite gentleness. "Then let me show you. Every day, for as long as you'll let me."

A tear slips free, hot against the chill air. Gideon catches it with his lips.

We stay like that for what feels like hours—still tangled, still wrapped around each other like the night built this balcony just for us. Eventually, he lifts me again, carrying me inside as though I'm the most precious thing he's ever held.

And maybe, for the first time in my life, I believe I am.

Chapter 20

Domestic Dream

Gideon

Naomi sleeps tangled in the linens, one leg kicked free, her breath soft and even. She's a riot of color against the white sheets—flushed cheeks, wine-stained lips, a smear of juice still clinging to her thigh like a love mark. I pace barefoot near the open balcony doors, espresso cooling in my grip, bitter and untouched. The ceramic cup feels too delicate in my hand. Like her.

Sunlight scorches across the villa's stone floor in thick honeyed bands, catching on the folds of the curtains and the curve of Naomi's bare shoulder. Cicadas screech in the olive trees. A tractor rumbles in the distance. But inside, time has slowed to a crawl.

My gaze keeps snagging on her. That mess of red hair fanned across the pillow. A hand tucked under her cheek like a kid. She looks peaceful. Fragile. Dangerous in a way that makes me want to wrap her in steel and never let her go.

Last night punches through me in hot flashes. Her thighs locked around my hips. Her mouth wrecked with pleasure. The way she begged. The way she let go. That moment she came apart, looking up at me like she could see every monster, every ruin inside me—and still chose to stay.

I don't believe in fairytales. But something split open in me under that moonlight. Something I can't put back together.

I drag in a breath. Rosemary, salt, her skin. It's all tangled in the air like a drug. I let myself pretend—just for a second—that I get to keep her.

Then the knock comes.

Three soft raps against the stillness.

I don't move. Just open my eyes.

The door cracks open. One of the staff hovers, not looking at me. "Signore. They're waiting for you downstairs."

The espresso hits the back of my throat like ash.

I set the cup down and walk away from the view. Naomi stirs, stretches, the hem of the sheets sliding higher up her thigh. I force my eyes away before I change my mind. No time for softness now. The mask goes back on.

The hallway smells like lemon oil and polished stone. The villa hums with heat and age—arched doorways, frescoed ceilings, echoes of a thousand secrets. I pass a sunlit courtyard where a gardener snips lavender, but it doesn't reach me.

The sitting room is a shrine to old money and older power.

Vito lounges like a monarch, crisp linen suit, gold rings gleaming. Dante scrolls through his phone with a glass of Barolo in hand. Claudia sits poised like a painting—flawless, deliberate, untouchable. Her dress is white. The irony is fucking blinding.

"You're late," Vito says, not looking up.

"Didn't realize we scheduled this ambush."

Claudia rises, smile razor-sharp. "Gideon. You look... well used."

I give her nothing. "Tuscany's good for the blood."

She glides over, kisses my cheeks—air, calculation, currency. She steps back and scans me like she's taking inventory.

"Your uncle's concerned," she says, all sugar and poison. "Things are moving quickly. Alucard's... motivated."

The name makes my spine go rigid.

"He always was."

Dante looks up. "We need stability. A formal engagement would send the right message."

I cross my arms. "She's here to be my PR stunt?"

"She's here to secure our legacy," Vito says. "Yours."

Claudia tilts her head. "We can be discreet. Your... hobbies don't have to interfere."

Naomi's face flashes in my mind—hair wild, feet bare, laughing in the vines, whispering against my throat.

"She's not a hobby."

Everything stills.

Claudia's smile dies. "Then you have a problem. Because I'm not stepping aside."

Vito rises, slow and deliberate. Straightens his cufflinks. "You know what you owe. We gave you your name back. Don't make us take it."

My hand curls into a fist at my side. Fingernails dig into my palm. I keep my voice level. "I've paid. But I'm not selling my future to cover old debts."

His eyes sharpen. "Then make her disappear. Or we will."

It hits like a body blow, but I don't let it show. I turn and walk out, heart pounding like war drums.

Back upstairs, there's a cream envelope waiting on the entry table. My name in Claudia's handwriting. Inside, a pressed orchid and a note written in looping script:

'Don't forget what's at stake. Some flowers can't bloom twice.'

I crumple it in my hand and toss it into the fireplace.

Naomi's voice cuts through the haze—soft, humming, alive. She moves barefoot across the tile, one of my shirts hanging off her frame.

She looks up and smiles, all light. "You're back."

I shut the door behind me. Watch her. Memorize this.

She comes closer, touches my jaw. "Everything okay?"

I don't answer. Just kiss her—deep and slow. Like an apology. Like a promise.

She doesn't ask again.

And I don't tell her that war is coming, and she's right in the crosshairs.

Naomi pulls back first, fingertips brushing my jaw one last time before she turns and heads toward the kitchen. Not some quaint little nook either—this is a chef's dream, all gleaming Carrara marble, brushed brass fixtures, and appliances so sleek they look like they were designed for a Bond villain.

She opens the fridge, squinting inside like she's scanning blueprints. "Alright," she murmurs. "Let's see what billionaire fridges look like when no one's performing."

I lean against the archway, arms crossed. "You know there's a full-time chef on standby."

She hums. "And?"

"And three staff members whose entire job is anticipating your every craving."

Naomi snorts, pulling out a carton of eggs and some smug-looking cheese that probably costs more than my first motorcycle. "Cool. I crave feeding my man. You gonna stand there looking pretty or help me find a damn spatula?"

I make my way over, but not without grumbling. "There's a copper skillet worth more than a Rolex in that drawer, by the way."

"Great," she says, cracking eggs into a bowl with practiced flicks of her wrist. "Now it'll have the honor of being used to make the world's sexiest scrambled eggs."

She's humming as she whisks, hips swaying to a rhythm only she hears. I grab a pan anyway, because I can't say no to her—even if I want to have a full-blown tantrum about her doing anything other than reclining like the royalty she is while the staff handles brunch.

"You really don't have to do this."

"And yet, here I am. Butter or olive oil?"

"Butter." I open the fridge and pass her a European block wrapped in gold foil. "The good kind. No shortcuts."

"Now you're speaking my language." Naomi tosses me a look over her shoulder. "See? We're already a domestic dream."

I lean against the counter, watching her pour the egg mixture into the skillet, swirling it slowly. Her movements are confident, intimate. She doesn't even flinch when I come up behind her, hands sliding around her waist, lips at the back of her neck.

"You're dangerous when you cook," I murmur.

She laughs, nudging me with her elbow. "Don't try to distract me with that voice, Gideon. These eggs are on a tight schedule."

"I'm serious." My hands flatten across her stomach. "You here. In my kitchen. Making breakfast while wearing my shirt and looking at home. That's a vision I wasn't ready for."

Naomi turns in my arms, eyes searching. "Hey," she says softly. "What's going on?"

I freeze.

She sees it.

"Something's wrong."

I try to mask it with a crooked grin. "Just had a meeting. The usual old-world mobster bullshit."

She folds her arms, egg forgotten. "Nope. Don't do that. Don't kiss me like that and then pretend everything's fine."

I press my thumb into the edge of the counter. My jaw tightens, but I say it anyway—because she deserves the truth.

"My uncle's here. And Claudia."

Naomi's eyes go sharp. "Claudia. As in—your fake almost-fiancée Claudia?"

I nod.

"And what do they want?"

"They want me to marry her," I say flatly. "To keep the peace. Strengthen alliances. Clean up the family's image. You know... all that patriarchal legacy crap."

Naomi blinks. "Wow."

"Yeah."

A beat of silence passes. The eggs start to sizzle too hard, and she turns, scrambling quickly to kill the heat and save the edges.

Then she sets the pan down, spins to face me, arms braced on the counter.

"Are we in trouble?" she asks.

The words hang in the air like smoke.

I want to say no. I want to lie so badly. But I can't—not to her.

"Not yet," I murmur. "But we will be. If I don't play this just right."

Naomi breathes in, then out. Calm. Grounded. Strong in a way I'll never stop needing.

"Okay," she says, lifting her chin. "Then play it right... so you can teach me how we can do it together."

Later, when the eggs are gone and the air has settled, I take her hand and lead her up the narrow staircase tucked behind the wine rack. She doesn't ask where we're going. She just follows, barefoot and curious, her palm warm in mine.

The rooftop terrace unfurls around us in quiet luxury. Stone warmed by the sun. A low wall wrapped in ivy. Lounge chairs that have never known rain. Beyond it, the Tuscan hills roll into forever, gold and green and sleepy with late-morning heat.

Naomi lets out a breath. "God, this view."

But I'm not looking at the view.

She turns, catching me watching her, and offers a soft, crooked smile. The kind that says I see you even when you don't want to be seen.

We sit. Not touching at first, just letting the silence stretch between us, thick and alive.

She curls her legs up beneath her. I stretch mine out. The cicadas hum. A bird dives across the sky. Somewhere far below, the kitchen staff is probably panicking over her egg sabotage.

"You ever think about just... running?" she asks suddenly, eyes on the horizon.

"Every day."

She glances over, surprised I admitted it.

"I thought you were too composed to fantasize about escape."

I huff a laugh. "I'm composed because I have to be. Doesn't mean I don't want to disappear sometimes."

"Where would you go?"

I think about that. "Somewhere no one knows my name. No history. No blood debts."

Naomi nods slowly. "Sounds lonely."

"Not if I take you with me."

She doesn't look away. "Then I'm in."

My throat tightens. I don't deserve her. I never did.

She shifts closer, leans her head against my shoulder. Her curls tickle my jaw. I breathe her in and feel something in me start to settle. Just a little.

"I can't promise you it'll be easy," I murmur.

Naomi hums. "I don't need easy. I need real."

I close my eyes. Let her weight against me be the one thing I trust today.

Later, when she's gone to shower, I return alone to the rooftop. The view hasn't changed, but everything inside me has.

I pull out my phone. Compose a message to a contact buried six layers deep under false names.

Need options. Contingencies. She's not leaving.

I hit send. Burn the thread.

Below us, the world spins, full of knives and masks and the ghosts of family legacies.

But up here, for a fleeting heartbeat, it was moonlight and honey.

And I'll burn every bridge before I let them take that from me.

Chapter 21

Tell Me Nothing, Show Me Everything

Naomi

The villa looks like a dream someone dared to make real—carved into the cliffs above Rome, all sun-warmed stone and ivy, balconies perched like secrets ready to be spilled.

And tonight? I'm freshly waxed, faintly tipsy, and way too aware of the fact that I'm not wearing anything under my dress.

My heels click against marble as I walk through the candlelit halls with Gideon beside me—a man who doesn't just enter rooms, he owns them. His tux fits like sin. His black mask only sharpens what's already dangerous about him—like war paint for the dangerously powerful.

Mine's more flirt than disguise: black lace and satin ribbon, a midnight-blue dress that clings to every inch he's claimed. And some he hasn't. Yet.

We're almost to the ballroom when he stops—one hand at the small of my back, the other brushing a curl from my shoulder.

His voice is low and lethal. "What are the rules, Naomi?"

I shiver. "No panties."

His hand tightens. Just enough to make me catch my breath.

"Eye contact," I whisper. "Obedience."

He hums, pleased. That hum is dangerous. A promise and a threat wrapped in silk.

"And if I tell you to stop?"

"Then I stop."

"And if I tell you to kneel?"

My heart stutters. "I kneel."

There's a pause. His fingers trail down my spine, slow and deliberate. Lighting me up.

"Good girl."

Two words. That's all it takes to send heat flooding low and deep. I nod—because if I try to speak, it'll come out a whimper.

He threads our fingers together. "Let's make them stare."

And we do.

The ballroom is dipped in decadence—gilded mirrors, candlelight, champagne laughter, and chamber music. It smells like wealth and whispers. All the masks in the room can't hide the hunger beneath them.

People turn as we walk in. Of course they do.

Gideon doesn't just exist in a room. He *happens* to it. And tonight, I'm part of the spectacle. On his arm. In this dress. In these heels. I feel like a secret weapon he's chosen to reveal. Something rare and deadly. Just for him.

I can feel the weight of eyes—some curious, some covetous. But I only look at him.

His fingers brush the inside of my wrist. I almost stumble.

"Eyes up," he murmurs without looking at me. "Stay with me."

I nod. Shaky but tethered. Always tethered to him.

He guides me toward the edge of the dance floor. Waiters in black move around us like shadows, trays of champagne and sugared figs floating past. I reach for a glass—he stops me.

"No drinking yet," he says, voice just for me. "I want you clear-headed. Responsive."

"I can be both."

"You'll be mine."

My thighs clench, the promise of that sinking in deeper than it should. We haven't even started, and I'm already aching.

Then everything shifts.

A silence moves through the room. Gideon's hand stills at the small of my back—he stiffens. Tenses.

I follow his gaze.

Two men just entered.

One wears a suit so sharp it could cut glass, his plum-colored mask perched like mischief. The other is all black: mask, clothes, stare. Cold and unreadable. Roman walks in like he owns the place—or doesn't care who does. His mask gleams gold. His grin is pure chaos.

"Well, fuck me slowly," Roman says, gaze sliding over Gideon, then landing on me. "Didn't know we were bringing the main course to the appetizer hour."

Gideon's jaw clenches.

The other one—Remi—says nothing. His mask is simple. His eyes are not. They don't look. They *assess*. Like I'm a puzzle he already half-solved.

Roman grabs a glass from a tray, like this is just another Tuesday. "She's prettier than the pictures."

"I don't recall inviting you," Gideon says.

"We didn't come for the food," Roman replies, smooth as silk soaked in sin. "Or the pomp. Or Father's parade of power brokers."

Remi's eyes stay locked on me. Calculating. "We came because *you* did."

Roman grins wider. "And because *she* did."

Gideon steps forward. Barely. But it's enough to put his body between mine and theirs. A wall of perfectly-tailored menace.

"Protective, are we?" Roman teases.

"You haven't told her," Remi says, soft and surgical. "About what tonight *really* is."

"Enough," Gideon snaps.

Roman lifts his hands like a man used to being tolerated, not obeyed. "We'll behave. Scout's honor. She's clever. She'll figure it out."

Remi adds, "If she hasn't already."

My mouth opens—to ask *what the fuck* I'm supposed to be figuring out—when Gideon shoots me a look.

Not harsh. Not cold. Just pleading. Quiet. Almost imperceptible.

Later, that look says. Please.

And I—stupid, infatuated, bleeding-trust me—nod.

Roman winks. "See you inside, darling cousin. Try not to bite anyone too hard."

Remi's gaze lingers on Gideon. Then me.

"Be careful with hearts," he murmurs. "They don't mend the way bones do."

And then they vanish into the crowd. Like smoke. Like a warning.

The music picks up again, like nothing happened. Like the air hasn't shifted around me. Like I'm not suddenly hyper-aware of everything Gideon isn't saying.

He takes my hand again, warm and firm, and starts to guide us deeper into the ballroom. But my steps are slower now. He notices.

"Naomi," he says, voice low, coaxing. "Don't disappear on me."

"I'm not disappearing," I say. "I'm... recalibrating."

His smile is tight. Strained. "Understandable."

The lights catch the edge of his mask just right, and for a second I think I see something raw in his eyes. Something close to fear. But it vanishes too fast, buried beneath practiced calm.

He pulls me close, leading me into a slow waltz before I can ask the million questions rising in my throat.

And God help me, I let him.

Because when Gideon touches me like this—possessive hand at my waist, the heat of his palm cradling mine—my brain doesn't work right. It goes soft. Feral. Hungry.

"You're shaking," he murmurs near my temple.

"You told me not to drink," I whisper back.

He chuckles, and it's real this time. Warm and deep and touching something in me that aches.

"Then let me give you something else to focus on."

The hand at my waist drifts lower—not enough to scandalize, but enough to make my pulse stutter. He sways us toward the shadows at the edge of the room, where the candlelight is softer and the crowd thins.

"I hate not knowing what just happened," I say, voice tight.

He spins me slowly. Brings me back in.

"I know."

"And I hate that you're not telling me."

"I know that, too."

Our bodies press together, the music folding around us like silk. I'm still mad. Still suspicious. But I can't pull away. Because whatever this is between us, it's stronger than my pride. Or maybe it's just deeper.

"Naomi," he says, voice rougher now. "You're everything I never let myself want."

My heart kicks against my ribs. "Then why does it feel like you're still hiding from me?"

He leans in, lips brushing my ear. "Because the truth could ruin everything."

That should terrify me. But it doesn't. Not as much as the idea of him shutting me out completely.

"Then ruin it," I say. "Just... don't lie to me."

He goes still. Completely still.

And then—softly, like the beginning of a storm—he presses a kiss just behind my ear. "I'll try."

It's not a promise. Not exactly. But it's more than I expected. Maybe more than he's given anyone.

The music swells, and we dance—bodies pressed too close, breaths shared like secrets—while the rest of the world watches from behind their masks.

But I'm not watching them.

I'm watching him.

And wondering—just how many layers of armor he's still hiding under that perfect tux and velvet voice. And how much I'm willing to strip away to get to the truth.

We slip away between dances. Not through the main doors, but a hidden corridor just beyond the draped velvet. Gideon knows this place too well—it doesn't surprise me. Of course he'd scout the villa before bringing me here. Of course he'd find the shadows.

He pushes open a door and guides me into a small side room—part wine cellar, part forgotten parlor. Cool air brushes my flushed skin. The faint scent of sandalwood and old stone fills my lungs.

He closes the door, locking it behind us with a soft click.

And just like that, the world disappears.

A woman in a pale white mask watches from the far corner, half-hidden behind a man in diplomatic silk. Her dress gleams like bone under candlelight. I don't know her name. But something about her stillness, her smile—too restrained, too sweet—puts my nerves on edge.

I turn before she can catch me staring.

But my skin prickles like I've just been clocked.

Chapter 22

The Silence Between

Naomi

Gideon's hand tightens in mine. He guides us to a balcony that curves around the ballroom like a watching gallery. Up here, we're seen—but not reachable. Close to the edge, cloaked in enough shadow that no one lingers.

He stands behind me. One hand at my hip, the other wrapped around my wrist, keeping my palm pressed to the balustrade. Possessive. Protective. Or maybe preparing for something he doesn't want to say.

I exhale slowly, trying to get my heart under control. The cool night air rushes up from below, scented with bergamot and jasmine, threaded with the distant echo of laughter and clinking glasses.

"They were watching us," I murmur.

"I know."

"Remi's still watching."

"I *know*, Naomi."

His voice turns to steel, laced with something more than irritation. Panic, maybe. Or guilt.

"Why were they really here?" I ask. "You didn't tell me there was more to tonight than a party."

A beat.

Then another.

He doesn't lie. He just doesn't answer.

And that silence? It tells me everything.

"They're your cousins," I press, searching his profile. "And they didn't come to dance."

"No, they didn't."

"Then why *did* they come?"

His jaw ticks. Something feral flickers behind his mask.

"To remind me of what's waiting."

"Which is?"

He leans down, lips brushing the shell of my ear.

"A choice."

His words are so soft I almost miss them. But I feel them—carved straight into bone.

When I turn to face him, the mask doesn't hide how guarded he's become again. Like he's already started locking parts of himself away. Preparing to disappear behind duty. Secrets. A name I don't even know how to spell.

Before I can ask what he means, the moment breaks.

An older man enters the ballroom below. Everyone turns. Bows. The energy shifts again—from indulgent to reverent. And for the first time, I see Gideon go pale.

He doesn't curse. Doesn't speak.

Just steps back.

"Who is that?" I whisper.

But he doesn't answer.

He's already letting go of my hand.

Already pulling on the mask I thought I'd peeled away.

The crowd parts like silk around the man now commanding the floor. He's tall—elegant in a way that feels rehearsed. Impeccably dressed in a deep oxblood suit, his mask a lacquered black crescent that gleams beneath the chandeliers. He walks like power has always been his. Like the ground knows to bow.

Even without an introduction, I know: this is *him*.

Gideon's uncle.

The man whose shadow even Roman and Remi seem to bend beneath.

The way Gideon stills—every muscle going wire-tight, his breath shallow like he's bracing for a blow—confirms it. And that... shakes something in me. Because I've seen Gideon dominate entire rooms with a look. I've seen people *shrink* under his silence.

But now?

He's the one shrinking.

Roman reappears at the man's side, all casual charm as he makes some sly quip I can't hear. Remi stands slightly apart, eyes cutting between his father and Gideon like he's counting seconds before impact.

And then the man speaks.

Not to Gideon.

To me.

"You must be Naomi."

My name sounds wrong in his mouth—too slow, too cold. Like he's testing the weight of it.

I hesitate, then nod. "I am."

"Brave girl," he murmurs, voice dipped in something that might be amusement—or threat. "Wearing his mark in public. Do you even know what it costs to be chosen by a Hawke?"

"Enough." Gideon's voice is like the crack of a whip—low, but deadly.

The man ignores it.

"Tell me, has he told you yet? What happens when this masquerade ends?"

My pulse spikes.

Gideon steps between us again, full shield now. "This isn't the time."

"No," his uncle agrees, smooth as ice. "It never is."

A sharp smile slices across his face. "But time's almost up, boy. And sooner or later, the girl's going to stop letting you hide behind her ignorance."

He turns to me once more. "I look forward to seeing how far you'll follow him when the lights come on."

And then he's gone.

Just like that.

The crowd exhales. Conversations resume. The music swells.

But I can't hear it. I can't *feel* anything but the hollowing in my chest and the tightening around Gideon's eyes.

I don't even realize my hand is trembling until he reaches for it.

I pull away before he can touch me.

And the look on his face?

It's not anger.

It's grief.

I don't remember walking away.

One second I'm beside Gideon in a ballroom full of strangers and shadows, and the next I'm outside, heels crunching over gravel, the cold Roman air biting through silk like punishment.

The villa glows behind me—too golden, too perfect. Like a memory I already know will rot.

My fingers shake as I brace them on a marble balustrade, the stone colder than bone. My chest feels too tight, like there's a scream wedged between my ribs that doesn't know how to claw its way out.

I hear him before I see him. The quiet slide of shoes behind me. The stillness that comes with his presence, like gravity has reasserted itself.

"Naomi," Gideon says. My name again, soft. Careful. Like he's approaching a wounded animal he knows might bite.

I don't turn.

"Is it true?" My voice is raw. Frayed at the edges. "What he said?"

He doesn't answer right away. The silence stretches. *Snaps.*

I whirl around. "Are you using me to buy time? Am I some pretty distraction while you negotiate whatever blood-tied bullshit's brewing beneath this whole curated Roman-god theater?"

His jaw flexes.

"That's not what this is," he says. Quiet. Too quiet.

"But it's not *not*, is it?" I laugh, but there's no humor in it. Just that high, hollow note of a woman realizing the ground beneath her might never have been solid. "You've been playing the part. Mister possessive. Mister I'll worship your stretch marks with my fucking teeth. But I was never in the room, was I? Not really."

"You were always the room," he says, voice shredded. "You were the only thing that ever mattered."

"Then why the secrets?" I fire back. "Why all the careful silences and tight smiles? Why do I know more about your Scotch preferences than I do about *this family you're at war with*?"

"Because I didn't want to lose this."

He steps closer. I step back.

"I didn't want to lose *you*."

"That's not fair," I whisper, tears pricking. "You don't get to say that like it's noble. Like lying by omission is some kind of sacrifice."

"I wasn't lying—"

"No. You were just *curating* the truth."

Silence.

He exhales like he's deflating. "I didn't want to drag you into this world."

I shake my head. "You didn't want me to *see* it. Because if I did, you knew I might not stay."

There it is. The real fear.

He's scared I'll walk.

And for the first time, I think I might.

"I can't do this if I'm just a pretty shield," I whisper. "If I'm only allowed to be your fantasy. I want the truth, Gideon. I want all of it."

His eyes shine—not with fury. Not desire.

With devastation.

"I don't know how to give you that," he says.

And in that moment, I know we're falling.

Not into each other.

Away.

I walk until the hush settles into my bones. Find a hidden alcove behind flowering hedges—roses, overripe and shedding petals like truths too long held.

I sit.

Not cry.

Just *sit.*

Eventually, he joins me. No touch. No plea. Just presence. Just a man folding his hands like they're prayers and maybe guilt.

"I'm sorry," he says. "For not telling you. For letting you walk into tonight blind."

I say nothing.

"You were right. I was protecting the idea of us. But that was a lie. I *am* this legacy. This fucking curse."

Still silence.

"I love you," he breathes. A whisper, a hope. "I love you in a way that terrifies me."

I almost believe him.

But love needs air. And we've been drowning in heat.

When I finally speak, it's soft. "Then why do I feel so alone?"

He breaks at that. Not with noise, but with stillness.

"I don't know how to stay," he says. "Not when staying means pulling you into the very world I tried to escape."

Then he leaves.

No goodbye. No promise. Just absence.

I sit there, roses drooping above. Still not crying.

But then—something *breaks.*

And I *laugh.*

The kind that scrapes from the gut. The kind that doesn't sound like me. The kind that comes when you're emptied out and hollowed. When love becomes silence.

And still—no tears.

Only night.

Only me.

I gather myself, half-mended. Shoulders squared. Mask askew. The chill night air nips at my skin, and Rome stretches out below like a sleeping god holding its secrets.

The ballroom is winding down. Quiet elegance, muted whispers, string notes like ghosts.

I round a corner—and freeze.

Gideon. Not five feet away. Speaking low. His hand on the arm of a woman—elegant, older, all pearls and poise.

Everything I'm not.

She smiles at him. He doesn't smile back.
But he doesn't move either.
I step back. One heel scuffs stone.
His head lifts—eyes scanning.
But I'm already gone.

Chapter 23

The Fault Is Mine

Gideon

The villa smells like sun-warmed stone and rosemary when I step inside, but the air is wrong—too still, too clean, like someone scrubbed away a mess and hoped I wouldn't notice. A citrus top note hangs too long in the entryway, not the usual undercurrent of coffee grounds and saffron. Every sense I trust for survival bristles, tuned to the imperceptible static of shift. A light near the alcove glows when it shouldn't—set to motion, but no one's passed in hours. A vase on the foyer table sits off-center. Caterina always keeps it dead even. Something has shifted in the foundation, and it isn't just the decor.

She's not here. Or rather—someone else isn't.

Caterina is always here by this hour. She hums as she moves, muttering to herself in soft Italian, grumbling about deliveries and overripe figs. She's nowhere. The kitchen is clean—*too* clean—every surface gleaming, not a single used cup in the sink. No heat coming off the stove, no espresso in the pot. Just the faint click of the security system's passive scan as I move through the entryway, sterile as a vault.

The absence hammers harder than presence. Something's off.

A breeze slides in through the open windows, ruffling the linen curtains like they're whispering secrets. Somewhere in the west wing, Naomi laughs. The sound's soft, muffled by distance, but sharp in contrast to the tension prickling across my shoulders. That laugh—light, unguarded—cuts through the quiet like an exposed nerve. It doesn't belong in a house that suddenly feels like a trap.

I follow the sound. The corridor cools as I near her suite, shadow creeping over the art-lined walls. The sun's low enough now to flatten the light, painting everything in amber and copper. Her door's ajar. The screen inside glows with movement.

Naomi is sprawled across the velvet chaise, curls loose and wild, one leg hooked over the arm. She's barefoot, wrapped in a cotton robe I bought her the second night we landed here. She's laughing, animated, holding her phone to her ear, the soft slur of familiar names—Zoe, maybe Maddie—tumbling past her lips like they still belong in a world untouched by all of this.

The air in her room is warm with orange blossom and skin cream. Cozy. Lived-in. The opposite of the dread knotting between my ribs. Even the way the light spills in—low and gold, caressing her legs like it has permission—feels wrong. Like the villa itself has turned traitor.

She's beautiful like this. Present. Unburdened. A world away from the girl who sobbed against my throat last night, nails digging into my back as she told me she wanted to stay. Who whispered thank you like it was a confession—like giving herself to me was some kind of reckless salvation.

I can still feel her breath on my neck, the arch of her back, the way she went still after, letting me hold her. Like I was the only thing anchoring her to earth.

Now she's laughing. And I am floating.

That version of her—raw, real—is seared behind my eyes. And this one, the one smiling now? She's the one I'm going to lose. Her safety is my salvation. And my fucking curse.

I turn away.

Vivienne is already there.

I don't hear her approach. She's always been better than me at silence.

"Caterina was sent home," she says from the hallway, voice calm and clipped. "Apparently, Claudia thought you'd appreciate the quiet."

I turn, slow. She's framed in the archway, arms crossed over her immaculate cream blazer. No clipboard. No tech. Just watching.

"She's not your handler," I say.

"No. But she's playing the role." Vivienne steps closer. "And she's already rewriting your script. Did you notice the staff? Half of them weren't here yesterday."

My jaw tightens.

"You let her in, Gideon," Vivienne adds. "Now the board's watching your every breath. And hers."

I don't respond. I don't need to.

"She's lovely," Vivienne says, not quite smiling. "That kind of lovely that makes powerful men do reckless things. Be careful."

Then she's gone, heels a whisper against the stone.

The study door clicks shut behind me with more force than necessary. The smell in here is different—dust and leather and old scotch, sharp and heavy. I drop my bag onto the desk and yank out the tablet, the leather warm from the sun, but it feels foreign in my hands. Too light. Too vulnerable.

I key in. The system stutters. One second. Then another. Just long enough for my gut to confirm what my instincts already screamed.

The logs open like a throat cut wide—raw, fast, spilling everything.

New IPs. External logins. Masked signatures. Cloaked observer tunnels.

Someone's inside.

Not just inside the villa. Inside my network. My perimeter.

The first mirrored feed loads.

Naomi.

The soft glow of her suite rendered in live detail—her body curled in profile, head thrown back in laughter, her robe slipping slightly as she shifts. She readjusts without thinking, fingers catching the lapel just before more of her breast slips into view.

My blood goes cold.

Someone else saw that.

Saw her in that robe. On that couch. Unguarded.

And she doesn't know.

The second feed is closer—zoomed from the floor lamp's perspective. I hadn't installed that. Didn't authorize any of it.

Her smile turns grotesque in the moment. Not because of her. Because it's no longer hers. No longer ours.

It belongs to whoever's watching.

My hand grips the edge of the desk. Fingernails bite wood. My lungs squeeze against the cage of my ribs.

I swipe the feed away, but the image burns behind my eyelids.

This is my fault. I brought her here. I should've known. Should've shut every door. Should've never let her trust me.

The tablet rattles against the stacked books when I shove it backward. Not enough. I want to hurl it. Crush it.

I want to scream.

Instead, I grab my phone. My thumb jabs a message into Ethan's encrypted channel.

Me: Check Naomi's file. Now.

I pace. Past the decanter. Past the shelves I haven't touched in months. I run my fingers over the spine of a history book I never finished, then yank open the bottom drawer.

A cufflink case rests inside, pristine and untouched. My father's initials engraved in gold. I used to think it meant legacy. Now it just looks like a fucking shackle.

The reply buzzes in.

Ethan: *Confirmed. They pulled her NDA from DevOne. Flagged her Slack history. They're building a case. Reputational. You're being boxed out.*

The words flatten everything.

This isn't just about leverage. They're positioning her as unstable. Untrustworthy. Someone I should've known better than to protect. They'll leak it. Let it trickle through whisper networks. She'll lose credibility, autonomy—everything she fought to build before she met me.

They're laying groundwork for a vote. If they move fast, they'll try to push me out—say I'm compromised, emotionally manipulated. Say I'm no longer objective enough to lead.

They'll destroy her to wound me. And if I don't act, she'll bleed while I watch.

My hand shakes as I set the phone down, and the sharpness in my jaw turns brutal. I can feel a molar creak, feel my pulse hammering against the hinge. The burn in my throat isn't from the whiskey.

I step back from the desk and yank open the bottom drawer.

A cufflink case rests inside—black velvet, gold initials. G.H.

My father's.

He wore them like armor. I wore them once. Right before my first deal closed in blood instead of ink.

Now they sit like a threat.

A reminder of everything I swore I'd control better.

But control's an illusion.

I slam the drawer closed.

Boardroom politics dressed as concern. My name under scrutiny. Her name dragged through the dark.

The whiskey burns as it goes down. My jaw clenches until my molars ache. My reflection in the glass looks like a man unraveling. I don't even recognize him.

She deserves better than this.

I wanted to keep her close. Safe. Now she's marked. A weakness. A target. And I—

I drop the tumbler.

It slips because my grip fails—not from shock, but from the slow, choking pressure building in my chest. It hits the floor in a clean, crystalline explosion. Shards skitter like shrapnel across the tile, catching light in erratic, dancing flares.

The sound slices through the room and something in me snaps with it.

My palm throbs. There's a thin slice of red rising along my lifeline. I stare at it—this one honest thing. Pain that's simple, explainable. Not like the rest of this.

I press my thumb into the cut and hold it there. Let the sting ground me. My jaw is so tight I hear something pop. The muscle near my temple spasms.

I clench my fist again. Harder.

A flicker of thought barrels in, uninvited and lethal:

If she were ordinary, I could let her go. Walk away. Survive it.

But she isn't. And I won't.

I brace a hand against the bar, shoulders hunched. Try to breathe through it.

There's no air.

I stare at it. At the glass. At nothing.

Her voice reaches me faintly from the hall. The call is over.

Silence again.

Then footsteps. Slower than usual. Careful. The kind that pause halfway down the hall, listening for something unsaid.

I don't turn.

The door eases open, no creak. Just the ripple of breath shifting space.

She doesn't speak right away. I feel her presence before I hear it—subtle and steady, like gravity adjusting around her. She takes in the shattered glass, the half-drained whiskey, the tight line of my shoulders.

She's reading me. Not the way most people do, looking for cracks to exploit. She's reading for tension. For heat. For the warning signs I taught her to notice.

"Gideon."

Her voice is low. Tentative, not out of fear, but out of knowing how close I am to snapping. She crosses the room, bare feet silent on stone.

She stops behind me. I feel her hand hover before it lands—right over my heart.

She says nothing at first. Just breathes. Slow. Deliberate. Matching the rhythm I've lost.

"You're vibrating like a live wire."

Her thumb moves slightly, not pressure—pulse. Matching mine.

"Gideon," she says again, softer this time, almost a whisper. "Just look at me."

I still can't.

Her fingers don't press—they settle. Weightless, warm. An offering.

A lifeline.

"What aren't you telling me?"

I almost say it.

Nothing.

Everything.

You. Me.

The words hover, sharp and unbearable, crowding my throat like glass. One breath too deep and I'll bleed.

I open my mouth.

And close it again.

Lie to her. Just once. Keep her safe. Tell her it's fine. That I'm fine. That we're fine.

But I can't make my voice behave. Can't make it lie for me the way it used to.

So I say nothing.

She waits.

Her palm stays against my chest for a heartbeat longer. Just long enough for her to feel the truth anyway.

When I still don't answer, she draws her hand back. Not all the way—just an inch. But something folds in her body. A softness that wasn't surrender. A shift that feels like retreat.

Her breath catches. Only slightly. But I hear it. Like something delicate cracking.

She steps back.

She leaves without another word.

This time, she doesn't close the door behind her.

Chapter 24

Fracture Lines

Naomi

I didn't close the door.

I always do—quietly, deliberately. A promise folded into habit. Tonight, I leave it ajar. The hallway beyond the study stretches ahead like a question I don't know how to answer. Cold air licks across my skin, raising goosebumps along my arms. The tile is cool and damp beneath my bare feet, like it's been holding its breath all day.

Behind me, the study stays silent. No footsteps. No shift in air pressure. Just the soft tick of cooling glass as the tumbler settles—or maybe shudders—against the stone. A chair creaks faintly, or maybe that's just my memory layering sound over absence.

My stomach pulls tight. Not pain. Not quite. More like dread with nowhere to land. The same slow squeeze I used to feel when my mother stopped answering the phone. Or when I found the first bug in my code and knew someone had slipped past me.

Gideon didn't follow. I listen anyway. Not just for footsteps. For anything. A sign. A breath. The clink of glass. Just silence.

I pass the arched window and catch a flash of myself in the reflection—hair mussed, lips swollen, collarbone marked. Claimed. I don't look broken. Just suspended. Like a decision half-made.

The warmth of my suite hits me as I step inside. The scent clings—orange blossom, my lotion, the mineral tang of his skin—but now it feels too thick. Like memory trying too hard to linger. The light has shifted again, fading faster than it should. Shadows creep like they've been waiting for permission.

The imprint of my body still dents the cushion.

I reach out and touch it—just two fingers, brushing the divot where my hip rested. The fabric is still warm.

Even the light turns on me now.

Like I never left.

Like the laugh that echoed off these walls wasn't already hollow when it left my mouth.

I didn't feel it then. The shift behind his eyes. Not in words. But my body registered it. Some part of me already knew.

I don't sit. I move.

Because stillness is permission, and I'm not ready to surrender.

The tablet waits on the side table. I hover for a second—just long enough to feel the twitch in my fingers, the resistance in my own breath. I don't want to find anything. Not really. I want it to be nothing. A blip. A leftover ping from something benign.

But I touch the screen.

My reflection stares back in the glass for a split second—distorted, stretched across code. My face doesn't look surprised. It looks resigned.

My hands move. Not shaking, but slower than usual. Each stroke purposeful. Lines of code unfold like breath, familiar, clean.

I dig—not recklessly, not invasively. Just deep enough to feel the tremor.

There it is.

An encrypted outbound call. Masked. Routed through a subchannel layered under the primary system—a signature I've seen once before. From Gideon's own secure line. Logged thirty-seven minutes ago.

Destination: New York.

My pulse stays steady, but something behind my ribs shifts. Tightens.

I go deeper. Peel back metadata. Scraped once. Then rewritten. My filter catches it before it fades.

Claudia Spinellie.

The name flickers and dies.

No message. No body text. Just a name buried like a trigger. Like insurance. Or a threat.

I lock the tablet and set it down carefully. My fingers leave faint heat prints on the glass. I watch them fade.

Her phone lights up once on the table, then goes still. She hasn't checked it.

ZOE: tell me you didn't just disappear into some man's trauma spiral again.

JADE: she's spiraling in silk rn. radio silence = red flag.

JOR: babe. say something. just one word.

ZOE: if i have to fly to italy and shake you, i will.

ZOE: no seriously. i'm looking at flights.

ME: I'm okay.

JOR: you sure?

JADE: girl that period is doing too much

ZOE: we're not letting you vanish again. even if i have to break into leviathan and leak his browser history

Me: noted.

Roman's voice returns—not loud, just low, curling in the back of my mind:

They'll dress you in silk and call it a cage.

I look down at what I'm wearing—midnight-blue silk, Gideon's choice. He'd handed it to me with reverence the day it arrived, peeled the price tag off like it offended him. I'd slipped it on and felt beautiful. Precious. Now it clings damply to my skin, the hem catching on my thigh where I've curled too tightly.

A flash of Roman's face surfaces—his eyes that day weren't cruel, but tired. Like he'd already watched too many women smile while the bars welded shut around them.

A soft knock.

I don't startle.

"Naomi."

Gideon's voice—velvet-wrapped warning. My name on his lips always sounds like a prayer made by someone who doesn't believe in salvation.

I don't answer.

The door opens anyway. Slowly. He steps in like he's crossing a blueprint someone else rigged to break, shoulders tight, jaw locked. The light behind him frames the tension in his posture—more warrior than lover.

His scent hits first—whiskey, sweat, the lingering smoke of whatever bridge he just burned. His right hand is clenched. When it flexes, I see a thin smear of red across one knuckle. A cut. Fresh.

His gaze finds mine across the room. And holds.

I see it then—the storm braced behind his control. The desperation buried beneath his power. He doesn't offer an explanation.

He offers *himself*.

He crosses the space like he's afraid if he doesn't move now, he'll shatter. His hand cups my jaw—not rough, but with a pressure that trembles at the edges. When his mouth finds mine, it's already parted like a question he can't ask aloud.

I let him.

Because some things don't need language. Some truths are spoken in pressure and breath and the scrape of stubble against skin. He kisses like he's claiming ground. Like if he owns this moment, the questions will burn out.

He tears my robe open. Lays me back. His hands map me like a coastline he already conquered but doesn't trust not to shift. His touch is frantic, reverent, afraid—each pass a search for reassurance he won't find.

His breathing is ragged, pulling heat between us like it's the only thing keeping him tethered. Mine stays steady, almost too much so, like I'm conserving energy for the questions I know will come later. My skin flushes under his grip, but the center of my chest feels cold—hollowed.

He groans when I arch into him. I don't echo it. My eyes stay open. Fixed on him, then past him. The ceiling. The lamp. Anything that doesn't lie.

When I come, it's sharp. Controlled. Like everything else about me tonight.

After, he wraps around me. Arms like armor. Breath warm against my shoulder. A rhythm I once believed in.

But I don't close my eyes.

I watch the ceiling. Trace the lines where plaster meets shadow. And I think about Claudia. About encrypted calls. About silence wielded like a weapon.

He sleeps.

The sheets are too warm. They cling to my thighs, damp and twisted, like they're trying to trap me in the echo of something that never quite felt like mine. His arm is heavy across my waist, the weight of it once comforting. Now, it pins.

I lie still, watching the slow rise and fall of his back. A muscle twitches near his shoulder blade, some dream flickering through his body. I could wake him. Ask. Demand.

But I don't.

My fingers brush the edge of the tablet on the nightstand, then pull back.

I stare at the ceiling. At the way the shadows have deepened into cracks.

I don't close my eyes.

I plan.

If he'd told me the truth—just once—I might've forgiven everything. The blood. The surveillance. Claudia. If he'd handed it to me raw, I would've cut my own palms catching it.

But he didn't.

I glance around the room—every luxury is a deliberate line in the script he's written for me. The silk robe puddled on the floor. The Cartier box now tucked in the drawer. The bracelet I stopped wearing two days ago without telling him. All of it gleaming. All of it calibrated.

A collar by any other name.

My fingers ghost over my sternum, remembering how it felt the first time he wrapped a real one around my throat. The weight of it wasn't fear. It was permission. But now I wonder if that power exchange was ever equal... or just choreographed.

Obedience looks a lot like worship when you stop asking questions.

And I've started asking.

The silk robe still lies in a heap across the tile. The tablet glows in standby. The door down the hall—the one I left open—is probably still ajar.

It used to mean trust. Now, it's a breach.

I told myself I wouldn't repeat my patterns. That I'd never again confuse possession with devotion.

But I let him dress me in softness and call it surrender.

Not anymore.

Chapter 25

The Choice I Won't Make

The city groans beneath the penthouse like something tethered too tightly, steel cables pulled taut and waiting to snap. It's late—later than I meant to arrive—but there's no real reason to rush anymore. Naomi's not waiting at the window, not pacing or curled up in the corner of the couch. Her absence doesn't echo. It lingers. Like perfume caught in the ductwork. Like warmth bleeding from a space already abandoned.

The lights stay low when I enter. I don't need them. Every inch of this place was built under my name, my scrutiny. The angles are perfect. The stone too cold. The glass flawless. It should feel like control.

It feels like a mausoleum.

She used to dance here. Once. Bare feet on marble. Laughing at a song I pretended not to like. Now, the same space holds only silence, too practiced to be peace.

Naomi's coat is draped over the back of a chair. She's here. Somewhere. The scent of her skin lives in the fibers. Jasmine, citrus, ozone. Memory dressed in silk. I find her in the living room, barefoot, one hand wrapped around a mug of untouched tea, staring out at the skyline like it might offer answers if she just looks long enough.

She doesn't turn when I enter.

She doesn't need to.

I can feel the tension radiating off her like heat from a blown fuse. Her spine is too straight. Her fingers grip the ceramic too tightly. Her breath barely moves her ribs.

"Naomi."

"Did you think I wouldn't find out?"

Straight to the bone. No pleasantries. No build-up. The storm doesn't roll in—it's already here.

"Find out what?" I already know.

She takes a sip of the tea. It's cold now. Untouched. Her hands don't shake. Mine do.

She turns then. Slowly. Her eyes are ringed with shadow, mouth soft with something that isn't sadness. Not quite. It's worse. It's resolve.

"Claudia," she says, quiet. "You didn't mention her when you left for Rome. But I found the metadata. The call. The routing key."

I exhale through my nose. Sharp. Controlled. Claudia's last words flicker in my memory—measured, pleasant, venom laced in protocol. My silence wasn't fear. It was survival. But Naomi doesn't care about survival. She cares about truth.

"She's part of the family business," I say. "This wasn't personal."

Naomi takes one step closer. Not threatening. Just enough to be in range.

"Wasn't it?"

Her eyes stay on mine. Wide. Clear. She's not trying to trap me. She's trying to see if I'll lie.

I don't.

"They expect me to marry her."

The silence between us folds in on itself. Becomes vacuum. A singularity.

"Why?"

"Legacy. Optics. The Hawke name. My father's will. There's more than one kind of leash."

She nods once, almost like she's not surprised. And maybe she's not. She's just disappointed.

"Do you love her?"

"No."

"Do you want her?"

"No."

"Do you want me?"

I hesitate. The answer is there—acid-bright and choking. My chest pulls tight. She deserves honesty, not reflex. But want isn't clean. It's never just yes or no. It's tethered to ruin, to guilt, to legacy, and still—

"Yes."

"Will you choose me?"

This is the moment. The one she'll remember. Not the nights I worshipped her. Not the promises I didn't speak. This silence will be the last word I ever say.

My mouth opens. Closes. The word is there. Lodged behind my teeth like a bullet I can't bite. My tongue won't move. My jaw's locked. My silence isn't noble—it's cowardice dressed in steel.

Naomi watches the failure form in real-time. The breath she takes is shallow, careful.

"Then we're done pretending," she whispers. "You chose already."

"No. I chose you. I always chose you."

Her face flickers. Hurt. Then nothing. She blinks once. Long. Like the effort it takes not to cry is costing her something she won't let me see. She sets the mug down. Walks past me without touching. Without breaking.

"Go ahead," she says. "Pretend this still means something. I'll play along, just this once. Lie with your hands if you can't with your mouth."

For a split second, I wonder if she still wants this—or if she's offering me a final mercy. One last sacrament before the collapse.

I follow. Into the bedroom. Into habit.

Once, ritual brought relief. Order. Connection. Now it feels like theater—motions strung together in the hope that muscle memory can revive something already dead. I move not with certainty, but desperation, dragging a ghost of intimacy behind me.

I bind her wrists with silk. She offers them without hesitation. Kneels because I asked. Because we built something holy in this posture. But it's a ritual now—one she no longer believes in.

Her eyes don't follow my movements. Her breathing doesn't sync to mine. She doesn't flinch, but she doesn't yield either.

I press into her like pressure can fix this. Like if I drive deep enough, I'll find the place she used to keep me. But she's gone. Her body's here, but she's somewhere I can't reach. And I know—before she says it. I feel it coming like a crack in the earth. My grip falters.

The rhythm's off. Her pulse doesn't rise like it used to. I kiss her throat and she doesn't tilt. Doesn't moan. Just breathes. Even. Steady. Like she's waiting for it to be over. I'm chasing something that doesn't live here anymore.

"Red."

It was the first thing she ever asked me about.

What would happen if I said it? Would you stop? Would you still want me after?

I told her the truth then. That I would never take her beyond what she could bear. That the word wasn't failure—it was faith.

But I don't think I understood what she meant. Not really.

And now she's using it not to save herself—but to save me.

It lands like a gunshot in a marble church. For a breath, everything slows. My vision tunnels. My fingers tremble—just once, enough. The cold starts in my spine, radiates out. My body knows before my mind catches up: I've lost her.

I freeze. The word doesn't echo. It detonates. My hands drop like I've been shot. The breath I was holding turns sharp in my chest.

Her voice is calm. Soft. But there's a hitch—barely there. A catch in her throat she swallows down like it costs her something. Like mercy shouldn't hurt, but it always does.

"I didn't safeword because I was afraid. I did it because I knew you'd keep going. Because you needed me to."

She unties herself. Smooth. Efficient. Places the silk on the bed. Folded. Not flung. She does it slowly. Carefully. Like she's placing a relic in a tomb. Like she's folding us. And I—folded too, just slower. A goodbye wrapped in fabric. Like she's folding us. Like it's an apology. Or a benediction.

She stands. Looks at me.

I don't move. Not because I'm in control. But because the moment I do, I'll shatter.

And then she leaves.

The door doesn't slam.

But it doesn't stay open either.

The room holds her shape even after she's gone.

The sheets still smell like her—sweat, salt, silk. My hands are open, empty. The silk she folded is a monument at the edge of the bed. I don't touch it. I don't move.

Not because I'm honoring her exit.

Because I don't know what comes after this.

I try to stand and the floor tilts. So I sit instead. Elbows on my knees. Head in my hands. A pose that used to mean prayer.

There's nothing to worship here. Not God. Not legacy. Not the bloodline choking my name.

Famiglia.

It tastes like rot now. Like betrayal sealed in vowels and ancient rules.

My phone vibrates again. Missed call. Roman this time. Third one tonight.

Claudia hasn't followed up. Which means she's letting it breathe. Letting me twist in the leash she left behind in Rome.

A deal with Venice stalled today—Remi flagged it, said we'd lose our foothold if I didn't handle it personally. I didn't even respond. I couldn't. Not when I'm still on the floor, trying to remember how to function without her breath in the room.

They'll say I'm distracted. That I'm weak. They'll be right.

And the worst part is—I don't even care. Not right now. Not when all I can hear is Naomi whispering *Red*.

I press my palms to my eyes. I want to scream. I want to tear at the seams of my skin until I find the part of me that let her go. The part that watched her unravel and said nothing.

The silence rings louder than her safeword. Louder than my father's voice. Louder than every vow I didn't speak.

The light from the hallway creeps in through the crack she left behind. Thin. Silver. Indifferent.

I reach for my phone. Open it. Type nothing. Close it. Open it again.

She said, 'Let him sleep. I won't.' I thought it was bitterness. It was warning.

If I move, it has to mean something.

If I speak, it can't be a lie.

But all I have right now is silence.

And she's already learned how to walk away from it.

Chapter 26

Rumor Mills And Maybach Rules

Naomi

The office is a crucible.

My phone buzzes once in my coat pocket. I don't check it. I don't need noise. I need clarity.

Everything about it feels manufactured for discomfort—the too-bright fluorescents, the chill of recirculated air, the whispery hiss of judgment slipping between cubicles. The elevator dings open like a warning bell, and the moment my heels click onto the marble, I know. They know.

Whispers follow me. Faces turn. Emails stop mid-keystroke. I swear I feel every syllable of the word *whore* pass between lips too cowardly to speak it aloud.

Mia is the first blade to draw blood.

She leans against the reception desk, polished and venomous. "Back so soon? I figured you'd stay in Europe—you know, where the Eurotrash don't mind sharing their toys."

Kelly snorts behind her, arms crossed like backup muscle.

I keep walking.

"Guess sleeping with the boss gets you more than just first-class flights now," Mia adds, louder. "New title. New project. New wardrobe."

The back of my neck burns. My jaw aches from holding. Still, I walk.

"Hey, Naomi." Mia's voice lilts mockingly behind me. "Be sure to wipe the desk down when you're done. Wouldn't want to catch anything."

My fingers tremble as I badge into the glass door. The office beyond feels too bright, too exposed.

I'm halfway to my desk when Toni's voice cuts through the tension.

"Mia. You always this obsessed with someone else's success, or is this just a particularly dry spell for your mediocrity?"

Gasps. A few stifled laughs. Mia stiffens. Toni doesn't blink.

"Move along," she adds, cool and dismissive. "Before HR gets wind of your extracurricular bullying."

Mia stalks off, her heels snapping their fury. Kelly follows with a glare. The air shifts slightly—less hostile, still heavy.

Toni walks beside me. "Ignore them. You earned your spot. Twice over."

I nod, not trusting my voice.

At my desk, the chair feels foreign. The login screen blinks like an accusation. My reflection stares back in the dark glass of the monitor—flushed, jaw tight, eyes glossed.

"You're not guilty of anything," I whisper.

But the silence that answers says otherwise.

The elevator dings again.

No one looks up at first—until they do.

Gideon Hawke steps onto the floor like he owns the air itself. Which, technically, he does. Charcoal suit, expression carved from ice, stride deliberate. He doesn't look left or right. Just walks.

Mia's already squaring her shoulders, lips parting in a saccharine smile.

"Mr. Hawke," she purrs, too sweet, too sharp.

He doesn't stop. Doesn't slow.

"Don't." One word, leveled like a gavel. His voice is low, lethal.

Mia blinks, her confidence flickering. "I'm not sure what you—"

"Don't speak to Naomi again." He doesn't raise his voice, but the floor still falls quiet. "Don't look at her. Don't think about her. You've already wasted enough breath humiliating yourself."

She flushes deep crimson, then pale. Kelly shifts uncomfortably behind her.

But Gideon steps closer. "And if you ever make another racial remark in my company—or anywhere under my name—you won't just be fired. You'll be flayed."

Mia gasps. "You can't—"

"I can," he says, and then, slower, colder, "I *will.*"

He doesn't look at her again. Doesn't need to.

Instead, he turns to me.

And that's when it happens.

The composure I've been holding like cracked porcelain finally fractures.

My eyes shine, glassy and too wide. My throat bobs once. My hand tightens around my badge lanyard like it's the only thing keeping me tethered.

Because he's defending me—but he's also reminding everyone *why* I need defending.

What I've been accused of.

What I've allowed.

I want to scream. Or cry. Or bolt.

But I just stand there, mute, blinking against the heat behind my eyes.

Gideon's gaze softens a degree. "Naomi—"

"Don't." My voice is sharp and quiet. I take a step back, enough to make space between us. "Not here."

He freezes. Just enough to make the entire room feel it.

Then he nods. Once.

"I'll wait in the car."

And just like that, he walks away.

The air doesn't move after he's gone.

It's like the entire floor exhales at once, but my lungs refuse to cooperate. The silence left in his wake is heavier than his presence. He defended me. Publicly. Brutally.

And somehow, I feel more exposed than ever.

Toni brushes her fingers lightly across my wrist, grounding me. "You okay?"

I nod once. Lying with silence.

My screen is still dark. I don't log in.

Instead, I gather my things—slowly, methodically. Purse. Phone. Pride.

"I just need air," I murmur, not sure if I'm talking to Toni or myself.

I don't take the elevator. I need the stairs.

Every step echoes with the sound of shame in designer heels.

When I push through the heavy glass doors at ground level, the Maybach is parked exactly where I knew it would be. Idling. Obedient. Waiting.

I turn the other way.

The sidewalk is hot beneath my soles, but the breeze is mine. Unsanctioned. Free.

I don't hear him get out of the car, but I feel it.

His presence moves like a shadow—soundless, sudden, overwhelming.

"Naomi."

I keep walking.

"Don't do this."

I stop.

Slowly, I pivot. Not because he commanded it, but because I allow it.

"You think you can throw your name around like a blade and then expect me to come running?" My voice is soft. Controlled. Deadly.

His jaw tics. "They humiliated you."

"You humiliated me." My eyes never leave his. "You made a public scene. Turned a rumor into a headline."

He opens his mouth, but I keep going.

"You want me in your car? Say the word."

A beat. The quiet between us stretches tight and trembling.

"Melrose."

I smile then, but it doesn't reach my eyes.

"You love that word. The control it gives you."

His silence is confirmation.

I step forward, slow and deliberate, until we're toe to toe.

"Fine," I whisper. "You want obedience? Then obey me first."

He blinks.

"If I get in that car, it's because I decide to. Not because you invoked some code. Not because you think I'm yours."

Gideon doesn't move. Doesn't breathe.

"And if I *do* get in that car..." I pause, lean in, let my lips ghost the shell of his ear. "I'm the one in charge. You understand me, Mr. Hawke?"

A flicker. Barely perceptible. But it's there—the shift. The slow, reluctant exhale of a man used to commanding every room, now waiting to be let inside one.

I step back.

His nod is small. But it's real.

Then I open the car door.

And get in.

The door shuts with a soft *click*, and the cabin seals like a confession booth.

For a few seconds, neither of us moves.

I cross my legs slowly, deliberately. Not for modesty. For precision.

"On your knees."

His gaze cuts to mine, sharp. Searching.

I don't blink.

Gideon shifts.

His hands curl against his thighs. His jaw locks. For a man used to commanding everything in arm's reach, the act of stillness is excruciating.

It's not graceful, not the way he usually commands space. This is reluctant surrender, an offering given under duress—but given all the same. The silk of his suit rustles against the floor mats as he kneels, broad shoulders bowed, head slightly lowered.

Still waiting for permission to look at me.

"Eyes."

They rise.

I let the silence settle like mist between us, because I want him to feel it. The weight of it. The reversal. The cost.

He kneels, and for a split second, my body betrays me—remembers. The way I used to trace the strong line of his throat when I was the one kneeling, his pulse steady under my fingers, his gaze molten with possession. Now, that same throat bobs—tight, uncertain, exposed. The symmetry tastes like power and ruin all at once.

"You made a spectacle of me," I say, voice low, the kind of quiet that cuts deeper than shouting.

"I protected you."

"No," I correct. "You marked me. Staked me. Like your reputation could buffer my shame."

He opens his mouth—but I raise one hand.

"Take one lick."

He stills. A heartbeat. Then bends forward and lets his tongue trace the soft inside of my thigh, reverent, trembling.

I don't flinch. Don't react.

"For every truth you give me, you earn one more."

He looks up at me like he's not sure if this is mercy or punishment. But I see the tension winding in his jaw. The restraint. The want.

"Why didn't you stop her sooner?" I ask.

His voice is wrecked gravel. "Because I didn't think you'd come back."

Another lick.

"Why invoke Melrose?"

"Because I didn't trust myself not to beg."

A third.

The sound I make isn't approval—it's satisfaction sharpened to a knife-edge.

He begs like the man who used to fix everything with silence and silk and the weight of his body on mine. But this time, I don't want gifts. I don't want orders or orgasms. I want the thing he's never learned to give. Truth, stripped of performance. Consequence without control.

"So beg now."

And he does.

Not with flowery words or groveling theatrics.

But with breathless restraint. With his mouth open, waiting. With his hands trembling in his lap.

"Please, Naomi. Let me make it right."

I thread my fingers into his hair and yank his head back just enough to remind him who's giving permission now.

"You don't get to make it right."

He shudders.

"You get to *try*."

Then I shift forward just enough that his breath ghosts over my own barely-restrained ache.

"But not yet."

I push him back with one toe. Just enough to make him *need*.

"You're going to earn me back in inches, Mr. Hawke. Understand?"

His nod is jerky. His breathing, ragged.

"Not with promises. Not with power. With presence."

He nods again. And I just watch him kneel.

Because for once, the world bends for me.

And this time, I'm not the one on my knees.

Chapter 27

God Left My Altar

Gideon

"Crawl to me." Naomi commands softly.

I don't hesitate. The carpet burns under me as I move obediently.

Her legs are still crossed when the phone rings. My hands are limp against her thighs, mouth close enough to beg for permission. She hasn't said a word since she made me kneel. She doesn't have to.

I'm already unraveling.

My knees press into the rug, nerves raw, tongue dry. The bruises from last night haven't even bloomed yet, but they ache like old confessions.

The ringtone splits the air like a bullet. Low. Controlled. But lethal all the same.

I don't move.

She tilts her head—not a command, not even disapproval. Just... watching. Measuring.

The second ring hums against my jacket on the armrest.

A third pulse. Then silence. Just for a beat.

Then it starts again—insistent. Like the past clawing at the present.

"You can answer it," she says, voice like silk over steel.

Her fingers twitch once. Not toward me. Not toward the phone. Just a slow movement, like she's brushing dust from silk.

"I won't stop you," she says.

Not cold. Not forgiving. Just... final.

That's all it takes to shatter the breath in my lungs. I should ignore it. I want to. But the pull of obligation, of blood—of *them*—wraps around my spine like piano wire. And I reach.

My fingers brush cold glass. I see her shift in the corner of my eye. Not away. Just... inward. Her spine straightens. Her chin lifts. The temperature in the room plummets, but I can't feel anything through the static.

I answer.

It's famiglia. Of course it is. One of the elders. Something urgent that can't wait, never *wants* to wait. Words like *blood* and *image* and *lineage* slither through the earpiece, slick with old power and older debts.

I speak. Brief. Controlled. Each word is a nail in something soft.

Naomi moves with the quiet finality of someone reclaiming her own skin.

My voice sounds alien in my throat. The words are standard—"Yes,“ "Understood," "I'll handle it"—but they taste like ash. I don't look at her. I can't.

Out of the corner of my eye, I see movement. Naomi rises from the couch behind me. Doesn't speak. Doesn't pace.

Her steps fluid and quiet, her back to me. I hear the whisper of silk sliding across her skin. Her fingers fasten buttons like she's done it a hundred times—calm, unbothered.

My knees drag forward an inch, like I can pull her back with proximity. My mouth opens again, trying to shape something—*Stay, I'll choose you, just don't leave like this*—but the syllables collapse behind clenched teeth. My throat locks. My body knows what I won't say.

She's fastening the final button, and my breath fractures like glass under pressure.

I'm shaking. Not from the cold. From knowing this is what it looks like when a god walks away from her altar.

I mouth the words: *Please. Don't go.* But no sound escapes.

She pulls her hair up, not bothering to look in a mirror, and steps into her heels with the precision of someone who's already decided.

I'm still kneeling. Crawling on my knees with my cell to my ears, following her.

I want to beg. But all that escapes is breath—shallow, jagged, useless.

She glances at me once. That's all. No accusation. No goodbye.

Just something far worse.

Disappointment.

The door closes behind her with the kind of softness that screams louder than any slammed goodbye.

I don't stand. Not right away.

My knees are numb. My palms press into the fibers of the rug she made me kneel on. The rug that still smells faintly of her shampoo—jasmine and something warmer, like spice soaked in heat.

When I finally hang up, the room is empty.

Her scent is still here—jasmine and sweat and skin—but I know that she's gone, like a trick of candlelight. The space where she sat is a ghost print, pressed into velvet memory.

I call her name.

Once.

The silence answers back.

I reach for my phone again. Tap her name. Thumb hovering. Then calling.

Straight to voicemail.

Again.

Again.

Still nothing.

I stumble upright, still half-naked, blood rushing to my ears. The air's too thick. I can't breathe through it.

I pace the length of the penthouse, moving through every room like she might be tucked inside one. As if she left herself behind in the folds of a throw pillow or the echo of a laugh in the kitchen. She didn't. She took it all.

"Rueben," I bark when he picks up.

"Sir?"

"Have you seen Naomi?"

"No, sir. Was I meant to?"

"I need eyes. Now."

"I'll get the team moving."

I hang up before he finishes.

The walls feel closer now. The city lights outside smear into abstract neon through the windows, like the skyline is weeping.

I think of Vivienne. She hasn't called. Hasn't checked in. She warned me about distractions. Now she's letting the silence answer for her. My reflection in the glass doesn't blink.

I drag on slacks, leave my shirt open, and make it to the terminal in the den. The chair still smells faintly like her lotion—almond and citrus.

I sit back, chest hollow, arms slack.

Then the message alert flashes.

Voicemail.

Timestamped two-eleven a.m.

I hit play.

Her voice is soft. Unyielding.

"I love you. But I won't kneel for a man who won't stand for me."

The sky shifts from violet to ash while I sit in the dark, replaying the voicemail in my head like it's the only language I understand.

By morning, I'm calling her again. Over and over. Voicemail. Silence. Dead air.

I message Zoe. Toni. Rueben. Even Cass.

None of them know. Or they're lying.

By midday, I'm in the car, headed to her building. I don't bother alerting anyone. I punch the security code myself. The doorman stammers, tries to stop me. I look at him once and he folds like a bad hand.

Her apartment is empty.

Not sterile. Not cleaned.

Just... paused.

Drawers still hold her clothes, but something in the air tells me she's not coming back for them.

I check her nightstand. Her laptop is gone. The burner phone I gave her is gone. No sign of a struggle. Just precision.

She didn't flee. She *left*.

My hands curl into fists at my sides. Rage pulses through the layers of fear.

This wasn't just an escape. It was *surgical*.

And there's only one family I know that trains that level of disappearance.

I call my uncle.

It rings three times.

He picks up. "Gideon."

"What did you do?"

A beat of silence.

"I beg your pardon?"

"You heard me. Did you touch her?"

"Is that what this is about?" The amusement in his voice ignites something savage in me. "Naomi's sudden...absence?"

"Don't say her name like you know her," I snarl. "If I find out you laid a single finger—"

"Careful, boy. I'm not your whipping post."

"You're famiglia," I spit. "And every time something precious slips through my fingers, it has your stink on it."

"I haven't touched the girl. I haven't even spoken to her."

"You swear it."

He exhales slowly. "I swear it. On your mother's name."

I want to believe him. But trust is a dead language in our bloodline.

"You lie well," I whisper.

"And you accuse poorly," he bites back. "She left *you*, Gideon. Maybe take that as the insult it is."

I breathe out through my teeth, blood burning in my veins.

"You always did mistake loyalty for control," he adds. "Maybe she finally taught you the difference."

I hang up before I break the phone.

Naomi's everywhere and nowhere. My home, my phone, my blood. And now she's... gone.

Naomi is gone.

And I have no one to blame but myself.

Her fingerprints might still be on the keys.

I log in. Drop the facade. Peel back the layers.

I built the backdoors she's slipped through. I trained a generation of white-collar predators to operate on this very system. I taught them how to disappear.

She didn't ask me how.

She just watched.

And now she's gone.

No ping. No location tag. Her cloud is wiped, backups clean. Every breadcrumb I'd taught her to look for—scrubbed.

She didn't vanish.

She *erased* herself.

Using my code.

I run the backdoor trace one more time—grasping at ghosts.

One IP flickers, flagged for a heartbeat: a public library on the outskirts of Oak Park.

Already wiped. Already gone.

She left it like a breadcrumb she knew I'd chase too late—wrapped in the very encryption she refined from my own code.

I open a browser window. Check her socials.

Empty.

The room spins. My forehead meets the carpet. I whisper her name. I don't recognize the sound it makes in my mouth anymore.

The clock ticks past three. Then four. I don't move until sunlight bleeds across the marble floors.

I try to shower. The heat scalds. I cut it off and stand under freezing water until my skin turns numb.

The robe she always stole is still on the hook. Untouched.

I bring it to my face. Try to smell her.

Nothing. Just linen and bleach.

I try to sleep, but I'm lost in code and by nine a.m., I'm in a suit.

I show up to the boardroom. No one meets my eyes. Someone—I think it's Brennan—starts to speak, but chokes on it halfway through.

"Mr. Hawke..." he says. That's it.

I don't answer. I don't sit. I leave them stewing in the air I've poisoned. The tie is crooked. My hair's still wet. I show up to the office and walk straight past reception without a word.

An intern—Carla, maybe?—steps into the hallway, files clutched to her chest.

She freezes.

I meet her eyes, and whatever greeting she meant to give evaporates.

She presses her back to the wall and waits for me to pass like I'm something that bites.

Maybe I am.

Toni intercepts me near the elevators.

"She's not coming back," she says.

I ignore her. Can't bear the sympathy in her tone.

I unlock Naomi's old office.

No mug. No framed photo. Just an empty chair, a quiet desk.

The indentation on the wrist pad is still there. I sit in her chair and rest my elbows on the desk like I used to when I watched her work.

The screensaver flickers. Just my reflection.

Eyes too sharp. Skin too pale. A man with nothing left to hold.

I tell myself I'll leave in five minutes.

I stay until the cleaners turn the lights off around me.

I taught her how to disappear. I just never thought she'd use it against me.

Chapter 28

Not Lost. Not Yours.

Naomi

The wind hums through the cracked shutters, carrying the scent of salt, jasmine, and diesel. A seagull shrieks somewhere in the grey-pink dawn, sharp and insistent like a judgment. Below, an old fisherman curses in rapid dialect, his radio hissing out a weather report between garbled jazz riffs.

I lie still. Breathing. Letting the silence press down like a second skin. My limbs ache faintly, like bruises beneath the surface of stillness.

This bed is narrow. The mattress is lumpy. The sheets coarse as sackcloth, threaded with the musk of salt and foreign detergent. It's a far cry from the Egyptian cotton I used to wrap myself in—Gideon's scent ghosted into every thread. Leather, clove, skin.

Now it's just me. My scent. My breath. My silence.

The cottage is set into the hillside, three streets up from the harbor. Crooked as a spine, with terracotta tiles and a roof that leaks when it rains. The toilet gurgles like it has secrets. But the power is steady, the title is in a shell name I created two years ago, and no one here knows my name.

Nadine.

I picked it because it sounds like something you'd forget after one glass of wine. Not exotic enough to remember, not plain enough to look twice at.

I stretch out my arm, letting it dangle over the edge of the bed. The morning chill climbs over my skin like memory. That last night—how he looked, naked and kneeling, and still not choosing me.

My throat tightens, but I don't cry.

It's been three weeks since I left him naked and kneeling in the penthouse. The days blur when you don't owe them to anyone.

I already did all my crying in the car, in the airport, in the anonymous hotel where I dumped the phone and scrubbed my identity clean like a bloodstain.

Now, I'm just... here. Breathing.

Tech has its perks. Salaries big enough to disappear if you plan ahead. I didn't buy the place to run—I bought it because I could. Because I wanted a door that only opened when *I* said so.

I rise slowly, my joints stiff, muscles complaining from days of tension that never quite eased. The tiles are cold under my feet as I pad to the window and shove the shutters open.

Light spills in, white-gold and blinding. The sea stretches endlessly and defiantly. Boats bob like lazy punctuation on a letter I haven't written yet.

No one here knows who I am. Or who I was.

And for the first time in a long time, I'm not under surveillance. Not even his.

I lean on the windowsill, forehead against sun-warmed wood, and whisper the name I'm not allowed to want.

"Gideon."

The silence that answers isn't cruel. It's just... final.

The coffee pot takes forever to boil. I count the clicks. I've learned its rhythm—seven slow drips, then a sputter. It's cheap, ancient, and louder than sin, but it works.

I drink it black now. No sugar, no milk. Every comfort stripped away on purpose. Pleasure can be a leash, and I'm not wearing one anymore.

My laptop's buried under a floorboard, but the burner phone sits beside the sink. I thumb it on, eyes scanning the screen. Nothing. Good.

But also—disappointing.

I set it down, screen-down, like it might betray me if left face-up. Old habits. Hard to kill. Especially the ones he taught me.

There's a USB drive in my bra. Always. It holds nothing explosive—just my script. My shadow. Log-ins, false names, the route I'm taking if I need to vanish again. It's encrypted twice over, with an access code only he'd know, buried under a phrase he once whispered in bed when he thought I was asleep.

A breadcrumb, not a lifeline.

I don't want him to come find me. I want to see if he knows *how* to look without trying to own what he's chasing.

I peel a sticky note from the back of the burner. A single number, written in my handwriting but shifted by cipher. It pings a dormant protocol he forgot existed. If he finds it, he'll know I'm not lost. I'm testing.

If he doesn't? Then I've answered my question.

I fold the note twice and burn it in the sink. The ash spirals up like incense, sharp and clean. My breath stutters once, then settles.

When I was with him, I always knew I could vanish if I wanted to. I just never thought I'd need to.

Now I know better.

And somewhere beneath all that knowing is a quieter truth: I'm not the only one who might be looking.

I wash the mug and dry it. Habit. Control. Precision.

The day starts like this: Erase. Breathe. Wait.

The baker calls me "Alma." I nod like it's always been mine.

The name sits weird on my tongue—too soft, too good. Like something you give to a child or a saint. But the papers say Alma Costa, and I wear it like armor, not skin.

He hands me a paper-wrapped loaf, warm through the wax. I thank him in the town's clipped dialect, my accent still rough around the edges. No one looks twice. That's the point.

Small towns protect their own, but they don't ask questions when you pay in cash and smile just enough.

I make my way back through the narrow streets. Salt in the air. Tiles in soft blues and broken ochre. Windows full of shutters and cats. It should feel like peace.

But peace is a language I'm still relearning.

At the base of the stairs, a girl sells fresh oranges from a wicker basket. She offers me one with a grin missing two teeth. I take it, drop a coin in her tin, and glance over my shoulder just once.

Just in case.

Inside, I peel the orange. The scent's bright, too loud for the silence in my apartment. I bite. The juice spills over my thumb, and for half a second, I imagine Gideon licking it off.

I blink hard. Swallow.

That girl, Alma—she doesn't think like that. She doesn't ache like that.

She disappears clean.

I pull the drapes. The orange goes in the bin.

I sit at the table, hands curled around my still-warm bread, and try not to remember how he used to call me his religion.

The modem blinks once. Twice. Steady green.

I keep my devices clean—no Wi-Fi history, no cloud sync, no real name tied to any of it. Everything I touch is anonymized, rerouted, masked behind layers I used to only read about.

But today, I break pattern.

Just for a minute.

Just long enough to look.

My fingers hover over the keys. I type with surgical care, bouncing through encrypted servers until I reach the backdoor I left in the Leviathan framework. The one Gideon taught me to build. The one he forgot I saw.

It's buried beneath three dummy firewalls. I access the node that lets me see what he's scanning. What he's searching.

My chest tightens.

Because he's not just searching.

He's tearing apart the internet.

My name is coded into dozens of queries, misdirected AI sweeps, dummy scripts that fail over and over. He's scraping everything—databases, IP leaks, language patterns in forums. It's obsessive. Beautiful. Terrifying.

He's trying to find me. He just can't.

And that's the point.

I stare at the dashboard.

He's using everything I gave him. Everything I was willing to be. But none of it can find the version of me that won't be claimed.

The part of me that learned to disappear.

I minimize the window. Shut the laptop. Unplug the modem.

Just because I miss him doesn't mean I'll go back.

I am not a map he gets to draw.

The message is nine words long.

I don't sign it. I don't timestamp it. I don't trace it to anything obvious. But I seed it in a way only he'll know where to look.

It's hidden in a dormant repository—buried deep in the codebase of one of Leviathan's satellite projects. A forgotten beta that was his pet obsession for three months before the board shelved it. He thinks no one remembers. But I do.

The phrase is simple:

"You still can't taste truth without trying to own it."

It's not a plea. It's not an invitation.

It's a cipher. A dare. A mirror.

He once whispered that line against my thigh, tracing it with his mouth like a secret prayer. I laughed, breathless, and said, *"You think possession is the same as knowing."*

He didn't answer. He just bit down.

Now it's his turn to interpret.

If he finds it, he'll know I'm watching.

If he understands it, he'll know I'm not lost.

But if he answers?

It better not be with a rescue. It better not be with control.

Because this isn't about what he'll do next.

It's about whether he's finally learning to let go.

The town is quiet after dusk. Not silent—just gentle. The kind of quiet that feels like it's holding its breath. Seagulls cry out over the harbor like they've lost something precious, and the boats sway like they're mourning. The air smells of brine and something old. Something like grief.

My flat is nothing special. Second floor. Terracotta tiles that don't remember footsteps. A window facing the sea I leave open just to pretend I'm breathing.

There's no music. No phone. No Gideon. Only the hum of stillness—and me, trying not to drown in it.

At night, I sit in the chair by the window with a blanket I don't need. I listen for a knock that never comes. I reach for my phone out of habit before I remember it's gone. I stare at the same blank wall and pretend it's a clean slate, not an epitaph.

I miss him.

Not the control. Not the way he made me feel owned.

I miss his silence. The kind that wrapped around us like a shield. That strange, broken man who looked at me like I was something holy and haunted all at once. The one I kept trying to fix—until I realized I was erasing myself just to make room for his salvation.

So now I sit. In this town where no one knows me. In this body I'm still relearning how to live inside. I journal when I can. Scratch words down with trembling fingers that miss the solidity of being held.

Sometimes I write one line over and over, like an incantation I don't believe yet:

Being alone is not the same as being abandoned.

But some nights, it feels exactly the same.

And I cry like I've been gutted.

And I stay anyway.

The café owner gives me my usual—no questions, no smiles. Just espresso and quiet. He doesn't ask where I'm from. No one does. In this village, privacy is the only language more fluent than grief.

Back in my flat, the air is sharp with sea salt and the faint sting of guilt. I open the encrypted laptop. Not the burner. The real one. The one I built from scratch using parts smuggled in under two aliases.

It boots in silence. And for a long minute, I just stare at the blinking cursor like it might blink back.

I shouldn't reach out. I don't need to.

But I do.

Just one line. No signature. No context.

A string of code disguised as a data fragment—buried inside an algorithm he designed for me, months ago. Hidden where only he would think to look. Where he taught me to hide.

Three words. His words. *Trust is earned.*

I embed it in the code and close the laptop. No alerts. No traceable IP. It'll ping one of his passive trackers buried in Leviathan's subroutine stacks—if he's still watching. If he hasn't shut himself down completely.

It's not a plea.

It's not a surrender.

It's a test.

I want to know what he does when he can't chase me. Can't fix what he broke with power.

Will he listen?

Or will he burn the system down trying to reach me?

I don't check my burner often. But when I do, I see the missed calls from Zoe—dozens in the first two weeks. Then one. Then nothing.

Toni hasn't called. She knows better. Her silence is its own kind of care.

Rueben... I half expect him to find me. But if he does, he'll do it quietly. If Gideon's looking for me—and he is—Rueben's the only one who might guess how deep I've gone.

Still, no one has found me.

And that's the point.

Each day I remain invisible is a scream into the void I know Gideon can hear.

But it's not about him anymore.

It's about what silence does when it's your own voice echoing back..

I miss them. Zoe's overpoured wine and sarcasm. Toni's knives and loyalty. Even the rhythm of the office, the ghost of who I was before I met him.

But I won't trade this hard-won freedom for their comfort. Not yet.

Maybe not ever.

Because this isn't exile. It's exile with purpose.

And purpose is the only thing keeping me upright.

I don't leave a trail.

But I do leave a key.

Buried deep in a closed server loop, behind an abandoned node Gideon once told me he built "just for fun." The only reason I remember it is because it was the first time I ever saw him laugh like a boy—unguarded. Human.

That's where I plant the line. Not a cry for help. Not a call home.

Just three words:

The first wall.

He'll understand.

If he remembers Tuscany—when we traced the cracks in a fortress wall and he said, *"Every defense begins with a wall. Every surrender starts with the hand that lays it down."*

It's another test.

Not to see if he can find me. To see if he deserves to.

Because I miss him.

God, I miss him.

The weight of his stare. The sound of his voice when it dipped low with want. The way his hands shook when I told him no.

I ache for him like phantom pain. A limb severed but still alive in my nerves.

But love that only survives in control isn't love at all.

So I wait.

I sip my coffee with shaking fingers and watch the ocean breathe.

I imagine him trying every door, chasing every ghost I left behind.

And I wonder:

Will he stop trying to own me long enough to finally see me?

Because if he does—really sees me—he'll know where to look next.

He'll find the second wall.

And maybe, just maybe, he'll be ready to take it down.

Chapter 29

Hacker vs Hacker: Penance

Gideon

The bunker smells like burnt circuits and sleep deprivation. Artificial cold hums through the vents, but my body is slick with sweat beneath this shirt. I haven't changed in three days. The fabric clings like it remembers every failure. Every almost. Every breadcrumb that led nowhere.

I haven't left this room since Tuesday. Or maybe it's still Tuesday. Time stopped mattering the second her signal resurfaced.

The walls are lined with screens, all aglow in soft cyan and static white. A halo of motion. Motion that isn't her. My team thinks they're monitoring anomalies. They think this is about data. They don't understand—they never did—that every packet of code she sends is a breath. Every bounce is a bruise she means for me to find.

There's a half-drunk coffee on the rack behind me. Cold. Bitter. I don't remember pouring it.

"Node out of Tuscany just activated," Leo says, voice careful like he's afraid I'll snap. "Could be a ghost. Or her."

"It's her."

My voice doesn't raise, doesn't crack. But my pulse spikes anyway. Tuscany. Where the tiles were always cold and she hated shoes and I hated how much she made me feel like I had a body.

A ping traces the route—Tuscany to Prague, then Iceland, then London. A rhythm she used once when we were in bed and I traced it on her spine, fingertip by fingertip, like code.

She's speaking. Not to them. Not to the world. To me.

I move closer to the screen. I can already feel it in my teeth—Naomi's code. Her signature. Her scent without the body.

The code unspools like a silk ribbon dragged across a blade.

It's not just hers—it's *her.* In the tempo. In the architecture. In the defiance.

Line two loops through an old IP signature I taught her to write when she still wore tank tops and sat cross-legged on my rug, chewing cinnamon gum and asking if firewalls could have feelings. Line five slows deliberately, like breath catching in a throat. Like hesitation.

By line nine, I forget to blink.

She's not hiding.

She's *haunting.*

Every line has fingerprints. Every function echoes something only I'd understand. A subroutine shaped like the curve of her back when she arched under me. A delay interval that mirrors the rhythm of her gasp when she came hard and tried not to beg. A junk variable named after the street we fought on in Barcelona, where she walked away barefoot because I'd said something cruel and she hated slamming doors.

I see her.

I *feel* her.

And fuck, it's worse than silence.

One line stutters mid-process. It triggers an old script—one I wrote for her, once. To feed white noise into her earpiece when she needed to disappear.

The noise dissolves. Chopin plays.

Soft. Off-tempo. Ghostly.

She left it clipped. Of course she did. The same unfinished refrain she always stopped before completing, like closure was a trap she refused to step in. She never told me why. I never asked.

Now, I think I know.

She's not asking to be found. She's reminding me what it *costs* to try and own her.

A notification pings on the second monitor.

Embedded message detected.

The script decrypts slowly.

Not because it's complex. Because it *wants* to hurt. Because she *wants* it to.

Each line unfurls like a breath held too long, like something pulled out of skin instead of code. A pulse. A wound. The kind of message you only write when you know it'll land like a fist.

It hits.

Right there—center screen, center chest:

You always trace from the outside in.

I stop breathing.

My hands go cold on the desk, but I don't move them. Can't. I just stare. Because it's her. And it's not just something she *said.* It's something she *knew.*

She whispered it once, smirking against my throat, the night I told her she'd mapped a search pattern wrong. She laughed like she wanted to be wrong. Like she knew it would make me look at her longer. She said it again when I was inside her. Just once. Just to see if I'd flinch. Back then, I thought it was clever. Flirtation. A line in a game we both liked losing.

But now?

Now it feels like *execution*.

My throat closes. Tight. Acid creeps up from somewhere low in my stomach, and I realize I'm clenching my jaw hard enough that my molars ache.

I want to speak. Ask why. Ask how she knew. But there's no one here.

Just the message. And the mirror she made it into.

Because she's right.

That's how I trace. That's how I *love.* From the outside in—around the perimeter, skimming the surface, prying it open like a vault until I feel safe enough to touch the core. By then it's already bleeding. By then it's already gone.

I didn't search to see her—I searched to contain the part of her that scared me. To bend the story back into something I could survive.

She knew.

God, she fucking knew.

My heart kicks in my ribs, fast and wrong. My palms are slick now. I wipe them on my jeans and it still feels like I'm underwater. Drowning in a message only she could write—and only I could deserve.

Behind me, Natalia's voice cuts in, blurry and miles away: "The route just spiked. Berlin. Reykjavik. Montreal. No stable origin."

I barely hear her.

Because the point wasn't stability. It wasn't direction. It was *intention*.

She's not leading me to her.

She's showing me what I look like when I lose control.

And what I see?

It makes me want to claw my own skin off.

A flicker across the top-right monitor.

Then another.

Then red.

Not Naomi's kind of red. Not her threadbare scarf or the lipstick she only wore when she wanted to win a fight. This red is harder. Harsher. Cold, coded violence.

I lean in. Every muscle pulled tight like my body already knows what my brain refuses to admit.

"New breach just hit from Bucharest," Leo says. There's something in his voice—uncertainty. Maybe fear. "It's not her. Rhythm's wrong. Aggressive. Like... like a clamp."

I already know.

I feel it crawling under my skin before the trace renders. The pressure. The shape. It's not an algorithm. It's a fucking fingerprint.

Not Naomi's.

Mine.

Or what used to be mine.

"It's clumsy," Natalia says from behind me, eyes flicking over the display. "Overwritten protocols. Military grade but messy. No encryption finesse."

Because finesse was never the point. This is brute-force legacy code. Teeth without a face.

And it's mine. Or was.

The system pings again. An old framework—reconstructed, sloppy, stitched together from tech I developed when I still worked in shadows. When I thought surveillance was love and control meant safety.

My hands curl into fists.

Sicily. The lab. The surveillance suite I dismantled piece by piece after Naomi first pulled away.

I burned it.

But he didn't.

"Patch the origin," I say. My voice is low. Too calm.

I already know who it is.

The signature hits the screen like a punch to the throat.

My framework. My skeleton. His hands.

Claudia hasn't returned his calls in days. That alone says more than any breach.

Vito.

I stop breathing.

"Everyone out," I say.

Leo turns, eyes wide. "Sir—?"

"Out. Now."

He hesitates. That's new. That's dangerous.

"Get the fuck out."

He moves.

So does Natalia. Quiet. Efficient. The room empties with the kind of hush you only get before blood hits tile.

And then I'm alone.

Just me. Just the monitors. Just the past I thought I'd buried, grinning at me through lines of code I wrote in a life I tried to amputate.

But amputations leave ghosts.

And now they're in *her* systems.

I stare at the code like it might take it back.

As if recognition alone could reverse impact. As if knowing it's my fault is enough to undo it.

It's not.

Vito didn't find her. **I showed him where to look.**

I trace her signal. Obsessively. Publicly. With a full team. Every sweep I launched left heat on the trail. Every node we pinged was a breadcrumb *he* could follow too. While I was decrypting memories and calling it love, he was watching. Learning.

Waiting.

He didn't breach her. **I did.** With every search. Every trace. Every time I told myself I was protecting her.

The bile rises so fast it burns.

I grip the edge of the desk hard enough my knuckles go bloodless. It's not enough. I want to put my fist through something. Through *me.*

How the fuck did I not see it?

All that noise I made about redemption. About finding her clean. Without power. Without control. But that's not what I did. That's not what I ever did.

I hunted her like a possession.

I *broadcast* her existence to every threat I ever tried to shut out.

My breath goes ragged.

She thought she was playing chess with me. Leaving me breadcrumbs. Daring me to follow the trail without falling back into patterns. To see her, not cage her.

But I wasn't playing.

I was *surveilling.*

And now the thing she ran from is clawing at her door—wearing my fucking code.

I bury my face in my hands.

I can't cry. I don't deserve to. I don't get to collapse when I'm the one who handed her map to the devil and called it affection.

The phone buzzes.

I don't reach for it.

My hands are shaking too hard anyway.

The sound cuts through the bunker like a reminder that I still exist. That someone is still out there watching this collapse in real time. That I'm not invisible, even when I want to be.

It buzzes again. Then stops.

The quiet afterward is worse.

I let the screen light up, bright and blinding. I can't bring myself to look at it—like the glow might peel back skin. Like whatever's on there will confirm what I already feel splintering behind my ribs.

But I look anyway.

It's my message. The one I sent earlier, trying to keep the fear clinical, the failure clean.

They're in her signal.

My thumb hovers.

And then—her response. Zoe's voice, as sharp as the first cut:

Even now, she's more loyal to Naomi's truth than I ever was.

And what are you in? Guilt? Power? Or grief?

My lungs seize. The question hits like she's standing in front of me with a scalpel and no anesthesia.

Because I don't know.

Because it's all of them. And none of them. And something worse.

My body folds into itself. I sit hard, like the weight finally dragged me down. I press the heels of my hands to my eyes until everything goes dark. Like maybe if I push hard enough, I won't see what I've become.

Buzz.

One more message.

She didn't vanish to escape. She vanished to be seen without being owned.

I drop the phone.

It clatters to the floor, face down. But the words stay. They've already etched themselves behind my eyes.

She vanished to be sn...

Because I never saw her. Not really.

I saw the version I could hold. The version I could fix. The version that needed me.

But the real her?

I made her disappear.

With love that suffocated. With touch that took. With protection that was always just another kind of leash.

I taught her how to hide. And then I forced her to use it.

I curl forward, elbows on knees, mouth pressed against the back of my wrist to keep from making a sound. My breath is uneven. Ugly. My chest aches like it's caving in.

This is what grief tastes like when you've earned it.

This is what power looks like when it devours everything you swore to love.

And now—

Now I don't get to chase.

Now I don't get to win.

All I get to do is *step back*.

Shield. Cover. Burn every fucking bridge that might lead him to her. Not to earn her back.

To make sure she never has to run again.

Even if that means she never looks back.

Even if that means she never forgives me.

My hands remember how to move before my mind catches up.

Keys click. Lines of code unfold. Commands launch.

Not to trace. Not to track. To cover.

To protect.

To erase the heat I left behind with every desperate grab I called a search.

This isn't a sweep. This is a funeral pyre.

I redirect resources, shut down external trackers, kill threads we opened weeks ago. Everything we pinged—nodes in Tuscany, Prague, Berlin—I smear them in digital blood. I scatter decoys. Wrap them in noise. Make the signal dirty, mean, unworthy of pursuit.

I spin a trail so chaotic even Vito won't touch it. Not because he can't crack it—because it reeks of failure.

Because it looks like the one thing he's trained never to chase: a trap with no reward. A woman who's already been claimed by the void.

Naomi, hidden beneath all of it, wrapped in ghost layers of code and silence, shielded by the one thing I never gave her before:

Distance.

Every node I shut down is an apology. Every misdirection is a vow.

I won't lead them to her again.

I won't be the man who tracks what he should have worshipped.

And if this means she never sees me again—never looks back—I'll take it.

I deserve exile. Not a second chance.

But if there's a god in the machine, he's quiet tonight.

So I do what I know how to do.

I build.

And I burn.

I code until my hands cramp and the servers sweat and the bunker smells like something dying.

I don't stop until the trail is gone.

Until she is safe.

Until I've made it clear:

This is not pursuit. This is protection. This is penance.

The bunker is quiet now.

Everything's still—except me.

I'm stripped down to nothing but breath and bone, muscles tight from hours hunched over heat and guilt. My shirt sticks to my back. The lights sting my eyes. The static in my ears has become a companion. A warning. A hymn.

And then—

I open the generator.

It's old. Primitive by now. I kept it as a reminder of who I was before I learned what power cost. Before I met her. Before I ruined her freedom by calling it love.

The cursor blinks at me, patient. Waiting.

I write.

Not like before. Not to impress. Not to provoke. Not to make her feel me watching.

I write like *her* now.

Deliberate.

Spare.

Honest.

No encryption. No manipulation. Just rhythm. Memory. Truth.

I echo her loop structures. Match her phrasing. I write in her tempo, not mine. I fold myself into her cadence, the way I once folded her body into mine.

At the center, one line:

You never trace from the inside out.

A pause.

Then:

I'm not chasing. I'm here.

Another breath. I hesitate. Then I write the part that costs the most.

If you see this...

My hands stop. Hover.

I type the rest:

...know I waited. Not for you. For who I had to become to be worth your eyes again.

I stare at the screen.

No flourish. No signature.

Just stillness.

I press send.

And for once—I don't wait for a reply.

The music doesn't play.

No server chirps.

The silence is complete.

But it's not empty.

It feels... right.

It feels like the first honest thing I've done in months.

Chapter 30
The Mirror
Gideon

The bunker's quiet. Too quiet. That unnatural kind of silence that only comes after you've bled something out of yourself and left the wound open to breathe.

The air tastes burnt. My eyes sting from too much code and too little sleep. I haven't moved in hours—haven't spoken since I sent that message. The one that didn't ask her to come back. The one that didn't expect a reply.

My fingers twitch against the desk like they don't know what to do without her signal.

I don't look up when the door hisses open. No one has clearance for that.

So when it happens anyway, it's not a glitch. It's an intrusion.

I smell Roman before I see him—cologne too expensive, presence too loud. He's not subtle. He never was.

"You look like hell," he says, voice echoing off cold metal and old shame.

I don't answer.

Remi follows behind him, quiet. Measured. He doesn't look at the monitors. He doesn't sit. He crosses his arms and studies me like a case file he's already solved.

"How'd you get past the locks?" I ask. My voice cracks halfway through. It's not a real question.

Remi shrugs. "You've been broadcasting grief like a bat signal. Thought you might need a mirror."

Roman steps in front of me, kicks one of the dead server boxes out of the way. It screeches across the floor like protest.

"What did you do?" he asks.

I don't flinch. "Everything I could."

He stares at me like that's not enough. Like it never was.

Remi pulls a flash drive from his coat pocket. Holds it between two fingers like a coin he's about to flip.

"You're not the only one who's been tracing her," he says.

And just like that, the silence dies.

He drops the flash drive onto the desk. No drama. No flair. Just precision.

I eye it like it's ticking.

"I intercepted a trace two nights ago," Remi says. "Encrypted route pinged off a legacy node in Bucharest. Tied to the same surveillance framework you used in the Sicily blacksite."

I go still.

He doesn't blink. "It wasn't your ping. Wasn't Naomi's either."

My throat tightens.

Roman paces behind him, arms crossed. Silent now. Letting her cut.

"The signature matches an old contact of Vito's. Military-adjacent. Russian-built, then fragmented and sold to private buyers. He's moving."

The weight in my chest goes cold. Not sharp. Heavy. The kind of pressure that doesn't pierce—it smothers.

Remi doesn't let up.

"I cracked the loop Naomi ran through Berlin. It wasn't just breadcrumbs. She was setting up counter-surveillance—cloaking her trail, misdirecting signal heat."

I nod. Slowly. "She knew someone else might be watching."

"She knew you'd lead them in."

The words land like a slap. He doesn't raise his voice. He doesn't need to.

Roman finally speaks. "She's better at disappearing than any of us ever gave her credit for. But she's not invisible anymore."

I look down at the flash drive.

"She left a window open," I say.

"No," Remi corrects. "You did. She just rerouted the fall."

I sit back. My whole body suddenly feels old. Too big. Too slow.

"And you've known where she is?" I ask.

His gaze softens, but he doesn't look away. "For three weeks."

The silence stretches between us—hot, thick, furious. Roman shifts, waiting for me to explode.

But I don't.

I just ask, voice low: "Why didn't you tell me?"

"Because you weren't the one she needed to see her. Not yet."

Roman leans against the console, arms crossed over his chest, watching me with that ex-military calm that always came before a kill shot.

"I get it," he says, voice low. "You thought this was about proving you could be different. Cleaner. A better version of the man who raised you."

I don't answer.

He steps forward.

"But you didn't become a better man. You just wanted to be seen as one."

I flinch. Just a flicker. But Roman doesn't miss it.

"Don't," he warns. "Don't do the thing where you intellectualize it and call it devotion. You loved her, yeah. I believe that. But you didn't love who she is. You loved what she gave you—purpose, resistance, ache."

I step back, but there's nowhere to go. The bunker feels smaller now. Tighter. Like the walls are leaning in to listen.

"You think she left because you lost control?" Roman says. "She left because control is all you ever offered. And that's not love, Gideon. That's inheritance."

For one second, I see something flicker in his expression. A ghost of something like regret. But it's gone before it can settle.

He steps in closer. Close enough that I can smell the citrus edge of his aftershave. Feel the heat behind the chill in his tone.

"If you show up at her door with legacy on your breath and dominance in your posture, she won't just shut you out—she'll disappear so hard none of us will find her again."

"Naomi doesn't need a fixer," he finishes. "She needs a man who knows what it means to lose power and still stay. You ready to be that man?"

I don't know how to answer.

And maybe that's the point.

Remi sets the flash drive back on the console, this time with quiet finality.

"No encryption," he says. "Clean coordinates. One-time trace."

Roman's eyes don't leave mine. "We're not giving you another."

I pick it up, feel the weight of it. It's light. Laughably small for what it holds.

It's her. The last piece. The last step between obsession and arrival.

My hands shake.

Remi's voice cuts through the silence. "You need to understand something. That location isn't a key. It's a threshold. If you cross it as the man who wrote that surveillance code, she'll know."

"She'll feel it," Roman adds. "In your posture. In your voice. In the way you look at her like she's something to be solved instead of someone to be met."

I close my hand around the drive.

Roman steps forward. "You get one shot," he says. It's not a threat—it's a truth. "If you bring dominance, she'll close the door." "If you bring legacy, she'll run." He looks me dead in the eye.

"You show up with anything but honesty, and she disappears for good. No trail. No echo. Just gone."

I want to argue. But I can't. Because they're not wrong.

They've already decided. This isn't a vote. This is a reckoning.

Remi turns to go. But he pauses at the door, hand on the frame.

"She didn't need you to change the world for her, Gideon," he says softly. "She just needed you to stop making her fit inside yours."

Then they're gone.

And I'm alone again.

Just me. The drive. And the version of myself I'll have to bury to earn what it points to.

The door clicks shut. Their footsteps fade. Only the low hum of the bunker remains—and the hollow sound of my own pulse in my ears.

I don't move.

The drive is still on the desk. Small. Insignificant. But it feels like a live wire.

My hand hovers above it, trembling.

And then—I just sit.

I don't reach for code. I don't speak. I just breathe.

Shallow. Broken.

The silence stretches, elastic and cruel.

And somewhere in that stretch—something gives.

The grief doesn't hit like a wave. It creeps. Starts in the chest. Crawls to the throat. Settles behind the eyes like a pressure I've spent my whole life denying.

I blink once. Then again.

The third time, the tear spills before I know it's there.

It's not cinematic. It's not beautiful. It's quiet. Ugly. A crack in a dam I didn't know I still had.

I press the heel of my hand to my face. Too late. The second one falls faster. The third drags a sound from my chest that doesn't belong in this body.

A sharp inhale. A choked breath. A whisper of something I never learned how to say aloud.

I bury my face in my hands. And I break.

Not because I lost her. Because I finally understand what it means to let her go.

Because everything I've done to try and win her back has only proven why she left.

And now— Now there's nothing left to prove. Just a question.

Can I walk toward her without needing her to catch me?

I sit in that question until the tears slow. Until the silence returns. Until I feel the weight of my body again.

Then I wipe my face. And stare at the flash drive.

Not like it's a mission. Not like it's a challenge. Like it's a mirror.

And when I stand— I won't bring power. Just truth.

Chapter 31

Permission To Stay

The square isn't big. Just a fountain, a few shuttered storefronts, some cobblestone that still remembers war. I walk through it every day at the same hour, arms full of bread and oranges, head tilted to catch the sun.

It's quiet here. On purpose.

I picked this town for its silence, its shadows, the way the sea is always just out of sight but never out of reach. I wanted a place where I could vanish without vanishing. Where I could breathe without being watched.

So when I see him—when I see *Gideon* standing across the square, hands in his pockets, stillness pressed into his spine like a warning—my body forgets what to do with itself.

He doesn't move.

He just stands there—one hand tightening in his pocket like he's fighting to stay still. Like every instinct in him is begging to reach for me, and he knows he no longer has the right.

I keep my eyes on him. Quiet. Cutting.

He swallows.

Tries to speak.

Fails.

The second attempt lands in pieces. "I—" He exhales hard, starts over. "I didn't come to take you back. I didn't come to... fix it. I came because I—"

He breaks off.

His throat works around the words like they're splinters.

Then, softer: "I don't know how to ask to stay. Not without sounding like I'm still trying to own something."

His voice—*fuck*. It's not even steady. It shakes. Just a little. Like whatever composure he walked in with is already peeling at the edges.

He takes one slow step forward. Careful. Barely more than a shift in weight. Like even *hope* is dangerous.

"I don't have anything left to offer but this. Just me." Another breath. "No mask. No script. No command."

His hands are at his sides now. Palms open. Exposed.

"I know I ruined it. I know I made you vanish. And I—" His voice cracks, raw in the middle. "I still don't know how to be a man who deserves to see you like this. But I'm trying. I swear to God, I'm trying."

That's the crack I wasn't ready for.

Not the words.

The *tremble* in them.

The fact that for once, he's not performing remorse—he's *drenched* in it.

So I stare.

Hold him in that silence.

Let him flinch under the weight of not knowing if he's already too late.

And then, with zero warning, I speak.

"You're not wearing a watch."

His brow knits like he doesn't understand why that matters.

But then he does.

And his voice drops to almost nothing.

"I didn't want to know how long I've been losing you."

I nod once. Just enough for him to see it.

Then I turn.

Walk.

Slow. Sharp. Unforgiving.

I don't say "Come."

I don't say "You're forgiven."

I just move.

And when I hear his footsteps behind me—*not chasing, not commanding*, just... *following*—

It's not relief I feel.

It's restraint.

Because this isn't a victory for him.

This is *permission to try*.

We don't speak.

Not through the narrow stone alleys, not when the bell above the chapel tolls noon like it knows what he did. Not even when we pass the bench where I usually sit with my coffee, pretending I've forgotten how to be touched.

He walks behind me.

Not beside.

Not leading.

Like he knows he doesn't get that place yet.

And I hate that part of me notices—*approves*—how small he's become. No power in his stride. No dominance in his posture. Just silence.

Just restraint.

Just him.

God, it should make it easier. But it doesn't.

Because even muted, he still pulls at something in me. Not lust. Not anger. Something deeper. Something like... gravity that remembers what it was like to fall.

I unlock the door. My fingers shake.

He doesn't ask to come in.

I don't invite him either.

But I leave the door open.

Not as permission.

As a test.

I set the bread on the counter. Unwrap the cheese. Pour two glasses of water—not because I want him comfortable, but because *I remember how dry his mouth gets when he's nervous.*

My body still remembers him. I hate that it does.

I hear the door close.

Softly.

A sound like surrender.

He's inside now. Quiet. Careful. Like if he breathes too loud he might lose the right to stay.

I don't look at him.

I don't have to.

I *feel* him behind me. The heat. The weight. That quiet thrum I used to crave like oxygen and now treat like a threat.

I hand him a glass without turning.

Our fingers don't touch.

He takes it with both hands. Drinks like it means something. Like it costs him something.

And I—

God, I almost ask if he's okay.

The words rise fast, stupid, reflexive. Muscle memory of comfort I used to give without question.

I bite them back.

Because he's not mine to worry about anymore.

Because I don't owe him soft.

But it hurts.

It *hurts* to hold that line. Because he's here. He *came*. And for one fractured second, I want to touch his jaw and say nothing and let that be enough.

But love without safety isn't love.

And I love myself more now.

So I stay still.

Watch him drink. Watch him *not look at me*.

And I wait.

Not for him to speak.

But for the part of me that wants to fold—to *die down*.

The room is too quiet.

Even the house feels like it's holding its breath.

He sets the glass down on the counter with both hands like it might break if he lets go too fast. Doesn't speak. Doesn't move closer.

And that's worse, somehow. Because the Gideon I remember filled every space. Every pause. Every silence.

This one… doesn't assume he belongs.

I slice the bread.

The knife scrapes against the wood like it's trying to speak for us.

He watches, I can feel it—like heat on my shoulder. Like breath. He used to do this when we were home late from a scene, both too wrecked for words. He'd sit on the floor behind me and watch me eat, like witnessing my hunger made him full.

I shake the memory off.

It clings.

I hand him a slice. He doesn't thank me. Just breaks it in half, slow, reverent, like communion.

God, everything with him was always *so intense.*

Even now.

Especially now.

He sits, not at the head of the table—where he always used to—but across from me. Diagonal. At a distance.

And I realize—

He's *trying* to be small.

To be quiet.

To take up less space than his name deserves.

And it should make it easier to breathe.

But all it does is make me want to reach for him and scream *Why now? Why not when I needed it?*

I say nothing.

Just tear a piece of bread. Let it sit on my tongue. Let myself taste the restraint.

We eat in silence.

But it's not empty.

It's the kind that *aches.*

Because this is the kind of silence that used to hum with command. Now it trembles with apology.

He doesn't ask to help clean.

Doesn't try to fix anything.

He just watches me stack the plate, rinse the knife, fold the cloth napkin I brought out for no reason except I wanted something beautiful between us.

I dry my hands on my thighs.

My palms still sting.

Not from labor.

From *not touching him*.

I wipe the counter one last time.

Not because it needs it.

Because I need something to do with my hands.

He's still at the table.

Still watching me like I'm a star he's not allowed to name anymore.

I say nothing.

Finally, he stands.

Doesn't come closer.

Just lingers near the threshold of the hall, fingers grazing the edge of the wall like he's tracing the outline of a question he doesn't have permission to ask.

I turn slowly and we lock eyes.

And for a moment, just one fragile, fractured moment, I swear he's about to drop to his knees.

Not to beg.

To *earn*.

But he doesn't.

He swallows whatever instinct flickered in his throat, lowers his gaze just slightly, and says:

"I'll take the couch."

And fuck, it shouldn't hurt.

But it *does*.

Because it's not cowardice.

It's *grace.*

It's him telling me he knows what he broke—and that this house, this silence, this air... doesn't owe him comfort.

I nod.

Just once.

He moves past me, careful not to brush my shoulder, like even static might be too much.

And when he settles on the couch—long legs bent, one arm behind his head, the other draped low—I see it.

He doesn't look like a man waiting to be invited in.

He looks like a man *hoping he's done enough not to be thrown out.*

I turn away before that image settles too deep in my chest.

Before it carves out something I swore I'd already healed.

I flip off the kitchen light.

The dark moves in like water.

I don't say goodnight.

But I leave the hallway light on.

Not because I want him to see.

Because I want him to know I *see him.*

And maybe that's enough.

For tonight.

It's almost midnight when the floor creaks.

Soft. Hesitant.

I don't move.

I'm curled on my side, facing the window, one arm tucked beneath the pillow like I can hold myself steady.

The air smells like ocean salt and memory.

My body is still, but inside, I'm wired. *Raw.*

The door opens.

Not wide. Just enough for the silence to slip through.

He doesn't say my name.

He doesn't say anything.

And still—I feel him there. Just standing in the doorway like a man who's memorized the shape of my absence.

"I'm not here to touch you," he says quietly. "Or take anything."

My fingers curl around the sheet.

"I just—" he hesitates. "I needed to see you... To make sure this wasn't some dream I built out of guilt."

I keep my back to him.

Because if I look at him now, I'll shatter.

"You should go," I say.

It comes out softer than I mean it to.

He doesn't argue.

Doesn't beg.

But then—

"Can I just..." His voice breaks. "Can I sleep on the floor?"

That's what *splits* me.

Not the question.

The way he asks it. Like it costs him something. Like he'd crawl into silence for me if it meant one less step backward.

I roll over.

Look at him.

Barefoot. Shoulders tense. Eyes hollow. He looks like a man who *knows* he ruined the one place that ever felt like home.

"I won't touch you," he repeats. "I won't say anything. I'll be gone before you wake up. I just—"

He swallows hard.

"I just want to fall asleep knowing you're real."

My throat closes.

Because I remember this man.

Not the billionaire. Not the Dom.

Because I remember the way he used to make space when I needed quiet. The way he'd sit at the edge of the bed, wordless, waiting until I was ready to let him in. I remember how it felt to be seen without being touched. Just... witnessed

I *remember* him.

But memory isn't enough.

And love, when wielded wrong, is still a weapon.

I nod once.

That's all.

His breath leaves him in one shaky exhale, like I just handed him something precious and painful.

He steps inside.

Doesn't look at the bed.

Just curls up on the rug, near the edge. One arm folded beneath his head, the other draped across his ribs like he's trying to hold himself in.

No blanket.

No pillow.

He doesn't ask for more.

And I don't offer.

Because I'm not ready to be warm again.

But I don't turn away either.

I watch him for a long time. His breathing. His stillness.

The broken, beautiful effort of it.

And when I finally close my eyes, it's not because I'm calm.

It's because I'm exhausted from *not touching him.*

I lie there long after his breath evens out.

Eyes open, staring at the ceiling like it might offer absolution. But there's nothing up there. Just white paint and the sound of him not reaching for me.

The silence is *deafening.*

Not because it hurts—but because it doesn't.

Because for the first time, there's no manipulation in the quiet. No bait. No game.

He's here.

And he's not asking me for anything but permission to exist.

And still—

My body knows him.

My breath hitches every time he shifts on the floor. A soft exhale. A rustle of fabric. A sound that used to mean more was coming—hands, voice, control.

Now it's only presence.

And somehow, that's worse.

Because I miss him.

Not the man who made me feel small when he was afraid. Not the one who watched instead of saw.

I miss the man I only ever got in flashes—glimpses between power plays and perfectionism.

The one who laughed once when I couldn't figure out a password, and said, *"Maybe you don't need to solve everything to be brilliant."*

That man? He's on my floor. Curled up like repentance. And I don't know what to do with that.

I turn on my side.

Face the window again.

Let the dark hold what I can't.

The moon hangs low. Tired. Complicit.

And I whisper, not for him, not even for me—but for the part of myself still watching from the inside out:

Don't you dare forgive him just because he finally stopped talking.

I close my eyes.

And finally—

Sleep comes.

But only just.

And not without cost.

Chapter 32

After the Ruin

Naomi

The light is pale when I open my eyes. Soft and stretched, creeping across the floor like it's afraid to disturb us.

I don't move.

Because somehow—*somehow*—our hands are touching.

Not holding.

Just... there.

Fingers resting in the space between us. Not clasped. Not seeking. Just *left behind*. Like even sleep couldn't finish what last night started.

He's still on the floor. Curled into himself. Chest rising slow.

And I—

I *watch him*.

I don't mean to. I just... do.

His lashes cast faint shadows on his cheeks. His jaw is softer now, the hard edges dulled by sleep and whatever ghosts he made peace with in the dark.

There's something almost cruel about it.

How still he is.

How *young* he looks like this—like a man who doesn't know how to perform yet. Like whatever version of him I fought to believe in might've been real all along, just buried under all the noise.

I brush my thumb against his knuckles.

Barely.

It doesn't wake him.

I almost wish it would.

Instead, I slip my hand back—slow, careful. My fingers remember too much. They twitch when the warmth leaves them.

He stirs.

Eyes crack open.

Bleary. Disoriented.

Then they find me.

And everything inside him stills.

He doesn't speak.

Just looks at me.

Waits.

I sit up slowly, every motion careful. "I'll make coffee," I say, voice hoarse.

He nods. Doesn't stand yet.

Doesn't move.

Like even gravity is permission he won't assume.

I disappear into the kitchen.

By the time he joins me, I've poured two cups. Set out the last of the bread.

Neither of us mention the floor.

Or the hands.

Or the fact that I didn't pull away.

We eat in silence.

Later—later, when the sun has settled into something golden and lazy—I pour wine. Just a little. Not for comfort. Not for ritual.

Just... to mark that we're still here.

Still breathing in the same space.

He sits on the edge of the couch again. Upright. Contained.

He doesn't sprawl. Doesn't command.

Just watches me like he's memorizing the shape of my restraint.

I pass him the glass. Our fingers don't touch.

He sips it slow. Like it costs something.

"The basil on your windowsill is thriving," he says finally.

I glance at him.

He keeps his eyes on the glass.

"I talk to it," I say.

He nods like that makes perfect sense.

Maybe it does.

Maybe we're both just talking to things that can't talk back.

He huffs a laugh. Barely. Just a breath behind his teeth.

Then: "There was a squirrel on the roof last night. I think he threw a nut at me."

I blink.

"...What?"

He shrugs. Sips again. "It hit the window. Felt personal."

It takes me a second.

Then—*fuck*—I laugh.

Quiet. Sharp. Reflexive.

It escapes before I can kill it, and his eyes dart to mine like it might be a trick. Like he's not sure he's allowed to enjoy it.

"I'm serious," he says, deadpan. "I heard him scamper away after like he'd made a point."

"You're really blaming a squirrel for starting shit?"

"I'm not saying it was strategic warfare. But I am saying it felt earned."

The corner of my mouth twitches again, despite everything.

He leans forward slightly. Not close. Just enough to drop his voice.

"I might have stepped on a snail. On purpose. Last time I was here."

I snort.

"You're a monster."

"Reckoning's come," he says, lifting his glass in salute. "Nature has spoken."

The moment stretches.

Warm.

Stupid.

Easy.

And so much worse because of it.

Because it shouldn't *still* be easy. Not after everything. Not after the burn and the break and the *fucking surveillance*. But somehow, sitting here with bread crumbs and vineyard leftovers, we slide into a rhythm that feels... lived in.

Not healed.

Just remembered.

I gesture toward the bell tower outside. "They ring every hour. Except midnight."

He tilts his head. "Why not midnight?"

I sip. "Apparently the priest has insomnia. The bells kept him up."

He smiles. The real kind.

It makes something inside me hurt.

I clear my throat. "I leave the basil out during storms. It likes the lightning."

"Of course it does," he murmurs.

"Meaning?"

He shrugs. "Just... sounds like something you'd do. Feed it chaos. Make it thrive."

That lands harder than I expect.

He must feel it.

Because he retreats into his glass again, suddenly quiet.

The air shifts.

Again.

Back into something careful.

We don't talk about New York.

Or the code.

Or how silence used to mean surrender, and now it means protection.

But I notice the way he holds his body smaller than before. Tucked in. Leaned back. One foot drawn up like he's afraid of taking space I haven't given him.

That's new.

And I don't say anything.

But I *let it matter*.

We don't finish the wine.

It sits untouched between us, like a truth we're both circling, too afraid to name.

I should tell him to go. I should end this now—while I still can. While my spine is still steel and my skin still remembers how to burn instead of reach.

But I sit.

And then I say—quiet, flat, out of nowhere—

"You ever break anything?"

He looks up. Blinks once. Like I asked him to solve a code he wasn't ready for.

"A bone?" he asks.

I nod.

He shifts. "Collarbone. Motorcycle accident. Stupid decision. I was sixteen."

He doesn't ask why I want to know.

Maybe he already knows.

I stare at the edge of the table. Run my thumb along the seam in the wood. Let the memory settle into my throat like something sharp.

"I broke my wrist when I was ten," I say. "During a fire drill. Fell down a flight of stairs."

I feel him watching me now. But I don't look at him.

"No one noticed," I add. "I didn't cry. Didn't scream. Just sat outside and waited for it to end."

The air shifts.

He doesn't speak.

So I keep going, voice lower now, like I'm slipping into a version of myself that still lives in that body.

"It clicked after. Every time I turned it too far. Hairline fracture that healed wrong."

I lift it, show him.

Flex.

Click.

It's a small sound. But in this room, it hits like confession.

He flinches. Barely.

I don't.

"I used to do it on purpose," I say, softer now. "Under the table. In class. During dinner. Just to prove I still could."

My pulse stings behind my teeth.

"I wanted to control something. Even if it was just the ache."

He says nothing.

Does nothing.

And for one wild, shattering second, I want him to reach for me.

I want his hands on my wrist, his mouth against my palm, something—*anything*—to prove this pain still means something.

But he doesn't.

He just sits there. Watching. Breathing. *Honoring it.*

Not fixing it.

Not absorbing it.

Just *seeing* me.

And it wrecks me.

Because I've never told that story before.

Not because I couldn't.

Because no one ever stayed quiet long enough to let me.

He nods, once.

His voice is careful when it comes.

"Thank you for telling me."

That's all.

No follow-up. No questions. No commentary.

Just a pause, just a moment, just the weight of being heard.

And it shouldn't feel like relief.

But it does.

I exhale.

Not a sigh.

A surrender.

Tiny.

Silent.

But real.

The quiet after that feels different.

Not heavy.

Not tense.

Just... full.

Like silence finally stopped punishing us and started holding space.

I gather the dishes. Slowly. One by one.

He moves to help—but stops halfway, like he remembers who he used to be and doesn't want to risk becoming him again.

I don't stop him.

But I notice.

It's the restraint that undoes me more than any apology ever could.

When the sink is empty, and the table cleared, I stand there like a fool with my hands damp and my heart louder than I want it to be.

He doesn't say he's tired.

Doesn't ask where to go.

Just gestures toward the couch.

"I won't take your bed," he says. "Or your silence."

That second part—

That's what lands.

Because *he sees it*. He sees what I've made of my quiet. That it's not a punishment. It's a boundary.

I nod.

Not because I approve.

Because I understand.

My phone pings once on the sideboard.

ZOE: you alive or just emotionally constipated and curled around a man again

JADE: god she's totally curled. probably let him breathe on her wine glass too

JOR: leave her alone she's building boundaries

ZOE: ok but if she starts defending him again i'm posting the screenshot

ME: i'm here. just dealing...

JOR: good. stay with us. Here if you wanna talk.

I linger a second before I delete my half written response. I want to tell them everything. I want to name what this is, what it means. But I don't have the words yet.

So I let the screen go dark. Let the silence answer for me.

Then I turn. Flick off the kitchen light. Walk the familiar path down the hall—past the coat hooks, the crooked frame, the little chip in the tile I never got around to fixing.

I hear him moving behind me.

Slow.

Deliberate.

Like even the weight of his steps might be too loud.

I don't close my bedroom door all the way.

Not for him.

For me.

Because some part of me needs to know he's still out there. Still real. Still close—but not *too* close.

I peel back the blanket. Slide in.

The sheets are cool.

The pillow smells like wind and salt and a little bit of lemon soap.

I lie on my side. Facing the door. Listening.

The couch creaks.

Then stills.

His breath evens out faster than I expected. Like this space—this quiet—is the safest thing he's known in years.

It should make me feel strong.

Instead, it makes my chest tighten.

Because I'm the reason he knows how to be small.

And I'm the reason he *has* to be.

I close my eyes.

Try to sleep.

But I keep listening to him breathe.

Quiet. Careful. Present.

He doesn't fidget.

Doesn't whisper my name.

Doesn't even shift.

Like he knows the ghosts in this house are mine now. And he's not allowed to touch them.

I want to cry.

I don't.

Instead, I press my palm to the sheet. The space between us.

And let myself feel the ache.

Not because I want him to break the silence.

But because—for once—I need to know he won't

Chapter 33

Trust Fall: The Cost Of Gravity

Gideon

The scent of garlic clings to the air, thick and sharp, curling through Naomi's small coastal kitchen like a question that won't be answered. Butter hisses in the pan. Lemon sizzles as it hits, bright and biting, too much too fast. My hands move on autopilot—grating cheese, stirring pasta, dragging time forward with every motion that avoids the one I actually want—reaching for her.

The windows are cracked open, letting in salt air and the rhythmic hush of waves against rocks below. Wind presses against the screen door like it wants in. I'm not sure if it's a comfort or a threat.

She hasn't said a word since she let me in. No welcome. No glare. No explosion. Just silence. And that's the worst part. The quiet is clinical, intentional, like she's studying me under glass. Not angry. Not cruel. Just distant. Like she doesn't owe me anything—and she's right.

Naomi perches on the couch, one leg tucked under the other, hoodie sleeves shoved to her elbows, a sea of tangled cables and warm light around her. Her laptop casts code across her skin, cool and flickering like a force field I can't breach. She's working. Or pretending to. Her fingers move with sharp precision, not frantic but focused. I don't know if it's distraction or discipline.

I set the pasta down on the table between us. Steam curls in soft spirals. I added a sprig of parsley like a coward pretending it's garnish and not guilt.

Something green. Something controlled.

She doesn't touch it.

I take my time cleaning up. Water runs hot over my hands. The sponge squeaks against the plates. A knife slips in my grip. I flinch. The blade doesn't cut me, but the jolt echoes. I focus on the repetitive rhythm of washing, stacking, rinsing. At least the dishes don't flinch when I fuck up.

By the time I sit, my palms are red and pruned, my shoulders tense. She hasn't looked up. But I can feel her watching in the peripheral edges of my shame.

I don't speak. I don't fidget. I just sit in the stillness and let it press its weight into my chest.

Minutes pass. Or hours. Time folds when you're bracing for impact.

Then, softly—

The laptop closes.

The sound is soft. But it hits like a verdict.

Naomi looks at me. No venom. No pity. Just quiet, clear-eyed calculation.

"What are you actually afraid of, Gideon?"

No bite to it. No sarcasm. Just clean truth, offered like a blade. I could lie. I could posture. But she deserves more than that. More than the curated version of me.

I exhale, and it comes out raw.

"That without control, I don't exist."

Her brow lifts slightly. Not surprised. Just waiting. She's letting me dig the grave myself.

"That if I'm not powerful, not needed, then there's nothing left but the rot underneath."

The words sit between us, sour and unpolished.

"That the dominance wasn't about the dynamic. It was about the armor. The image. The excuse."

She doesn't interrupt. Just watches.

"And worse than all of it?" I force the next words past the lump in my throat. "I think I led them to you. My family. They found your new name. I was too slow. Too confident. Too selfish to pull back."

I almost call Roman. Then Remi. But they'd only offer solutions.

I call Ethan instead.

He answers on the second ring. "Is she okay?"

"I don't know."

Silence hums between us. Then—

"You're not calling for strategy, are you?"

I press my thumb to my temple. "No. I'm calling because I don't know how to be the man she needs. Not anymore."

Ethan exhales slowly. "Then stop trying to be anything. Just show up. No power plays. No plans. Just Gideon. Nothing else."

The line clicks off.

And maybe for the first time, I actually listen.

My voice falters. Shame doesn't shout. It burns slow—like acid behind my ribs. I almost say it. The excuse. The thing that would make the guilt easier to swallow. I didn't know. I never meant to. But she's looking at me like she already knows.

So I swallow it.

Because this time, silence is the only honest thing I have left.

She stands. Slowly. No rush. No heat. Just presence.

The floor creaks under her bare feet. She steps close. Her gaze pins me, sharp as a scalpel.

"You don't kneel to hide," she says. "You kneel to show up."

Her voice is soft, but there's steel braided through it.

She moves past me without touching. Walks to the center of the room and turns.

The air presses down. Not heavy. Not cruel. Just honest.I think about all the things I used to say to fill this kind of silence.All the ways I used to perform devotion instead of feel it.I say nothing now. And somehow, it feels louder.

She stands there, a whole cathedral made of fury and grace.

She's breathtaking. Not in the polished, posed way the world sees her, but in the way light breaks around her silhouette. Solid. Soft. Unshakable. Like she built herself out of scar tissue and intention.

I want to fall into her knees. Into her hands. Into whatever space she'll give me—if she gives me any.

I step forward like a sinner who's forgotten how to pray.

And then, I kneel like a man who's burned every altar but still begs for absolution.

Each step is a slow undoing. Like every inch of distance I close scrapes away the man I used to be. The one who led with fear. The one who mistook control for connection.

I lower myself to the floor.

The rug is soft beneath my knees, but nothing about this feels easy.

I let my hands fall open on my thighs.

Drop my gaze.

Breathe.

No collar. No command. No absolution. Just knees on a rug—and a hope I never earned.

Just this.

Her. Me. And the hollow place where power used to live.

She doesn't move.

But I feel her gaze settle like weight across my shoulders.

The silence turns sacred.

My chest rises and falls. Slower. Steadier.

The air tastes different here. Briny and electric.

Her presence wraps around me like a wire, hot and sparking, but she doesn't close the distance.

She lets me stay there.

On my knees.

Stripped of the armor. The performance. The lies I used to live inside.

Then—a shift. Not a sound. A presence.

She steps forward. Close enough that the heat of her skin brushes my breath. She doesn't touch me. But I feel her watching.

I lift my eyes slowly. Only to her waist. Her thighs. Her breath stirs the air just above me.

I don't look higher. Not without permission.

"Look at me, Gideon."

Her voice is velvet-wrapped steel.

I obey.

Her eyes cut straight through the version of me I used to be.She doesn't smile. She doesn't soften.And still—I want her to see me.Not the man who broke her. The one kneeling now.

She's beautiful. Fierce. Radiant in her restraint.

I feel like a man being granted vision after centuries in the dark.

"Say it," she murmurs.

"I'm yours."

She doesn't blink. "And?"

My throat closes, but I force the words through.

"I need you to forgive me. But more than that—I need to earn it. I'll spend the rest of my life learning how. If you let me."

Something flickers across her face. Something deep. Something dangerous.

"You don't earn me by kneeling."

I nod. Not because I agree. Because I understand.Because kneeling was never about surrender. It was about staying still long enough to mean it.

My heart cracks.

"You earn me by staying down until you know what it means to rise the right way."

I remember what she said, once, when we were still circling each other in shadows:

That love without safety isn't love.

I didn't understand it then.

I do now.

I don't kneel to vanish.

I kneel to be seen.

To be nothing but this.

Mine, if she lets me.

Hers, even if she doesn't.

I close my eyes.

Let it wreck me.

I used to think I owned her silence. Now I know—it owned me.

And still, I stay.

Knees pressed into the floor.
Body stripped of defense.
She hasn't said I belong.
She hasn't said I should go.
And that silence? It's not mercy. It's a mirror. And I finally don't look away.
And if she walks away—I'll still be here.

Chapter 34

Waiting and Willing to Worship

Naomi

He hasn't moved.

The silence wraps around him like a second skin, salt-damp and trembling, but he doesn't break. Doesn't twitch. Doesn't even lift his head.

And for a long moment—I just look at him.

Because this isn't about dominance. Or forgiveness. Or any script we used to follow.

It's about whether he means it. Whether I believe it.

So I wait.

Because I want to know if this is still performance—or if the man kneeling before me is finally done pretending.

The wind outside shifts, brushing over the porch like breath held too long. My fingers curl at my sides. The air between us hums with heat that has nothing to do with summer and everything to do with the ache I've carried since the night he left me shattered and gasping and alone.

But I'm not gasping now.

I step toward him.

One quiet pace. Then another.

He stays down.

Good.

I stop just short of touching him. The smell of lemon and garlic lingers on his skin. His shirt is soft and wrinkled. His jaw is tight, lips parted like he's mid-prayer. I wonder if he thinks this is still a test.

It's not.

It's a reckoning.

I lift my hand and run my fingers through his hair.

He exhales like I punched the breath out of him.

"You're not mine by default, Gideon."

He flinches at the sound of my voice but doesn't move.

"You're not mine because you kneel, or because you're sorry, or because you finally realized your last name doesn't make you God."

Silence.

"You're mine," I murmur, "only if I say so."

His breath catches. Shoulders tense.

"And if you do?" he whispers. "Say I'm yours?"

I circle him slowly. Let my fingers drift across his collarbone. The top of his spine. I don't push. Don't claim. I just trace. Slow, steady contact.

"If I say you're mine," I say, "then you follow."

I don't take ownership lightly. Not now. Not again. If I call him mine, it's not to cage him. It's to carry what that means.

"I will."

"No titles."

He nods.

"No commands."

Another nod.

"No assumptions."

His voice is sandpaper: "None."

I kneel beside him—not submission. Proximity.

And when I kiss his temple, it's not forgiveness. It's permission.

I touch him like communion. No rush. No hunger. Just reverence, as if his skin remembers the altar he forgot he was made for. Slow, sacred, deliberate. His temple, where sweat gathers and clings. His chest, where breath stutters and slows. The scar on his hip he never talks about.

He's warm and real and present. Flesh, not armor.

And with every place I press my fingers, I feel it:

He's unraveling in real time, quietly coming undone under nothing but reverence.

Not because I broke him. Because I'm seeing him, and he's letting me.

And when I rise, he follows only when I crook a finger.

I lead him to the bed—not as a guide, but as a priestess with her chosen penitent

He follows without a word. Not submission. Devotion.

I don't speak. I just look at him until he understands: this only happens if he's willing to be worshipped. Not owned. Not mastered. Just seen.

He strips slowly. I let him.

When his hands move to the waistband of my sweatpants, I still them with mine.

"My pace," I say.

"Yes."

I undress myself, layer by layer. Hoodie. Tank. Cotton panties with a rip in the waistband I haven't sewn. I don't hide. I don't perform. My skin is mine.

And his gaze—when I finally step into it—is nothing but awe.

He reaches for something in the nightstand. A small box. Inside: the collar.

He offers it, palms open.

My heart stutters.

I take it. Not to wear.

To weigh.

"I won't wear this unless we both do."

He looks up.

No confusion. No protest. Just a breath that breaks like something holy.

"Okay," he says.

We don't fasten it.

We place it on the pillow between us—a relic, a vow, a proof of silence willingly kept.

The worship isn't one-sided. It's every moment he waits for my touch. Every breath he holds when I don't offer more. Every time he lets me stop exactly where I want to.

Not because I'm submitting. But because I don't owe him more than this—and he never asks.

But because I want him to see what real power looks like:

A woman who knows what she wants. And a man willing to give it without keeping score.

That's when it happens.

The tears come.

Silent. Hot. One after another. Not because I'm broken.

Because for the first time, I'm whole enough to feel it all.

The ache. The rage. The grief I buried under control. The cost of loving someone and letting them love you back.

He holds me through it. Doesn't try to hush me. Doesn't flinch. Just breathes with me.

Like he finally understands what it means to stay. He doesn't reach for more. Doesn't push or plead. Just presses his face to my thigh like he's praying. And I let him stay there. Not because we finished. Because we didn't need to.

And when we lie there, wrecked and reverent, there's no bargaining in his eyes. No neediness, no demand, no echo of all the ways men once reached for my body like it owed them something.

This isn't that.

This is choosing.

This is worship.

A goddess and her witness. A lover and her altar. A woman remade by choosing to be known.

I think about something I once said. About love without safety not being love at all.

I didn't just say that for him. I said it for me.

And tonight—it feels true. Finally, truly, bone-deep true. It's not about who holds the power.

It's about who's willing to share it.

He stays. And I let him.

We lie there in the hush of it. Not speaking. Just breathing. His face is still against my thigh, but it shifts—up, just slightly, to rest against my stomach. One arm wraps around my waist. The other fists the sheet like he's trying to ground himself in something real.

I let my fingers slip into his hair again, slower this time. Not guiding. Just... there.

"You smell like salt," he says softly, voice muffled.

I smile. "So do you."

He lifts his head, just enough to see me. His eyes are tired, wrecked, reverent.

"I used to dream about your scent. Couldn't remember it. Just remembered needing it. Like it was the only real thing left."

That undoes something in my chest.

I trace the curve of his cheekbone. "You listened better when you were quiet."

His lips curl slightly. "Trying to be a fast learner."

We fall back into silence, but it's warm now. Not electric. Not brittle. Just... peace. Our bodies drawn together by instinct, not heat. His nose nuzzles into the crook of my neck. My legs tangle with his.

I feel his hand on my hip. Light. Not coaxing.

"Naomi."

I hum.

"Can I touch your face?"

My heart skips.

Not because of nerves. Because of *how* he asked. No script. No game. Just the ache of a man holding back until he's sure.

I nod.

"Yes."

He moves like prayer. Like every inch of me is sacred. His hand grazes my waist, then the dip of my spine. His lips press under my jaw, slow and soft, not to claim but to ask. And every time he touches me, he waits for my breath to say go.

I turn to face him fully.

Our eyes meet.

"I want this," I whisper.

And this time, when he kisses me—it's not to take.

It's to worship.

He kisses me slowly. Then softer. Then not at all—just breathing me in like he's afraid I might vanish again.

"Can I ask you something?" he murmurs.

I nod against his shoulder.

"How have you been... taking the edge off?"

He's bashful as hell. I feel the heat of his blush even in the dark.

I grin. "You mean how have I been getting off without you here to boss me around?"

He groans. "Not what I said."

"Not *not* what you meant."

He hides his face in my neck. I press a teasing kiss to his hairline.

Then I lean back just enough to look him in the eye.

I let the silence stretch. Just long enough to make him squirm.

"Bottom drawer. Bedside table."

He moves. Opens it. Finds it.

Holds it like it hums secrets.

"This one?"

I nod. "Go on."

He returns, slow and certain, setting it down on the bed between us like an offering.

Then he kisses down my sternum. My ribs. My belly.

"Tell me if you want to stop," he says.

"I won't."

And when he picks it up—he doesn't rush.

He shifts between my knees, kisses the inside of one thigh, then the other. His breath is warm, steady, reverent. Then the toy hums softly to life in his hand.

He doesn't go straight for the obvious. He teases the backs of my knees, the soft crease of my hip, letting it buzz lightly over my skin until I'm half-laughing, half-melting.

When he finally moves between my legs, it's slow. Focused. He drags the rounded tip over my inner lips, circling, pressing, easing in patterns I don't recognize but my body clearly does. My hips arch instinctively. His hand rests on my thigh—not holding me down, just anchoring me.

"Right there?" he murmurs.

I nod, already breathless. "Yes. Don't stop."

He adjusts the vibration. My thighs shake. I bite my lip. Moan. He watches all of it—like it's a language he's spent his whole life learning just to hear me speak.

My orgasm rolls in slowly. No crash, no scream. Just a trembling release. A heat that blooms and coils through me until I'm undone—quiet, raw, open.

And when I open my eyes, he's still there.

Kneeling between my legs, lips parted, gaze wrecked.

Watching like it was his own miracle.

He's watching like he's memorizing. Not to own. To honor.

He brushes his lips against the inside of my knee. Gentle. Grateful. Then trails them higher, pressing a kiss above the curve of my thigh.

"Can I taste you?" he whispers, voice frayed, reverent.

My breath stutters.

His hands slide slowly up my waist. "Can I touch you?"

I reach for him, my fingers threading into his hair, grounding us both. He leans in, pressing his mouth to my hip like he already knows the answer but needs to hear it anyway.

His voice drops to something deeper, rougher—want and awe tangled together.

"Can I make love to you?"

My pulse spikes. The space between us pulls tight.

My mouth opens. No sound comes.

Because I want to say yes—I just haven't caught my breath yet.

Yes is already in my chest. But my throat won't let it out.

I want to say yes—

But this time, I won't give in until I feel it all the way through.

I owe myself that much.

Chapter 35
The Cost of Legacy
Gideon

I should've known better than to believe I could have this.

Her.

The way Naomi looks at me now...soft, steady, eyes blazing with something dangerously close to trust—feels like standing on the edge of a blade. One wrong move and it could cut. She should've walked away. After every truth I spilled at her feet, every confession pulled from my ribs, I expected retreat. Recoil. Distance.

But she didn't flinch.

She stepped closer, her voice a whisper against my mouth: "Yes."

And in that single word, she offered me everything I never dared to want.

Her lips seek mine again, soft and certain, fingers threading into my hair as if to anchor me here—like she's the one holding *me* together. My pulse thrums.

Not from lust. From something sharper. Deeper. Reverence I don't know how to hold.

I kiss her like a man starving. Like this might be the last moment I'm allowed to touch her before the world claws her from my grasp again.

Naomi breaks the kiss only long enough to whisper against my mouth, "I trust you, Gideon. All of you. Even the parts you tried to bury."

For a moment, I forget how to breathe. My hand tightens around her waist.

"You shouldn't," I rasp.

“But I do.”

Her lips brush mine, soft as silk. She tastes faintly of the wine we abandoned hours ago, of cinnamon and something uniquely her—sharp and sweet and intoxicating. My pulse kicks against my throat.

I don’t deserve this. But I won’t refuse it.

Naomi shifts, straddling my hips as she pushes me back against the bed, her thighs bracketing mine, skin warm against skin. The sheets twist beneath us, cool cotton against overheated flesh. Outside, the city hums faintly through the penthouse windows—horns, sirens, the distant thrum of life moving on. But in here, it’s only us. The whole world pressed into the space between her breath and mine.

“Lie back,” I say gently, “or sit on my face. Your choice.”

Her breath catches.

“You keep offering that like it’s a favor to me,” she mutters.

I grin against her inner thigh. “It is.”

She huffs. “Saint Gideon.”

“Still on the altar, baby. Just waiting.”

She straddles my chest, knees bracketing my ribs. Her fingers grip the headboard. And when she lowers herself onto my mouth, slow and certain, I swear my soul leaves my body.

She tastes like fucking heaven.

I grab her hips and let her ride my tongue. Not fast. Not greedy. I want her to feel every second of it. I want her to know she’s worshiped. Kept. Fucking adored.

Not with urgency. With awe.

□Every sound she makes is a psalm. Every tremble, a sermon.

She gasps. “Gideon—“

“That’s it,” I growl, against her wet cunt. “Come all over my fucking mouth, baby.”

She does. Her whole body shudders. Her thighs clamp around my head. I ride it out with her, groaning into her skin, wrecked and worshipping.

When she collapses onto the bed beside me, I kiss her hip. Her belly. Her breastbone. I settle over her like a prayer draped in skin.

“I could die like this,” I whisper into her neck.

She hums. “Don’t.”

I kiss her slow. Deep. Her nails rake lightly down my back.

"Then let me live inside you."

And she grants me the honor.

I sink into her slowly, almost trembling with how much I need it. She's so wet for me I slide in smooth, but tight enough that my jaw clenches as I bottom out.

"Fuck," I breathe. My forehead presses against hers. "I missed you."

Her fingers tangle in my hair, pulling me closer, her lips brushing mine. "Show me."

Oh, I will.

I start slow. Not because I want to, but because I have to — because if I let go, I'll lose my goddamn mind. She's gripping me so tight I feel her around every inch like a fucking vice, pulsing, dragging me deeper every time I move.

My voice is ragged in her ear. "You feel so good, baby. So fucking good."

Her breath hitches, nails digging into my back, her body already chasing more.

"Harder," she whispers. "Please—harder."

I obey.

I fuck into her deep, strong, every thrust driving her up the mattress, every sound she makes punching heat straight through my spine. My lips drag across her jaw, her throat, tasting the salt of her sweat, the sweetness of her skin. She's everywhere. All I can feel. All I can fucking taste.

"I'm sorry," I groan against her neck, my words breaking as I move inside her. "I'm sorry for everything I put you through. For pushing you away. For making you doubt."

She pulls me even closer, wrapping her legs around my waist like she can't stand any space between us. Her voice breaks against my skin, breathless: "Don't stop."

"I'll never stop again," I promise, teeth scraping along her collarbone.

Her body starts to tense beneath me—tightening, spiraling. She's close.

"Come for me, baby. Show me it's mine. Give it to me."

She shatters beneath me with a choked cry, her cunt clenching around me like she's trying to pull me deeper, keep me there. Her thighs lock around my waist, back arching off the bed.

But I'm nowhere near done.

I don't pull out. I don't stop.

I drive her through it, dragging out her orgasm, forcing her to feel every pulse, every thrust. She's still gasping when I shift her hips up and start again.

"More," she breathes. "Gideon, again—please—"

"Greedy fucking girl," I groan. "You want to come again for me? Huh? That what you need?"

"Yes—yes—please—"

And I give it to her.

I angle my hips, grinding into the spot that makes her breath catch every time, her cries turning into breathless little sobs of pleasure as I pound into her. She's soaking me, wet and slick and perfect.

"Take it," I growl. "Take every fucking inch. You're mine, Naomi. My perfect fucking girl."

Her breath catches. "Oh my god—Sir—fuck—Gideon—I need you to come inside me."

I lose it. "Fuck—baby—I'm right there—"

I'm so close, my release coiled tight in my balls, ready to snap—

And that's when the door crashes open.

The sound rips through the room like a gunshot—sharp, splintering. The world jerks sideways.

My body moves before my brain fully catches up. I slam my hand down, covering Naomi's bare chest instinctively, shielding her as my head snaps toward the door.

Three men. Black tactical gear. Masks. Weapons drawn.

Not street muscle. Trained extraction unit.

"Stay down, Mr. Hawke," one orders, voice flat, precise.

I freeze. My pulse spikes. My mind already racing.

Vito.

Fuck.

Naomi stiffens under me, breath caught in her throat—but she doesn't scream. She doesn't panic. She moves.

One of them lunges for her.

She twists, elbow driving straight into his ribs, hard enough that he stumbles. The man grunts but catches her wrist mid-swing before she can strike again.

"Easy, sweetheart," the second one says, voice low. "Vito said he wants you breathing."

Her teeth bare. "Touch me again and I'll break your fucking hand."

The first man chuckles under his mask. "Vito didn't say what condition you had to be in."

The third man keeps his rifle trained directly on my chest.

Every option flashes through my mind...Three on one. Naomi in their grip. Guns.

No clean exit.

If I fight, they'll take her. If I don't—

My stomach knots. My jaw clenches.

I meet Naomi's eyes—wild, burning—and shake my head once. No.

She snarls, twisting hard against the man holding her. "Gideon, don't you fucking dare—"

I cut her off, voice low. Controlled. "Don't. Let me do this."

Her breathing is sharp. Furious. She's calculating, even as her chest heaves, her wrists strain.

"Survive," I whisper. "Then burn them."

She freezes—just for a second—then nods. A soldier conceding the field. For now.

They're already on me. Ripping me up off her, forcing my arms behind my back. Zip ties cinch tight around my wrists.

"Package secured," one of them radios. "Extraction moving."

Naomi lunges, pure rage sparking behind her eyes. The man restraining her yanks her roughly back.

"You don't want to do this!" she shouts.

The second man leans in close, his voice dark. "We really do."

As they shove me toward the door, I lock eyes with her.

Wild hair. Bare skin. Face flushed from sex and fury. Unbroken. Calculating.

She's not afraid.

"I'll find you," she says, voice low, steady, dangerous.

I swallow. "I know."

They drag me out into the hall. The door swings shut behind me, cutting off the last glimpse of her.

They think they've won. They took me. Now I'll take everything.

The hallway closes in around me. My pulse stays steady, but my hands flex against the restraints.

I test them. Hard zip ties. Tight, but not unbreakable.

The moment I'm far enough from Naomi—out of their immediate line of fire—I shift my weight, ready to strike. Two steps, maybe three, I can drop the one on my right first, get to the second before—

A voice cuts through the tension like a blade. Smooth. Lazy.

"Ah, ah... I wouldn't, if I were you."

Vito's voice.

I freeze.

He steps from the shadows, flanked by more of his men. Calm. Smiling. His eyes gleaming with the kind of sadistic patience only a man who believes he's already won can wear.

"You've got no leverage here, Gideon," he says softly. "Not tonight. If I decide to pull the trigger... her life ends before your heart even finishes its next beat."

I clench my jaw, muscles tight, forcing myself to stillness.

Not yet.

Not while Naomi's life hangs in the balance.

Vito smiles wider, stepping closer like a man welcoming home a prodigal son.

"Welcome home, Gideon."

He pauses—just long enough to let the blade sink deeper—before delivering the final twist.

"It's time to prepare for your wedding... to Claudia."

Oh, fuck.

Chapter 36

From Haunted To Hunter

Naomi

The door slams behind them.

For one breath, my body goes still. My chest is tight, skin flushed from everything Gideon just gave me, everything we finally let happen. The sheets are probably still warm, a reminder of where his body pressed into mine.

They took him.

I stare at the door like I can will him back through it. My jaw clenches, fists curling into the sheets.

For half a second, panic claws its way up my throat, sharp and hot. But I shove it back down where it belongs.

Of course my first instinct is to panic... but the second is rage.

You don't get to fall apart. Not yet. Not here.

I force my breath out, slow and sharp, anchoring myself. My hands shake as I yank on a pair of leggings and one of Gideon's t-shirts that still smells like him — soap, cologne, heat — like everything they just stole. His smell hits me like a slap.

A reminder of what's at stake.

Good. I want him on my skin while I burn their world down.

I grab my phone off the dresser, my thumb already flying across the screen. Zoe answers halfway through the second ring.

"Naomi? What the hell it's 3am!"

"They took him." My voice sounds distant. "Vito's men. They got into the penthouse."

There's silence on the line, but I hear her breathing. Processing.

"Are you hurt?"

"No, but we don't have time. I don't know who in his network is compromised."

Her voice sharpens. "What do you need?"

"Meet me at our spot. And bring that thing I left with Sir Nickolas."

There's a pause. Then her tone shifts — steady, hard, exactly what I need right now. "Got it. I'll see you when you land."

I end the call and grab my laptop bag from the corner of the bedroom, tossing it over my shoulder as I slip out the back door. The salty breeze of the ocean hits my face, sharp and cold under the moonlight, and for a moment I let the sting ground me.

No damsel. No victim.

The old SUV waits where I left it, tucked under the covered drive. I climb in, hands already steady as I fire the engine. The headlights slice through the narrow winding road that leads off the coastal property.

This is why I bought the house out here. This is why I had the exit plan. Just in case the nightmare ever reached this far. The private airstrip comes into view as I round the final turn, security lights blinking against the dark.

The plane's already waiting. My contingency fund made sure of that long before any of this started. I don't hesitate when I park.

Just step out and strut straight toward war.

The plane ride back to New York feels like a bad dream.

I don't sleep. Can't. The steady hum of the engines grates against my nerves, but I keep my breathing even, my eyes locked on my laptop screen, scanning systems Gideon probably never meant me to have access to.

The moment the wheels hit the tarmac, I'm already dialing Toni.

She answers mid-keystroke, breathless. "Naomi?"

"I need backend access. All of it. You still at Leviathan?"

"I'm in Ops. What's going on? Are you—"

"They took him."

Her breath catches. "Shit."

"Don't freak out." My voice is sharper than I intend. "I don't have time to explain. But I need you. Quiet access. No one can know."

Toni hesitates for half a second. She's scared. Good. She should be. But she's loyal. She exhales. "Okay. I'm in."

I smile grimly. "That's my girl."

The safehouse Zoe setup downtown is quiet when I arrive. The air is heavy, thick with the scent of strong coffee and old takeout. Zoe's already pacing by the window, one hand on her hip, the other flipping the USB drive I left her months ago between her fingers.

"You're late," she says the second I step inside, her tone sharp, but her eyes sweep over me—assessing, cataloguing. Making sure I'm whole.

"I'm here now," I reply, voice tight.

She tosses the USB onto the table with a clatter and grabs her tablet. "I've been warming up your war toys. Everything's prepped."

I don't waste breath thanking her. We both know what's at stake.

Instead, I drop my bag on the table and flip open my laptop. The old metal table rattles under the weight. Zoe already has her tablet linked, the drive plugged into her secure hub. The glow of the screens illuminates her sharp grin.

"So," she says, stretching her neck, "he dicked you down so good you're about to commit war crimes."

I snort despite myself, dragging a hand through my hair. "It's not about that."

"Oh, honey, it's always about that." She spins the tablet toward me, bringing up the interface we built together months ago. "You want to fire up Scylla?"

The name pulses on the screen like a heartbeat.

Scylla—my monster, my failsafe. The thing I built when I couldn't trust anyone. The thing I built for exactly this moment. The monster I fed with every worst-case scenario I hoped I'd never have to face. The system I built in secret, knowing one day, I might need to go to war.

"Boot her," I say. My voice stays even, but my chest tightens as the servers hum alive.

Lines of code race across the monitors as Scylla's engines spool up.

Zoe's eyes gleam. "She's still hungry."

"Good," I whisper. "So am I."

She glances sideways. "Toni's feeding in backend credentials as we speak. Board communications, private ops logs, financial shells—everything."

I nod. "Perfect. We run this silently. I want full access before we step foot in Leviathan."

Zoe leans back, her voice quieter now. "You know you don't have to do this alone, right?"

I meet her eyes. "I know. But I'm still doing it."

She exhales a laugh. "Yeah, that's my Syntax Siren."

We leave the safehouse behind and head straight for Leviathan. Every block we drive toward the tower feels like we're crossing another line that can't be uncrossed.

We move fast, slipping through the maintenance corridors we mapped months ago — when we were playing at hypotheticals. Worst case scenarios. Except now, it's real.

Zoe glances over as we move. "You want to tell me why we're not calling Gideon's team?"

"Because someone flipped," I say, my voice low. "And until I know who, I'm treating everyone as dirty."

Her mouth pulls into a sharp grin. "Paranoid Naomi. My favorite version."

"We don't have room for mistakes."

We reach the cold server room, the hum of equipment vibrating under my boots. I connect my rig into the isolated line Gideon showed me once — late one night, after too much wine, when I teased him into revealing where his real secrets lived.

The screens blink to life, washing us both in icy blue.

Zoe watches me work, her fingers flicking across her tablet to disable surveillance feeds. "You want me to pull Toni?"

"She stays put," I say. "She's giving us access to the Board's restricted partitions."

"God, you're terrifying when you go full psycho hacker."

"I'm not even warmed up."

Her smile grows sharp, wicked. "Remind me not to piss you off."

"Noted."

The deeper we dig, the dirtier it gets. Gideon built Leviathan like a fortress, but even fortresses have cracks. And I know where every one of his keys are hidden.

Hours blur as my fingers fly across the keyboard. Logs, shell companies, offshore accounts—Vito has his hands deeper than I expected.

Then I see her.

Vivienne fucking Gray.

Payments. Wire transfers. Communications logs.

I exhale slowly. "Found her."

Zoe leans in, scanning fast. "That bitch."

"She sold him out."

"She sold *you* out."

"She sold out everything."

I copy everything. Bank records. Transcripts. Contracts. Enough to dismantle Vivienne's life and everyone tied to her.

Zoe shakes her head. "You know we're not just going to fire her, right?"

"Oh, we're not firing anyone," I whisper. "We're going to bury her."

She whistles softly under her breath. "Syntax Siren strikes again."

Toni chimes into the comm line, voice low. "I just patched into the family asset server. Do you want everything?"

"Yes."

"Naomi—what you're doing..." She hesitates. "This crosses lines."

"We're past lines."

The data floods my screen. Private airfields. Transport logs. Secure real estate holdings hidden under layered shells.

And then—I see it.

Gideon.

They moved him to an off-book estate. Rural. Isolated. Family property tucked under multiple dummy corporations.

"They've locked him in."

"They're planning something bigger," Zoe says. "This isn't just leverage."

"They're forcing him back under Vito." My voice breaks for half a second, but I lock it down. "He's trying to make Gideon their puppet again."

My chest tightens, breath catching sharp for half a second. "They want him to marry that bitch Claudia."

Zoe's eyes sharpen. "That's not going to happen."

"No," I whisper. "It's not."

I close the laptop with finality, my pulse steady now. The clarity I've been waiting for finally settling into my bones.

"There's a moment where everything stills. The rage. The code. The fear. Just breath. Just choice.

"I'm going.""

Zoe grabs my arm, eyes flashing. "You're not going in alone."

"Yes, I am."

"Bullshit."

I squeezed her hand once. Firm. Final. "If I don't come back, burn it all."

Her voice goes flat. "Burn it."

"Burn everything."

Chapter 37

Queen On The Offensive

Naomi

The phone buzzes once. I already know who it is before I answer.

Roman.

I take a steady breath and swipe to accept, holding the burner tight to my ear as I drive toward the estate.

"Naomi," his voice is tight, low, already defeated. "Don't do this."

"I'm already doing it."

"You don't understand what Vito will do. If you push him—"

"He already took Gideon. He already crossed that line."

There's a beat of silence. Roman exhales. "He'll kill our cousin if you back him into a corner. You know that."

"I know exactly what he'll do." My voice sharpens. "That's why I'm not giving him the chance."

"Naomi—" he starts again, but I cut him off.

"I'm not asking for help, Roman. I'm telling you where this ends."

He sighs. "Then we can't protect you from what comes next."

"I never needed your protection." I hang up.

The road winds forward as the gates rise in the distance. They expect me to show up afraid.

Let them.

The guards at the outer gate barely glance at me as I pull through the checkpoint. My SUV glides forward like I belong here — like I'm one of them.

I'm not.

The estate spreads out ahead, a silent sprawl of wealth and power. The road curves up through manicured hedges and white stone walls, designed to impress anyone arriving for the first time. They expect awe. Deference. Submission.

I roll my shoulders, forcing the tension out of my muscles as the driveway opens up to the mansion. Massive columns rise into the overcast sky, a little too much like a courthouse. Or a tomb.

The SUV eases to a stop.

Two men flank my door before the engine even settles.

One taps the window. I lower it slowly, letting cold air rush into the cabin.

"Name," he demands, like I'm here for a job interview.

I tilt my head slightly. "Naomi Walker."

His eyes flick over me. He wasn't expecting me to sound like this. Calm. In control.

"You're alone?"

"Yes." I give him a smile — just enough teeth to remind him I'm not prey. "You should be grateful for that."

He doesn't appreciate the joke. He nods once to the other man, who opens my door.

I step out into the chill, smooth and unhurried. My boots click sharply against the stone drive. The wind carries the faint scent of salt from somewhere far off the coast. Expensive silence.

The first guard motions. "Come with us."

The front doors open as we approach. Polished mahogany, gold accents, all the predictable excess that comes with old blood money. The lobby smells faintly of cigar smoke and fresh varnish. The floor under my boots is marble, cool and gleaming, with some old-world crest I don't bother looking at.

Vito's taste is exactly what I expected: heavy-handed and desperate to remind you who's in charge.

Too bad it's not him.

I hear the click of polished shoes before I see him. Vito stands at the top of the grand staircase, hands folded like a man receiving a guest instead of orchestrating a kidnapping. His smile is smooth, practiced, but his eyes glint sharp as a blade.

His voice drips down the staircase like oil. "Well. You made good time."

I walk in with my chin up, every step deliberate, like I own the ground under my boots. The guards hover, expecting nerves or fear.

They won't get it.

I meet his gaze with a smirk. "Don't bother playing gracious host. You're not qualified. And I'm not impressed."

Vito descends slowly, savoring the moment. "You impress me, Naomi. I thought you'd send one of Gideon's people. Or perhaps simply run. You're not exactly built for this."

He wants me small. Nervous. Out of place.

I give him none of it.

"You keep making the same mistake."

"Oh?" He cocks his head, amused. "And what's that?"

"You think any of this makes you untouchable."

A flicker of curiosity crosses his face. Brief. Then gone.

He gestures lazily, snapping his fingers. "Bring him."

My stomach tightens, but I keep my breath even.

Gideon appears a moment later between two men. His wrists are zip-tied, his head low, but his feet move under him. His lip is split, and there's a bruise spreading along his jawline. His eye is swelling, but when he lifts his head, his gaze finds mine instantly.

My stomach drops sharp and cold. For half a second, my breath catches. Fear claws up fast — hot, wild — but I shove it down before it can take root. Not now. Not here.

The guards beside him jolt him forward roughly, one of them shoving an elbow into his ribs for good measure. Gideon grunts, stumbling slightly, but never breaks eye contact with me.

The flash of violence punches my gut, but I lock it down again, tighter this time. They want me shaken.

They won't get it.

There's pain in his eyes, but something else too. Something steady. Something proud.

I keep my hands at my sides.

I don't run to him. That would be what Vito expects.

Instead, I force my voice to be calm. "You don't need to parade him like a trophy. This isn't about him anymore."

"Isn't it?" Vito smiles again, taking slow, measured steps closer. "He's the reason you're here, is he not?"

I don't give him the satisfaction of answering. Instead, I open my bag and pull out the slim tablet Zoe and I prepared.

The guards stiffen, but I lift my hands slightly. "Relax. No weapons." I tap the screen. "Just information."

Vito watches, eyes narrowing as the nearest monitor flickers to life.

The financial networks light up first: offshore accounts, hidden subsidiaries, names he thought were buried. Years of quiet laundering, blood money shelled out into foundations, political contributions, real estate trusts scattered across multiple continents.

The numbers scroll across the screen like a confession.

"Cayman. Zurich. Singapore, Trinidad and Tobago." I say softly. "You hid them well. You should have hidden them better."

He doesn't speak, but I see it — the brief tightening of his jaw.

I swipe again, feeding the next file into the stream.

Surveillance footage now. Vivienne Gray, sitting across from one of his men, handing over Leviathan's internal data like it's a goddamn gift basket.

"Your mole's been busy." My voice stays even. "Feeding you corporate strategy, board decisions, asset shifts. Months of betrayal."

From the corner of my eye, I catch Vivienne stiffen near the back of the room. Her face drains of color. She wasn't expecting to be exposed like this.

Good.

Another swipe. Recordings of private calls. Bribes paid to regulators, politicians, foreign officials. Wire transfers with handwritten signatures. Blackmail files. The digital noose tightening with every screen.

"You don't survive this kind of exposure," I say softly. "Not even you."

Vito tries to smile, but it falters at the edges.

"You're bluffing."

I tilt my head. "I'm recording this conversation right now. The evidence is already pre-loaded into my offshore server cluster. Any attempt to detain me triggers a full public release to the SEC, DOJ, Interpol, and a very curious Wall Street Journal editor who would love nothing more than to make your name his career."

Vito's voice tightens. "You won't pull that trigger."

"Vito..." I step forward, lowering my voice until it slices through the air like a wire. "You don't understand. I already have the gun to your head. All you have to do is give me a reason to pull it."

The silence thickens.

The men behind him glance at each other. Doubt, sharp and spreading.

For the first time, I see it — the crack. The realization crawling under his skin that he's not in control anymore.

I keep my voice even. "You release him. Right now. Or your entire family burns. You won't survive the first headline. The second will bury you."

His eye twitches. His lips press into a thin line. The smile is gone.

He exhales slowly, as if trying to salvage dignity from the wreckage. "Cut him loose."

The guards hesitate. Vito's voice sharpens. "Now."

They move fast after that.

The zip ties fall away. Gideon staggers slightly but stays upright. The moment his arms are free, I move — stepping beside him, steadying his weight against my shoulder. His breath is warm against my ear, rough and quiet — but alive. Still mine.

"You shouldn't have come."

I whisper back, my voice a blade. "You're mine... and I don't like other people touching my things."

We move toward the doors together, my arm tight around his waist, his steps growing stronger with each one.

At the threshold, I pause, glance back once. Vito stands frozen. His empire bleeding out at his feet.

"You thought I was prey and you were wrong." I let my voice drop with a low chuckle. "I bet you wish you'd left me alone."

I hold his stare for a breath longer, let him choke on his silence. Then I turn, guiding Gideon out with me, not looking back. My kingdom now.

BREAK ME FIRST

Chapter 38

The Price of Peace

Gideon

Naomi's breath stirs against my skin, soft and warm, her hand still resting over my chest like she's anchoring me there. The weight of her fingers moves slightly with every exhale, light but grounding, as if she knows the moment she lets go I might vanish.

Her skin smells like lavender and sweat. The faintest trace of her perfume lingers under it, clinging to the sheets wrapped around her bare legs. The morning light cuts weak lines through the heavy curtains, barely touching her face.

I let my eyes trace every inch of her. The way her hair spills across the pillow, her lips slightly parted, her brows relaxed. Her body loose in sleep for the first time in days. She fought for me. She walked into fire for me. She built the storm that cracked the walls I once thought were impenetrable.

My ribs ache when I shift under her hand. The dull heat radiates out from each bruise, a sharp pulse that makes my jaw flex. The split in my lip reopens slightly as I move to sit up, but the sting is small. Manageable.

The war isn't over yet. Not until I finish it.

I press my lips to the back of her knuckles, careful not to wake her. She doesn't stir. I slide out from beneath her slowly, steadying my feet on the cold floor. My bare toes curl briefly against the polished wood. The temperature change is sharp, sobering.

As I stand, I let my gaze fall over her one last time. The soft, rhythmic rise of her breathing. The calm. The trust.

She saved me.

Now I end this.

I pull my shirt over my shoulders, biting down against the pull of tight muscles. The bruises across my ribs protest with every breath, but pain sharpens my focus. My fingers fasten the last button as I cross to the door. The small creak of the handle sounds loud in the stillness, but Naomi sleeps on, undisturbed.

The door closes with a gentle click behind me. The world on this side of it feels colder. Not empty—but functional.

The adjoining suite is already alive. The table glows faintly under the light of the screens, the hum of encrypted servers running like a second pulse beneath my own. Burners sit neatly lined up. A row of silent soldiers.

I tap the first connection. The secure line hisses briefly as it locks in. Ethan's voice is waiting, sharp, awake, steady.

"You're late."

"I'm right on time."

The video feed stabilizes. His face glows pale against the monitors behind him. His fingers are already moving, fast and exact, pulling up files, cross-checking data as if this war hasn't kept him up for days.

"We're in position across the board," he says. "The offshore accounts are locked. Zurich's frozen. Cayman and Singapore are down. The Trinidad shells collapsed overnight."

"The legal arms?"

"Rerouted and tangled. Anyone trying to untangle the asset trails now will bury themselves before they touch anything real."

"Good." I pause. "Corporate holdings?"

"They've already started to bleed. Leviathan's secondary structures are scrambling." His fingers move across another screen, green confirmation ticks appearing. "They'll fight each other trying to stabilize what's already gone."

"They'll cannibalize their own."

"They always do." His eyes flick back to me. "The Board will fracture within the day."

I exhale, letting the rhythm of the operation steady me. It's clinical. Predictable. Exactly how I designed it.

My thumb slides to the next file. Names populate the screen. My family's enforcement tree. Enforcers, fixers, private security heads. The men who carried Vito's reach like blades for years.

"The lieutenants," Ethan says.

"Yes. Quiet removals. No bodies. No noise."

"Selective or full?"

I scan the list again, my chest tight but cold. I see their faces—men I've known since childhood. Men who smiled at dinners while orchestrating extortion behind closed doors. Men who thought themselves untouchable.

I tap the screen once. "Flip who you can. Silence the rest."

Ethan nods. "Already started."

His hands glide across the keys, and I watch the extraction alerts populate in real time. I can almost see the dominoes falling—hotel suites breached, private flights grounded, men lifted from their beds and black bagged before sunrise.

Some flip. Some vanish.

I don't blink.

One by one, the branches collapse until only one name remains on the center screen. Vito.

Ethan's fingers pause above his keys, hovering. "He's isolated. Do you want me to dispatch a team?"

"No."

He watches me quietly. He doesn't ask why.

"Personal."

"Location's secure," Ethan says. "My people already swept the perimeter. You're clear to approach."

Before I close the laptop, I open the private line to Roman and Remi. Their faces fill the screen, eyes sharp, but not surprised.

"It's time," I say.

Roman exhales. "You're really doing it."

Remi speaks first. "It should have been done a long time ago."

"I'm not taking the family," I say. "Dante can have what's left. If you want to stand with him, stand with him. But this? This ends with Vito."

Roman nods once. "Do it."

I close the laptop softly, the weight in my chest sinking lower, heavier now. This isn't rage. Not anymore. This is purpose. Control. The final severing.

I slide my jacket over my shoulders and feel the press of the weapon tucked inside. Compact. Balanced. The silencer attached, cold against my ribs.

The elevator ride down is silent. The tires slice through wet asphalt as I pull away, the city still half-asleep under the dull early light. Raindrops collect in scattered bursts across the windshield, the wipers sweeping them away like thin layers of fog.

The estate rises out of the forest edge like a stone relic—remote, forgotten. The iron gates swing open as I approach, unlocked, waiting. My tires crunch through loose gravel, each slow rotation humming beneath me as I coast forward.

The windows glow faint behind thick curtains. No sentries. No guards. No escape routes left.

The house breathes warm air against me as I step inside. The scent of leather, cedar smoke, and old scotch folds into my lungs like heavy fabric. The fire crackles softly across the grand room, long shadows dancing against rich wood paneling.

Vito sits alone, waiting by the fire, one leg crossed, fingertips steepled under his chin. His mouth curves faintly as I approach, but there's no victory behind it.

"You've finally learned who you are, Gideone." His voice slides through the room like silk wrapping around a knife.

My steps echo as I close the distance. My hand settles inside my jacket, fingers curling around cold steel.

"No, Uncle." I answer softly. "I finally learned who I choose to be."

His eyes flicker as he leans forward, still grasping for leverage. "You were supposed to be my legacy."

"You were supposed to protect us. My mother. Me."

His voice sharpens. "You think she saved you? Your mother made you weak!"

I step closer, lowering my voice into a blade. "No. She taught me how to code. Mother taught me that there are other ways... a different type of family, and it made me crave freedom."

The guards drag my father in, his hands bound, his face already pale beneath sweat-soaked skin. His breathing staggers when he sees me, eyes wide, desperation pouring out of him like blood from an open wound.

"Gideon, figlio mio—please..." he whimpers, voice cracking, falling to his knees as they shove him forward.

Vito watches, lips curling into something bitter. "You won't do it," he sneers. "He's still your blood."

I stare at my father, the man who watched my life burn from the safety of his silence, the man who let my mother drown under this family's weight. My voice stays even. "He made his choice long before I made mine."

My blade slides free with a soft whisper of steel. The light catches its edge as I cross the space between us. My father trembles, babbling prayers, tears streaking his face as he begs for mercy neither of us deserves.

The blade drives in clean beneath his ribs, angled sharp. His body jerks against me, breath hitching as I lean in, watching the panic bloom in his eyes.

"Look at me," I whisper.

His gaze locks onto mine, wild, panicked—and then the light drains from them, slow and irreversible, until there's nothing left but glassy emptiness.

I let his body slump to the floor. The blood pools quickly, spreading like dark silk across the polished marble.

Vito's face drains of color, his breath quickens, and for the first time, I see it—real fear. The kind of fear even monsters can't hide from.

I walk toward him, my voice colder than the rain outside. "The Calabrese family dies with you and this coward."

The blade flashes again, this time slicing across Vito's throat with one brutal, clean pull. His hands scramble for his neck, eyes wide, mouth opening in silent screams as blood spills over his expensive suit.

I stand there, watching the life drain from him, watching him drown in his own blood, until his body goes still and the only sound left is the crackle of the fire.

The flames spit softly behind me, casting flickering shadows across the polished blood. I turn away, stepping into the rain as cold wind slaps across my face. My boots cut clean prints into the gravel as I walk toward the gates.

The city glows ahead, lights humming under a bruised sky.

The phone buzzes in my pocket, vibrating against my ribs.

The blood's still drying on my hands when it hits. Her words. My anchor.

Naomi's message is simple.

Come home.

My lips twitch. Not a smile. Not quite.

I'm free.

I belong to her.

And this time? It's not surrender. It's not desperation. It's choice.

Chapter 39

Crown and Consequence

Naomi

The blinds glide open on their silent track as the sun breaches the Manhattan skyline, soft amber light slipping across marble floors and spilling onto the edge of the low platform bed. The sheets beneath me remain smooth, crisp Egyptian cotton. Cool where my skin doesn't press into Gideon's warmth.

I blink into the morning slowly, exhaustion clinging to my limbs like silk. The air carries the faint clean scent of his laundry detergent mixed with him—subtle spice and the sharp undertone of cedar soap. Everything about this penthouse feels curated, deliberate. No clutter. No softness except what he allows. Except me.

His fingers trail along the curve of my waist, slow and steady, like he's watched the light find me for some time. His voice comes low, thick from disuse and sleep.

"You never looked more dangerous."

My lips pull into the faintest smile, but I keep my eyes closed for another breath, savoring his palm flattening against my stomach, his thumb sweeping back and forth over my skin. The city hums outside the glass walls, traffic distant but constant, alive beneath us.

"I thought I was supposed to soothe you back to health," I murmur.

"You are. You just haven't figured out which part of me needs soothing yet." His voice rolls like rough silk, the edge always there, even softened by morning.

I open my eyes, turning to catch his face in full light. The bruises faded into pale shadows near his jaw and ribs. The cut on his lip nearly disappeared, but I remember where it split because I kissed it through every stage of healing.

His gaze drags over me like a touch. Possessive, reverent, never frantic. This man almost died. I almost lost him. And now he looks at me like I'm the only thing in this penthouse worth worshiping.

"You need to eat," I say, brushing a hand through his hair, fingers catching in the soft waves.

"You're avoiding."

"I'm prioritizing," I correct. "You need strength before I throw you into my mess."

A ghost of a smile tugs at the corner of his mouth, but he doesn't fight me. "Our mess."

The intercom buzzes before I answer, a sharp chime slicing through the lazy intimacy. Gideon doesn't move to stop me as I pull free of the sheets and slide out of bed, the silk of my robe cool against my skin as I pad barefoot across the floor.

The private elevator doors open as I reach them. Zoe steps out first, oversized sunglasses still on despite being indoors. She carries two drink trays and enough attitude to fill the entire penthouse.

"I brought fuel for the hostile takeover," she says. "And croissants, because world domination requires carbs."

Toni trails behind her, tablet in hand like a weapon, already skimming through documents. Jade steps in next, flawless as always, in bone-white slacks and an emerald blouse that costs someone's salary. Jor follows last, phone to her ear, issuing quiet instructions to someone unfortunate on the other end.

I close the door behind them as they sweep into the living room like my personal war council. Zoe tosses me a latte before I even ask.

"Drink. You're about to eviscerate billionaires."

Jade drops her bag on the marble counter and pulls up the projection file with a flick of her wrist. "The board's split straight down the middle. The opportunists smell blood. The cowards smell risk."

"They don't know which way to jump yet," Jor adds, sliding her phone into her pocket as she eyes me. "Which is why you're walking in to make the choice for them."

Toni lifts her head long enough to flash me her dry, unbothered expression. "All files scrubbed, forensics tight, digital audit sealed. Vivienne's backdoor stays closed."

Zoe grins. "And I pulled every trace of her side deals. You'll walk in with receipts."

The weight of what's ahead settles in my chest—not fear, but awareness. That hum beneath your skin before a fight. Not physical. Worse. Corporate. Controlled. Power living in silences, in gazes held too long, in who blinks first.

"This isn't just another hack," I say softly, voicing the piece that's sat under my rib cage since I decided to do this.

"No," Zoe agrees, coming up beside me. "It's better."

Her hand wraps briefly around mine, grounding me. "You're not stealing anything. You're claiming what you already built."

Gideon's presence fills the space behind me before I even turn. His hand settles gently at the small of my back, warm, steady, a silent anchor. He doesn't need to speak, but I hear it anyway: he trusts me to handle this. To finish it.

I glance up at him. "You good to sit this one out?"

"I'm exactly where I'm supposed to be," he says, voice quiet but absolute.

The girls move like a machine, pulling files, updating slides, reviewing worst-case scenarios. Jade briefs me on legal pathways. Jor reviews the talking points she prepared for external shareholders and PR fallout. Toni pulls real-time updates from internal servers. Zoe checks every file three times before sealing the packages we'll present.

The hours melt as we sharpen every angle until no fracture stays exposed. No weakness.

By the time we finish, nothing remains to fear.

Only execution.

The executive floor of Leviathan's tower greets me with chilled air and the sharp click of my heels on polished marble. The boardroom doors gleam ahead, two guards flanking them, barely glancing at me as they open. I step into the room with my head high, pulse steady.

The weight inside shifts immediately. Half the board members stiffen; the others watch with thinly veiled calculation. None speak first. That's telling.

Gideon remains by the door, silent, unbothered, letting his presence work without interfering.

I approach the head of the table. My files land with a soft, deliberate thud as I slide them forward.

"Let's begin."

The presentation unfolds with surgical precision. Financial records. Vivienne's offshore dealings. Digital evidence. Communications with Vito's family. Layer by layer, I peel back every lie she thought would stay hidden. The room grows colder as I speak, the board silent beneath the weight of truth they can't refute.

Vivienne sits at the far end, face pale but composed—barely. She opens her mouth once, but my gaze cuts her off before she forms a word.

"You didn't just compromise this company," I say, voice even but edged. "You opened us to predators who would've gutted Leviathan and buried everyone inside it for personal gain."

I pivot to face the rest of the board. "And I stopped it."

The words hang for a beat. Jade pushes the vote documents forward. Board members shift, eyes darting, but the path stays clear. The wolves know who holds the leash.

One by one, they sign.

Vivienne's resignation finalizes within minutes. Security escorts her from the room without a word.

When the final signature lands, I exhale. Not relief—control.

The chair at the head of the table sits empty for only a moment before I pull it out and take my seat.

The war ends.

Hours later, after the weight of boardroom stares and signed documents fades into the background, I return to the penthouse, and the girls burst in before I even set my bag down.

"You were magnificent." Zoe practically shouts it.

Jade toasts with champagne already in hand. "To Naomi Walker, Queen of Leviathan."

"Don't worry," Jor adds with a grin. "I scheduled your first press statement. Minimal bloodshed."

"And I prepped next quarter's earnings audit," Toni says, lifting her tablet. "You're welcome."

Laughter rolls easily between us. The adrenaline finally drains from my veins. Victory tastes like dry champagne and the warm presence of women who carried me through the fire.

I find Gideon standing by the glass wall, the city glittering behind him like a thousand promises.

I step into him, wrapping my arms around his waist as his hands cover mine. He presses a kiss to my hair, murmuring against my skin.

"You burned their kingdom."

I lift my gaze to meet his, my voice soft. "We built our own."

His lips find mine, slow at first, then deeper, hotter, until heat coils tight between us again. This isn't survival. This isn't power. This isn't control.

It's us.

Ours.

Behind us, laughter bubbles up from the living room, pulling me back with a gentle tug. The girls lounge across the wide sectional, shoes off, drinks in hand, their energy easy now—looser than it's been in months. They pretend not to watch us, but I feel the weight of their eyes as I slip from Gideon's embrace.

Jade catches my gaze first, her mouth curving into something sharp and amused. Zoe follows with a slow grin, eyes flicking between us like she's about to start trouble—and she absolutely is.

"Look at him," Zoe says, drawing out the words as she props her elbow on the back of the couch. "He actually exists. In the flesh."

Jade hums her agreement. "And not hard on the eyes either. You might actually be worth the trouble, Gideon. We'll see."

He steps into the room behind me, unbothered by the weight of their attention. Calm. Watchful. Dangerous when he needs to be—but not now. Now, he just looks at me like there's no one else in the room.

"I've been told I clean up well," he offers, voice smooth but edged with humor.

"Oh, we can see that," Jor says, lifting her glass with a smirk. "But the question is: do you cook?"

Toni doesn't even glance up from her tablet. "He better."

I turn just enough to catch the faint smile pulling at his lips, his hands sliding casually into his pockets. That quiet confidence never wavers.

"I do."

Zoe leans forward, grinning. "Perfect. You own the kitchen — go prove it."

Without another word, he moves toward the open-concept kitchen, rolling his sleeves with practiced ease as he starts pulling ingredients like he's done this a thousand times before. Like he's always belonged here.

The girls settle at the massive marble island, their teasing shifting into something warmer now—still protective, but softer around the edges.

"You know," Jade says, lowering her voice like she's letting me in on a secret, "this is the first time we've actually seen you relaxed."

I slide onto the stool next to her, my gaze drifting to Gideon as he starts whisking eggs like it's second nature. "I guess he makes that easier."

Jor watches him for a moment, eyes narrowing playfully. "Well, as long as he keeps making you this happy—and keeps making us food—I suppose he can stay."

Zoe grins wide. "Temporary probation granted."

From the kitchen, Gideon glances back with a raised brow, catching every word.

"I'll take that under review," he says, deadpan, and even Toni cracks a small smile.

The scent wraps around me — warm garlic, sharp herbs, and beneath it, him. A man who could orchestrate bloodshed with the same quiet precision he now uses to whisk eggs. The contradiction should terrify me. It doesn't.

And they all see it. That's what makes them settle. They know what kind of man he is—and they know I chose him anyway.

When the plates finally hit the island, the girls dig in immediately, laughter circling us like a warm current. And for the first time in a very long time, I let myself fully breathe.

This, right here, feels like peace.

Earned. Scarred. Ours.

Not chains. Not sacrifice.

Just peace.

Chapter 40

The Weight I Carry

Gideon

The city breathes beneath me like it always has.

Manhattan pulses outside the glass, the skyscrapers glittering like they've always belonged to me. The endless hum of traffic filters up faintly from streets far below, steady, constant—just like the empire I built was supposed to be. Unshakable. Clean. Controlled.

Exactly how they trained me to see it.

Behind me, the low mechanical hum of servers fills the penthouse. A faint glow bleeds across the marble floors from the rows of monitors still processing the final kills. Wire transfers executed. Shell companies terminated. Black accounts closed. What was once Vito's empire inside the famiglia—dismantled piece by surgical piece.

The last keystroke clicks beneath my fingers. Done.

And yet—my chest stays tight. My jaw clenches. The weight doesn't lift.

I stare at my reflection in the towering glass wall. I barely recognize the man watching me back.

The heir.

Not Vito. Not the man they feared in boardrooms. The one my father molded. Cold. Methodical. A master of the machine who knew how to move lives around like numbers on a balance sheet.

The man my mother prayed I wouldn't become.

I swallow hard, pulse heavy against my throat. The nausea curls low in my stomach, sharp as a blade.

I don't hear her footsteps at first. I just feel her.

The shift in the air behind me. The warmth she carries with her. The faint trace of her perfume—something sweet, barely there, but sharp enough to cut through everything else.

Naomi.

Soft steps cross the marble floor. She's barefoot. Wearing my shirt again—long enough to skim her thighs. She moves through my space like she owns it, like she's always belonged here. Because she does.

The quiet between us stretches.

She says nothing. Just watches.

I catch her reflection in the glass. The way her head tilts slightly, eyes narrowed just enough—not judging, not fearful—just steady. Waiting.

The pressure behind my ribs twists tighter.

"Come sit," I manage, my voice hoarse.

She crosses the space slowly, unhurried, folding herself onto the edge of the sofa with that same quiet grace that has always undone me. Legs tucked beneath her. Calm. Watching me with that focus that strips me bare.

I don't move at first. My hand scrapes through my hair. My skin itches like I'm being peeled apart. The words jam behind my teeth.

Naomi waits.

Her silence isn't cold. It's patient. She knows.

"This isn't your usual boardroom debrief," she says finally, voice soft, a dry curl at the edge of her tone.

Somehow, that tiny flicker of humor makes my throat squeeze tighter. I let out a dry breath that could almost pass for a laugh—if it didn't sound so fucking broken.

"No," I rasp. "Not even close."

The server lights blink steadily in my peripheral vision like they're mocking me. The empire within the wires—stripped. Killed. And still not enough.

The words scrape out like splinters.

"My father raised me for this."

Her gaze stays level. She doesn't blink.

"I was never supposed to leave the famiglia." My voice tightens. "They groomed me for quiet power. Not like Vito, not the street blood. I was built for offshore networks. The silent systems no one could trace."

I glance toward her, but her expression remains open. Present.

"I made it all invisible. I made them untouchable."

The burn rises sharp in my throat, and for a second I swear I can't breathe.

"After Vito killed my mother..." My voice fractures there.

Naomi's eyes flash, but she says nothing. She lets me bleed it out.

"I told myself I stayed to dismantle their grip," I push forward, hands flexing into fists at my sides. "But the deeper I went, the harder it was to pull back. The money moved faster. The walls got higher. I convinced myself I was protecting us. That I was keeping my distance from Vito's rot."

My breath hitches, my chest aching.

"I justified every compromise. Every deal. Every bribe passed hand to hand, every politician bought. Every favor traded in back rooms while my name stayed clean."

I swallow hard, my jaw locking as memories flash:

London underworld clubs. Shanghai wire transfers. Ministers trembling beneath my gaze while their countries burned.

"But it was a lie," I admit, my voice cracking. "I didn't stay clean. I was complicit. Every life moved like pieces on a board—like they didn't matter."

The weight presses harder against my ribs. My stomach twists, and for a second, my knees threaten to buckle beneath me.

"When Vito tried to pull me fully back under, I almost let him." The words come low, raw. "I almost became exactly what my father wanted."

The air feels thick, suffocating.

"And after we took Vito out—" my throat seizes as I say it, "I could've taken the famiglia for myself. Sat in my father's chair. Finished what they spent years grooming me to inherit."

My fists clench. My voice drops to a rasp.

"I wanted to."

Naomi's eyes soften—just slightly—but she still doesn't speak.

"I gave it to Dante."

I finally look up fully, my gaze locking with hers.

"Dante's not blood. Vito adopted him. But he has something I don't." My breath shakes. "Honor. A line he won't cross. A code my father never taught me."

The silence presses in like a vice.

"I could've ruled," I whisper. "Instead, I burned it. And handed the ashes to someone better."

But even after all that, even after burning everything down... the weight stayed. Not until you came.

I close my eyes. Force out the last part that feels like my bones splintering.

"Then you came."

The words barely make it out. My voice cracks wide open.

"I knew of you before I ever saw you. Your reputation. Your mind. That's why I hired you." My throat tightens as my eyes drop to the floor. "But then... then I saw you."

I glance up again, my chest pulling tight. "That night at Asylum. You walked into that room like you already owned every man inside. Untouchable. Unbothered. And I broke the second I saw you like that."

Her breathing shifts—just a slight hitch—but she stays still. Unflinching.

"I told myself I wouldn't pull you into my world. That I could want you quietly. That I wouldn't destroy you like I've destroyed everything else."

My voice shudders as the truth cuts through me.

"But I couldn't stay away. You were gravity."

The shame slices hot through my gut, twisting my stomach into knots.

"You didn't stumble into this war, Naomi. I pulled you into it. Every threat you faced, every risk you took—it all started because I was selfish enough to want you. Even knowing it could break you."

The burn climbs into my throat now, and I can't swallow it down.

"I wanted you before I ever deserved you."

"You were never the danger. You were the choice I was too afraid to make."

The final words fall into the quiet like a blade.

"This isn't a plea. This isn't manipulation. It's just the truth. If you walk away after this, I won't stop you."

The room closes in around me, heavy as a fist against my chest.
She watches me. The only person who ever sees everything—and stays.
And all I can do now is wait.

Chapter 41
Code And Collar
Naomi

He sits there, still and silent, waiting for my verdict. Not as the man who once orchestrated empires, but as the man who's finally torn himself bare for me.

The weight of his confession lingers in the air like smoke. Heavy. Raw. Real.

I feel it coil low in my belly — not fear. Never fear. Just the deep pulse of what it means to love a man capable of becoming a monster who instead chose not to.

I step toward him.

Slow. Measured.

His breath hitches, but he doesn't look away. His gaze stays locked on mine, burning with something that almost looks like... dread.

I stop in front of him, close enough to feel the tremor running beneath his control. My fingertips graze his jaw, forcing him to tilt his face up to me.

"You finished the reckoning, Gideon." My voice stays steady. "Now it's time to write what comes next."

His throat works around a swallow, but he stays silent, giving me all the space.

I let my fingers trail down to the collar of his shirt. "You've given me the truth. And I choose you." I lean in, my breath brushing against his lips. "But not as we were."

His eyes flicker. His hands tighten against his thighs.

"No more secrets. No more confusing control for protection that steals my choices." My voice sharpens, but never rises. "If you want to kneel for me, you kneel because you choose to. Because we both do."

"Yes." His voice breaks on the single word. "Anything."

I pull back just slightly, studying him.

"We rebuild the rules. Together."

He nods once, breathless.

I walk past him then, gliding toward the small drawer inside the private playroom we rarely entered since everything fell apart. The space smells faintly of leather, citrus polish, and him. I've kept this drawer locked for months. Waiting. Hoping.

I open it and pull out the two items inside.

Two slim, matching black leather collars. Custom-made. Clean. Elegant. One for him. One for me.

I carry them back, the soft weight of them grounding me as I kneel gracefully between his legs.

His breath stutters. "Naomi..."

My fingers trace his throat first. I let him feel the slow burn of my control, the gentle pressure of my fingertips just under his jaw. His pulse pounds against my touch, rapid but steady.

"I'm not here to own you." My voice lowers. "We offer this to each other."

He nods once, unable to speak.

I slide the collar around his neck, fastening it snug but loose enough to breathe. My thumb presses lightly against the latch.

"You are mine by choice," I whisper. "Only choice. Only consent."

Tears glisten in his eyes. Not shame. Not fear. Release.

I feel my own chest tighten as he gently lifts my second collar from my hand. His fingers shake as he places it around my throat, careful, reverent, steady.

"You are mine," he echoes, voice raw. "By choice."

The weight of it settles between us like oxygen finally filling both our lungs.

I rise slowly and offer my hand.

He takes it instantly, rising to his feet, waiting. Open. Bare.

"We negotiate everything, Gideon. Our terms. Our rules. No more control used as armor. We communicate. We check-in. Always."

"Yes."

I press my palm to his chest, feeling the thrum of his heartbeat beneath my touch. "We will use colors."

His eyes darken, but not with dominance. With surrender. "Yes."

"Green means safe. Open. No fear."

"Green." He repeats softly.

"Yellow means pause. We check in."

"Yellow."

"Red means stop. Always."

"Red."

I smile softly, my thumb sweeping along his lower lip. "And you will use them."

"I swear it."

The silence between us shifts then—less heavy now. It hums with anticipation, electricity buzzing between our bodies.

"Strip." My voice turns into silk, smooth but undeniable.

He moves instantly, unbuttoning his shirt with the same precise hands once used to dismantle empires. Now they tremble only for me.

When his clothes hit the floor, I let my gaze rake over him. The bruises from Vito's torture have faded, but the faintest traces remain—a map of what we survived. What he survived.

I guide him toward the padded bench near the wall. He kneels slowly, hands behind his back, spine perfectly straight as he waits for me. Not because he's been ordered. Because he wants to.

I secure his wrists behind him with soft leather cuffs—tight, but not harsh.

He exhales as I fasten him into position, his chest rising and falling with a rhythm that matches my own heartbeat.

"I trust you, Naomi." His voice cracks. "Completely."

The words slide into my bloodstream like heat.

I trace the edge of his collar again, letting my breath fan against his ear. "And I trust you, Gideon."

I trail a featherlight touch down his sternum, over the hard plane of his abdomen, letting my nails tease his skin. His body responds instantly, sharp and hungry but controlled, waiting for my permission.

"You don't hold the reins anymore," I whisper. "But you've never looked more powerful than you do right now."

His breath hitches, like my words alone just gut-punched him. His chest heaves, muscles tight beneath his skin, his cock flushed, hard, desperate.

I slide my hand up the smooth leather around his throat, my thumb pressing lightly beneath his chin, forcing his head up to meet my gaze.

"You're ready for me, aren't you?" My voice is low, deliberate, the silk-wrapped steel he craves.

"Yes," he breathes, voice hoarse already.

"Good," I murmur, eyes dragging down his body. "Because I'm not here to give you what you want. I'm here to take exactly what I want."

His jaw clenches, but he doesn't dare speak.

I let my robe slip off my shoulders, watching his eyes darken as I stand above him completely bare. His breath shudders as his gaze hungrily drinks in every inch of me, but he stays where I've put him — kneeling, open, waiting.

I circle him slowly, making sure he feels me, smells me, hears nothing but my heels against marble, my breath brushing against his ear as I lean close.

"You don't come," I whisper. "Not unless I give you permission. If you do..." I let my nails drag lightly over the back of his neck, watching him shiver, "you won't like the consequences."

"Yes, Naomi," he rasps.

"That's my good boy."

The words hit him like a pulse straight to his cock. His head drops slightly, cheeks flushed, already unraveling.

I grab his chin, forcing him to look back up. "Keep your eyes on me."

He nods, desperate.

I lead him onto the bed, pushing him back with a palm to his chest. He lies there, fully exposed, his body straining, barely holding it together. His cock is throbbing now, leaking, standing hard against his abdomen.

"Look at you," I purr. "So fucking hard for me already. You've been holding it together for days, haven't you? Sitting there like a good little soldier, cleaning up your empire while all you wanted was this."

He lets out a broken sound, his chest heaving. "Please..."

"Please what, baby?"

"Please... let me have it. Let me feel you. I need you."

I crawl down between his legs, settling on my knees, my hands gripping his thighs to hold him open. His cock twitches when I blow a soft breath across the flushed tip, watching precum bead up, already slick and dripping for me.

"You need it that bad?" I tease, letting my lips barely ghost along the head. "You're leaking for me. So fucking desperate."

"Naomi... please, I can't—"

"Oh, you can." My voice drops. "And you will."

I let my tongue drag flat across the underside, slow and filthy, savoring the way his entire body jerks beneath me. Then I swallow him, taking him deep, forcing him to slide straight to the back of my throat on the first stroke.

He cries out, head dropping back against the pillows, fists curling into the sheets.

"Fuck—oh my God—Naomi."

I moan around him, letting the vibrations make him shake harder. My spit coats his cock, slick and messy, dripping down my chin as I pull back and swallow him again, deeper this time. My hand twists at the base, pumping in rhythm with my throat.

The sounds coming out of him are wrecked. Guttural. Unhinged.

"Eyes on me," I growl when he dares close them. "You watch me ruin you."

He forces his eyes back open, glassy and wide, lips parted as he gasps for breath. The tears are already starting to build in the corners.

I bob my head faster now, hollowing my cheeks, letting spit drip down as I work him brutally, sloppily, loving every second of how undone he is. His hips jerk but I slam my palm into his stomach, pinning him down.

"Stay still."

"Naomi—Naomi—" His voice shatters on my name.

His entire body trembles, his abs tightening, his thighs flexing under my grip. He's right there, teetering.

I pull off with a wet pop, his cock flushed angry red and glistening.

"Not yet," I purr, dragging my tongue across the tip, lapping up the mess I've made. "You're not allowed to come. Not until I say."

He whimpers, completely broken. "Please, Naomi… please… don't stop… I need—"

"I know exactly what you need," I smirk, stroking him once, squeezing hard enough to make his whole body convulse. "And you'll get it when I decide you've earned it."

His head thrashes, voice cracking. "Fuck—Naomi—please—I'm begging you—"

"You look so pretty when you beg." I lick a long stripe up his shaft, letting spit dribble from my lips back down onto him, spreading the slick with my hand as I pump him slow, cruel. "And you're going to keep begging."

Finally, when his body is quaking, pushed to the edge of breaking, I crawl back up his body, straddling him.

"You want to come inside me, don't you? Feel me clenching around you while you lose your fucking mind."

"Yes. God, yes."

"But you don't come until I tell you to."

"Yes, Naomi. Please… please let me…"

I sink down onto him, slow and deliberate, taking every inch, locking my gaze on his as he arches beneath me, breath completely wrecked.

"Oh my fucking god," he breathes.

I ride him slow, rolling my hips, feeling him throb inside me while he struggles not to lose it. His hands fist into the sheets again, his entire body trembling.

"Don't you dare come."

He shakes his head frantically, tears spilling freely now, breathless.

"Naomi… I—I'm trying… please…"

"Good boy," I pant. "Hold it. Just like that. You're going to take everything I give you."

I ride him harder, grinding deeper, letting the wet slap of skin fill the room. The heat builds between us, unbearable, overwhelming.

His voice breaks as he sobs. "I love you. God, I love you."

"I know," I whisper, leaning down to kiss him, swallowing his broken moans. "Now come for me."

He explodes beneath me, his entire body jerking violently, crying my name, voice shredded and raw as release tears through him.

I ride him through every pulse until he's completely spent, trembling, wrecked.

When it's over, I lower myself against him, pressing my lips to his temple as his breath slowly steadies beneath me.

His voice breaks one last time. “Thank you.”

I stroke his hair gently, our collars brushing against each other as we lay tangled together.

“This isn't surrender,” I whisper quietly. “This is devotion. This is ours.”

Chapter 42

Epilogue - The Freedom We Chose

Gideon

The city glows beneath us.

Not as something to control. Not a chessboard waiting for my hand. For the first time, it simply breathes—and I breathe with it.

Tonight, the world belongs to her.

I watch Naomi move through the penthouse, still lit by the afterglow of Daedalus' launch. The scent of champagne lingers faintly in the air, mingling with her perfume—amber and honey and something sharp beneath it that always makes my pulse spike. Floor-to-ceiling windows frame the Manhattan skyline, glass humming faintly with the distant thrum of traffic far below. Our empire glittering quietly under her feet.

My woman. My salvation. My queen.

The party played like a symphony—Zoe keeping things unpredictable as always, Toni already planning her next audit of Daedalus' security protocols just for sport. Jade sealed a dozen interviews before Naomi even finished her first champagne, and Jor whispered an obscene investment offer into her ear that made her laugh in that way that guts me every time.

But all of it—the headlines, the applause, the empire—is nothing compared to this moment.

Because tonight, I get to take her home.

She moves through my space like she owns every inch of it—because she does. And God help me, I want her to own me just the same.

The silk of her dress glides along her thighs as she walks, catching the light with every step, her curls spilling like liquid gold down her back. The way she moves now—it's not just confidence. It's command. My pulse kicks harder, heat blooming low and insistent.

Naomi stops in front of me, tilting her head slightly, reading me the way only she can. A small smirk tugs at her mouth as if she can already see the way my body tightens under her gaze.

"You're already hard for me, aren't you?" she murmurs, voice like silk over steel.

I exhale, the confession pulled out like a string. "Always."

Her hand finds my chest, warm and sure, fingers splayed right over my pounding heart.

"Do you trust me tonight?" she asks, voice soft but pulsing with that electricity that always undoes me.

My breath catches. My pulse spikes beneath her touch. The anticipation hums like a live wire beneath my skin.

"Completely."

Her fingers slide up, curling gently beneath my jaw, guiding my face toward hers until her amber eyes fill my vision. That quiet command lives in her gaze now—the same one that once stripped me bare in a club in New Orleans. The same one I have been falling into ever since.

"Good," she murmurs, voice silk-wrapped steel. "Because we're going back."

The breath leaves my lungs in one sharp exhale.

"Asylum," I say, my voice lower now, thick with everything unspoken between us.

"Asylum," she echoes, her lips curving, but it's not a threat—it's a promise.

The pulse of Asylum hits the second we walk in. Heavy bass. Heat. The air thick with sweat, leather, perfume, and something darker that always coils under my skin. But this time, it doesn't swallow me whole. Not like before.

Naomi's hand is wrapped tight around mine as we move through the crowd. Her grip is steady, anchored, like she knows exactly where she's taking me. And God help me, I want to be led.

Six months ago, I came into this place looking to disappear—to bury myself in something brutal enough to numb me. I didn't know I was walking straight into her. Into the one thing that would undo me completely.

Now? She owns every inch of me.

Her dress is liquid against her skin, deep crimson catching every flicker of light as we move past bodies grinding, hands roaming, sharp cries swallowed by pulsing beats. Her curls tumble wild down her back. My throat tightens just watching her move. My queen.

We weave through the alcoves like we're hunting, and in a way, we are.

Naomi's voice was in my head the whole ride over. Whispering against my ear.

"Tonight, you're mine, Hawke." She slipped the weight of the muzzle into my jacket pocket before we left the penthouse. "My game. My rules. Think you can handle surrendering for real?"

Like I'd ever tell her no.

She finds our space—deep crimson curtains, familiar, waiting for us like a throne room dressed in sin. The massive chair in the center pulls at me instantly. Where I first claimed her. Where she first broke for me. And now, where I'll kneel.

She turns, eyes raking over me.

"Strip."

The word lands like a fist straight to my chest. My cock jerks even before my fingers move. I strip fast, efficiently, until I'm bare and pulsing, my breath coming faster with each layer peeled away. The air kisses my skin, cool and sharp.

"Present."

I drop to my knees, spreading my thighs, back straight, hands behind me—open. Offering.

Naomi circles like a predator, one finger trailing over my shoulder, my chest, down the tight line of my abs.

"Look at you," she murmurs. "All that strength... now right where you belong. Trembling for me."

I shudder at her touch, the smallest graze setting every nerve on fire.

"Color, Gideon?"

"Green. So fucking green," I rasp. "Please, Naomi."

She smiles, dark and pleased, bending to nip my ear.

"My needy boy. You ache for this, don't you? To be owned. To wear my marks. To be mine."

A whine escapes my throat before I can stop it. My cock throbs, dripping against my thigh.

She moves to the table beside us, lifting the muzzle with deliberate care. The weight of it makes my breath catch before it even touches me. Black leather molded into the shape of a jackal's snout—sleek, feral, studded along the jawline with small silver spikes that gleam under the red lights.

A beast's mask. Built for me. For her.

She runs her fingers over the sharp edges, like she's admiring her own creation. "My beautiful wolf," she murmurs. "Time to cage those teeth."

The leather is cool as she fits it to my face, tightening each strap with slow, practiced ease until it locks into place. My breath filters through the narrow slits, hot and fast, my world shrinking to the pulse of my heartbeat and her scent in the air.

"There you are," she purrs. "My beast. Caged. Perfect."

The rush hits hard—control leaving me completely as she circles again, her nails ghosting across my chest, my thighs, my leaking cock that jerks helplessly at every pass.

"You know, I could keep you like this forever," she hums. "Bound. Gagged. Desperate. You wouldn't last a week."

I groan, straining toward her even as invisible restraints hold me still.

"Not tonight, though," she whispers. "Tonight, we celebrate."

Her hand cracks across my ass—sharp, perfect—and my breath stutters behind the muzzle. Another slap. Then another. My skin warms under the steady rhythm of her palm.

She drags the blade next, the tip biting just enough as it traces shallow lines over my hip—marks for her and only her. Every nerve is on fire, my body vibrating, desperate and wide open.

The flogger comes next—light and maddening, feathering over my cock, my thighs, teasing me right to the edge without mercy. My breathing turns ragged, broken, reduced to animal noises behind the muzzle.

Naomi watches me unravel, her voice a low purr.

"You're so far under for me already, aren't you? My fierce wolf... reduced to a shaking mess just for my touch."

I'm gone. Gone for her.

She leans in, voice hot against my ear.

"Beg me, Gideon."

"Please," I choke. "Please, Naomi... need you."

Her laugh is pure sin, the sound sliding straight through me.

"Good boy."

With a click, the muzzle slips free. My breath drags in sharp and greedy as she cups my face, pulling me up until I'm standing, shaking, fully exposed.

She guides me backward onto the throne, climbing into my lap like she's claimed the whole damn world. Her dress rides up her thighs as she straddles me, lowering herself onto my cock in one slow, devastating slide.

My head drops back with a broken groan.

She moves with purpose, hips rolling as her nails scrape down my chest. My hands grip the arms of the chair, knuckles white, fighting to let her lead, to let her own every inch of me.

"Stay still," she commands, voice breathless but hard. "Don't come until I say."

I bite back a moan, hips twitching under her control.

Naomi rides me, relentless, dragging me closer and closer to the edge with every brutal, perfect grind. My muscles lock. My breath breaks. My vision tunnels to nothing but her.

"You're mine," she whispers, voice cracking with her own release building. "All of you. Always."

"Always," I choke.

And when she finally gives me permission—when she whispers "Come for me, my wolf"—I shatter.

The orgasm crashes through me like a tidal wave, stealing my breath, my sight, my fucking soul. She follows seconds later, nails biting into my skin as her body clenches around mine.

When the world slowly rebuilds itself, Naomi collapses against my chest, breath warm against my throat, both of us slick and trembling.

Her lips brush my jaw as she whispers, "You were perfect."

And I am. Because I am hers.

The tremor rolls through me as the last wave of release fades, my breath jagged, my body spent. Every muscle in my legs shakes, and for a second I think I might actually collapse.

Naomi doesn't let me.

She moves before I even fully register it. Sliding off my lap, reaching for the small tray of aftercare essentials she prepped before we even arrived, because she always thinks ahead. Because she always knows.

The leather muzzle comes off first, her fingers careful, slow, practiced as she unbuckles each strap and lifts the weight from my face. My jaw aches from the tension, but the cool air kissing my skin makes me exhale.

"Easy," she murmurs, voice softer now, all command melted into care.

A chilled bottle of water pressed into my hand. A cool cloth wiping sweat from my chest, my shoulders, my face. Her touch is steady. Reverent. She never rushes. Never leaves me floating too long.

"You're shaking," she says gently, but there's no concern behind it—only knowing. Only love.

I can't help the hoarse laugh that scrapes out. "You did that."

"You needed it," she counters, lips quirking. "You always do."

Her hands keep working as my breathing starts to even out, the ringing in my ears slowly fading back into the pulse of Asylum's low, primal soundtrack. All around us, the alcoves hum with breathy moans, sharp cries, wet sounds of pleasure layered over the bass.

But all I feel is her. Her hands, her voice, her calm.

Naomi presses her lips to my temple. "Color?"

I swallow, still catching up. "Green."

The word lands like a small surrender of its own. She smiles against my skin, and her fingers squeeze mine.

"Good boy."

I close my eyes at the sound, my chest tightening in ways that have nothing to do with the sex.

I don't even realize my voice cracks until the words scrape out. "I never thought I'd survive all of this."

Naomi stills, but only for a breath. She knows exactly what I mean. The famiglia. Vito. My father. The weight of all of it.

"But you didn't just survive," she whispers, brushing my damp hair back from my forehead. "You made it out. We made it out."

I open my eyes, locking onto hers. "I was never supposed to have this. Any of it."

Her expression softens, eyes shining. "That's because you were never taught what freedom actually was."

I let out a breath, raw and unguarded. "You are my freedom."

Her lips curve. "We're each other's."

The pulse between us shifts again. Softer. Steadier. The current that always existed but never gets any less powerful.

I swallow hard, fingers tightening around hers. "Obsession wasn't surrender. Not really."

"No," she agrees, her voice a thread of silk. "It was seeing each other for exactly who we are. And choosing it."

"Every time," I whisper.

"Always," she answers.

And as the pulse of Asylum continues around us—moans and music and shadows—we stay locked there, in our own private gravity.

Chosen. Not broken. Not owned. Free.

Acknowledgements

To my Ink Sis P.H. Nix — the best accountability partner a girl could ask for. The Munch King is yours; may the bibs stay wet and the beast be fed. Thank you for cheering, pushing, and threatening me in all the best ways.

To Jordyn — you read the original version, loved it first, and still had the nerve to jinx me with the 50-chapter curse. We only made it to 41, but I'll make it up to you in the bonus scenes. You know I will.

To Kris, my alpha reader — your comments live rent-free in my head, my docs, and probably my dreams. Thank you for seeing this story before the shine.

And to you — the reader who took a chance on a girl like me. Thank you for giving Naomi and Gideon space in your heart (and on your bookshelf). I hope they wrecked you just a little.

This book broke me in all the best ways.

Thank you for letting it break you, too.

About the author

Fortuna Lux is a real-life queen of steam, an unapologetic provocateur spinning wickedly erotic tales for readers who crave love stories with a dark and daring edge. Known for crafting dominant, dangerous heroes and the strong, sensual heroines who bring them to their knees, Fortuna doesn't just write about pleasure—she understands it. Her stories are an intoxicating mix of power, passion, and peril, designed for those who like their romance as untamed as their imagination.

When she's not weaving tales of sinful seduction, Fortuna can be found perfecting her rope work, exploring the great outdoors, and tending to an ever-growing collection of houseplants. She believes in fearless exploration, both on and off the page, and thrives in the company of fellow romance rebels who embrace the unconventional.

A little more about Memo Rable, one of many alter egos:

Memo Rable's stories are portals—intricate, immersive, and unapologetically dark. Inspired by the boundless lore of *Dungeons & Dragons*, the emotional chaos of *The Sims*, and the moral quandaries of *Fallout*, Memo crafts worlds where choices have weight and consequences bite.

A lover of rich storytelling, Memo thrives in narratives where reality bends and nightmares bleed into waking life. Whether weaving eerie psychological horror, twisted devotion, or brutal adventure, every tale is an invitation to step into the unknown and see what survives on the other side. Much like the best games, Memo's books aren't just meant to be read—they're meant to be played.

Where to Find Me – And Stay Wrecked

Love filthy, emotional chaos with brains and bruises?

Want first looks at exclusive content, bonus scenes, unfiltered thirst traps, and chaotic reader debates over who broke first?

Join the reader lair. I don't bite.

(Unless you beg.)

Private Facebook Group — Naughty By Fate – The Luxverse Reader Group

Exclusive chaos for Fortuna's readers: thirst posts, polls, memes, spoiler threads, early access, and sometimes emotional damage.

https://www.facebook.com/groups/fortunalux

Reader Discord — Naughty By Fate

If you want to scream in real time, post unhinged TikToks, or analyze kink psychology at 2AM...
This is where the real chaos lives.
https://discord.gg/jUmzkxZ84C

Made in the USA
Columbia, SC
27 June 2025

59938730R00159